KSc

Ajala

and the
Witches of Blood Underworld

This is ARC — Advance Readers Copy — Don't mind the errors, just enjoy the story and leave your review on my website, facebook, thriller.

01 = 07 = 2014

Ajala
and the
Witches of Blood Underworld
Copyright © 2014 Xsz-I I'

ISBN: 978-0-9927826-0-3

Ajala

and the

Witches of Blood Underworld

Xsz-I I'

Ajala series could be liken to an ancient Yoruba proverb which says,

"Bi omode ko ba itan,
A ba aroba,
Aroba ni baba itan."

Translated, *in the absence of history, fable will be available for children to learn and fable in itself is de facto grand history.* However, all the characters, organisation and incidence portrayed in this novel are either products of the author's imagination or are adapted from ancestral fables. Any similitude to real persons, living or dead, is purely coincidental.

With unalloyed love
this book
is
dedicated to
the bright memory
of
my beloved Mother,
Grace Ibiduni Areola, nee Owolabi.

Also by Xsz-I I'

Ajala and the Kidnapee of Aye

Forthcoming:

Shigidi and the sacrificial Victim

Eve's Wedding

Information and updates on

www.iiixsz-ibooks.com

Facebook 3ixi Literary Services

Email: books@iiixsz-ibooks.com

Order from: **www.iiixsz-ibooks.com**

Printed in United Kingdom

Thanks to

Lavinia Bulgaru, my beloved wife, for
riding along with me.
Your love, wisdom and strength have
encouraged me
To do the best I can do and to
continue pushing
To be the best I can be.

Chapter One

T HE sight of rectangular puddling mud shacks, unveiled a typical African village called Eboru. One of the dispersed groups of isolated and untouched settlements situated atop a plateau in the midst of an overwhelmingly thick, vast, mesmerising terrain that was naturally embedded with awful jungle and undulating mountains.

Unbeknownst to the civilised and sophisticated world, within this vast, pristine, nature embedded jungle, was a remote, overawed and uncharted West African territory, teeming with divers terrestrial and aquatic species and also home to about a dozen tribes that have had no exposure to civilisation. These uncontacted groups of superstitious, crude and indigenous tribes lived mainly from hunting, fishing, breeding and cut and clear agriculture. They regarded the tiniest settlement of Eboru amongst them as their sacred land, and most importantly, the land of which all these isolated and dispersed tribal settlements claimed ascendancy.

It was customary for all these tribes to make pilgrimage to Eboru every year *as the oracle* might reveal, just to offer their annual rituals to the gods according to their ancient religious system. Hence, the name Eboru, *ritual accepted,* as these lost tribes believed that only in Eboru could their oblations be accepted by the gods and their ancestors, whatsoever. During this yearly traditional pilgrimage to Eboru, as these tribespeople came with their offering for the gods and the ancestors, they also would bare gifts for the king of Eboru and the Babalawo, *the possessor of secret ancient knowledge and wisdom,* the official Ifa oracle custodian of Eboru, who also according to tradition was the royal priest of Eboru and the chief priest of these lost tribes. These tribespeople were very concerned about Eboru's traditional affairs surrounding their Babalawo, *the possessor of secret ancient knowledge and wisdom,* because his official position amongst these lost tribes was indeed a lofty one and could be said to be the backbone of their tradition.

1

Commonly, their shacks' floors were also constructed of puddled mud and in the passage of every of their mud house, it was customary to have a family leisure area and also dining area, molded into the puddled mud floors right from the time of construction. In a corner of this passage, there was a recumbent mould to the shape suitable for the paterfamilias, but this was usually sited in a well-ventilated area. In the rooms there were wooden or bamboo chairs, tables and wooden beds or straw or leather mats for use. The windows and doors of these rectangular puddling mud shacks were made of bamboos and wood, the windows and doorways' prop made of slender, but durable wooden post, tucked into the mud at the time it was still soft enough.

These lost tribes, like most primitive societies, were polygamous and this was outrightly a matter of choice or sometimes, circumstance. Nevertheless, no matter what they reckoned that families should stay together as one and close-knitted as the *immovable* mould of their dining and leisure seats, with neither malice nor prejudice *en famille*. This reference in their adage to the features in the passage of their homes was perhaps prompted for the stronger reason that this was the main place for family gathering and deliberations, *id est.,* a very important and remarkable family rendezvous suitable for mnemonic reference to uphold family unity.

Quarterly, special leaves of purple colour property and aromatic pleasantness were mashed in traditional mortar by the materfamilias, with adequate water quantity added. This mashed pulpy mass would then be used to scrub the mud floor, up to the knee length of the wall's level. This was done not only for indoor beauty and aromatic redolence or balminess of this particular leaves, but also for sanitising purposes to prevent epidemic outbreak. The floor would be swept of these leaves' crumbs after everything had dried. However, by that time the floor would have turned purple-like in colour, giving off some soothing and pleasing aroma and sight appealing too *by the virtue of these leaves*.

Open gardens were common features to most of these mud houses and these were a kind of domestic husbandry, home to crops – *according to their seasons* – to be used fresh for immediate needs of the family. Therefore, to prevent goats, sheep and cattle destroying the growth of these open gardens, these plants were sprinkled with water polluted with the droppings of these domestic ruminants – *a process which had to be repeated after a tropical African rainfall –* and as soon as these animals perceived their droppings on the growth of these gardens, they quickly turned away from feeding on them.

Also, it seemed mores to these lost tribes inhabiting this isolated territory to have one or two tropical fruit tree, growing at the front or sometimes at the rear side of their shanty and threadbare mud shelters. Primitively constructed rocking chairs, made of malleable branches, surrounded by stools made out of boles, were common sight under these trees. These were rendezvous for the paterfamilias and materfamilias or an elder en famille to communicate before bed time, moonlight tales, past histories and tribal decorum, as passed from generation to generation to the young ones. When it wasn't moonlighting, the older ones used this homely park for merriment of indulging in undiluted palm wine and smoked game meat with friends or family members. As for the children among these isolated and primitive population, this could be said to be their only form of classroom education. In fact, families or clans could request the supreme griot of these lost tribes for a visit to answer questions about their past histories, fables or prophecies and he might respond by sending the official griot or one of his protégés. This occasion was normally held under these trees during moonlighting.

These dispersed lost tribes' settlements as well as their time worn mud shacks were linked by narrow footpaths that navigated their ways through the bushes, hills, rocks, mountains and forests, as shaped by the feet of indigenes, but in some places, it was more or less climbing to get to another tribal settlement than walking.

Their rectangular mud shacks were effectively and admiringly thatched roof. However, some small, roundly built, doorless mud hut shrines were heavily covered with palm fronds. These mud hut shrines were homes to the gods of the land. Their shapes weren't only to differentiate between the homes of the gods and that of the humans, but also to designate that these roundly built homes for the gods weren't the original shelter of the gods, hence their round shapes, which meant that the home of the gods was immaterial and somewhere away in the heavens, therefore, infinite. But these shrines, sheltering idols representing different Orisha, *primordial beings – that they believed created the Earth and also from whom all living things emanated –* were located at different strategic places all over the settlements of these tribespeople.

3

The whole people of these lost tribes were penchant for all their beliefs, their Orisha and also for Eboru *village*. Therefore, apart from these roundly built shrines, statues of different bizarre figures were common sight as open shrines – *sometimes clothed with palm fronds, littered with different types of offerings and often strewn with palm oil all over, as blood libation* – for the people to offer rituals to which god they revered, as they might desire and without compulsion. Though, without any form of notice to show which deified statue designated which Orisha, yet these tribespeople knew their gods, even as much as they knew one another and also knew the right ritual to offer each Orisha every morning and evening or as much as they would like.

It wasn't unusual to see domestic animals tethered to these idols or simulacrums, as live offerings to the Orisha, *primordial beings*. Though, as the gods don't eat, it was customarily accepted that only the needy and the hungry were favoured by the Orisha to unfasten such offerings for their *own* use. Otherwise, the Orisha was believed would strike dead whoever covetously trespassed on their offerings.

These roundly built shrines must be consecrated by the Babalawo, *the possessor of secret ancient knowledge and wisdom*, before any of the tribespeople were to access it for ritual purpose or during the seasonal celebration of any of these gods. Sometimes, the Babalawo might have to journey to the other tribal settlement for this ritual importance, if Ifa oracle should reveal such or according to the seasonal celebration of such god or gods.

Amongst these tribespeople, trade was by barter and major bartering had to be made in the presence of the king, chiefs and elders – *as a seal of legal agreement* – on a particular day of the week designated for such routine by tradition, after the parties involved had agreed and resolved to convey their transaction as they might desire. Nevertheless, neither the king nor his trade council – *who would be sitting around him at the market centre on such days as witnesses* – were allowed to dictate the measure of bartering *to these parties involved*. Of course, it should be transaction as they deemed proportionate, appropriate and satisfied with. Though, if the parties involved weren't sure or satisfied with their bartering exchange, they were obliged by tradition to present their case to the king and his trade council to determine the appropriate measure for their bartering.

4

There was no form of taxation among these lost tribes, and the king himself had his own occupation and worked hard like any of the indigenes as tradition demanded. However, people would bring gifts to their king voluntarily much more than he did ever need. Therefore, taxation could be considered as freewill giving and according to tradition, the king had to share these gifts with every needy family of these tribespeople.

It was capital punishment – *as carried by most of these lost tribes' crimes* – to pacify Ogun, *the primordial being who was believed by these tribespeople to be their patron of smith,* with the blood of whoever disregarded or reneged on concluded trade by barter transaction, either made in the presence of the king or not, and the head of such victim would be displayed on his or her family's mud wall. Thus, there adage before and after every barter transaction was, 'Once bartered, it's forever sealed,' which meant no retraction.

However, it wasn't rife to see human head tucked on the mud shack walls of these lost tribes, but when this happened, it was some kind of ignominy for such victims and for their clan and also a deterrent to the tribespeople to avoid the same crime committed by these victims. So to say, these tribespeople were almost crime free and lived in peace and tranquility of their traditions and customs.

These remote tribes had a special cheap material as their common covering, created by carefully sliding a sharp needle-like thorn through the tissue of palmetto fronds, making it into a long fine hirsute. This bristle-like material would then be plied on thin ropes that could be fastened round the waist and breast line *for women* and stretched to dry in the sun. A covering used to protect mainly the private part and also could be used round the arms, neck and the shanks. Most of these tribespeople dyed this common covering to give more of variety in fashion and style. Also, certain colours were sometimes associated with a particular clan. This particular covering in its simple form shouldn't be washed by water, even when touched by water or rain, it marred its natural beauty and therefore could only be restored by washing it in undiluted palm wine, but when dyed, the dye had to be repeated for better luster.

However, the powerful and the rich among these tribespeople, according to their status and influence, used the hair of animals or the mane of lions or leather loincloth, instead of this material. Many who could afford leather loincloth did adorn themselves with it. Their shanks, arms, wrists and waists were the usual places normally adorned after covering their dignity. Nevertheless, whatever they wore scantily covered their bodies. Sometimes crafted shells, gourds, cowries, colourful feathers, beads, bones, horns and bamboos were commonly used as bling-bling. Some of these lost tribes had bandana of either animal leather or strip of rope, holding in place on their foreheads one or two shells or gourd or horn, according to their ancestral preference. They had a headwear of feathers, horns, shells, quills and scales. The wives of the rich, rulers and influential women fashionably distinguished themselves by enhancing their covering with costly beads, particularly, their waist adorned with much of these beads to augment their feminine figure.

Oftentimes, children could still be seen roaming around in nudity, but at adolescence they were obliged by custom to cover their dignity with this common material provided by their parents. Indeed, before adolescence all males should have their modest gourd penis sheath to hide their manhood. Traditionally, it was a taboo for children to see turgid penis, therefore, boys were made to accustom to wearing gourd penis sheath from childhood. However, penis sheath were also worn either for ritualistic purposes, ceremonial, ancestral or allegorically to convey a certain hidden meaning *as indicated by the design on them, shape or size.*

The shape of a gourd penis sheath might also indicate social do of wooing a woman into nuptial agreement. There was an annual sexuality festival amongst these primitive tribespeople, where men would serenade nubile female counterparts by dancing and displaying in their fascinating gourd penis sheaths of different shapes and sizes, using their well-oiled muscular bodies too as point of attraction. The nubile ladies would afterwards inform their parents to consult with the family of a prospective groom of their choice, whose gourd penis sheath they personally found most alluring.

In turn, the following year nubile women also would serenade their male counterparts with their engraved gourd boobs and bum sheath of different fashion, sizes and shapes and their male counterparts, or rather love struck admirers *too* would have to meet with their parents to consult with the family of prospective brides they found attractive. Afterwards, interested lovers would have to be interviewed by their family elders for their final decision to tie the knot.

The kings of these tribespeople and their chiefs and elders cover themselves with animal skins, plumaged beautifully according to status and influence. One could only know who was a chief or an elder in the mode of different kind of traditional fly-whisks in their hands, with elders having their kind of brown fly-whisks, while chiefs wore beads of different types as tradition allowed them and also were having the same white fly-whisks, as the king. As customary amongst these tribespeople, most adults normally carried a flabelliform object, like segment of a circle, made of either leather, straw or feathers to fan themselves or drive away flies and also could be used to shield the head from the excruciating hotness of the sun.

The hunters stood as the kings' bodyguards, under the sole command of the king through the 'OluOde', *generalissimo of the hunters.* They were said to be the descendants of renowned men and women. They had special padded animal skin jackets and aprons of juju, sewn with fetish materials like shells, horns, small gourds, bones, feathers, cowries and so on. Some of these jackets and aprons were drenched in blood of different animals they hunted down, as this was believed would refresh the potency of the juju. These heavily built and towering hunters had various iron-made weapons of different shapes and sizes and ranks were exhibited according to tribal preference, by either or the combination of the number of feathers, shells or porcupine quill on their bandana headdress.

The 'OluOde', *generalissimo of the hunters,* of Eboru, who was also the overall head of the hunters among these lost tribes, was having his headdress full of beautiful, colourful feathers and cowries *as a model of his highest ranking.* The king of Eboru's intimate bodyguards, who were chosen out of these hunters, were distinguished by their flat, well cowry-lined, waist-tight leather band. Whoever wanted to see the king would have to come through them. No one was closer to the king of Eboru more than these bodyguards except the wild animals of the throne *of Eboru.* These were said to be tamed supernaturally by the ancestors *according to these tribespeople* to protect the sacred throne of Eboru.

At Eboru, the king's palace was situated at the extreme end of the settlement, protected day and night by these hunters from all sides, as some of them were never to be far from the presence of the king. These hunters weren't protecting the palace because Eboru could come under enemy attack from the other tribes, but majorly from stray wild animals that often attacked the people. Therefore, all over the tribes, presence of these hunters were common sight in strategic places, most especially at nights.

The griots were like scribes, however, they had to commit everything to memory in their own coded and blended poetic flow, histories, every event and ancient prophecies of these lost tribes. These had been practiced from time immemorial successfully. The griots' members or clans were always present at every palace proceedings and often were always abreast of whatever occurred amongst these lost tribes. These groups were headed by the supreme griot and shadowed by the official griot, who would eventually become the supreme griot of these lost tribes someday. The importance of these groups in the tradition of these tribespeople couldn't be underestimated because they held in their brains the oral heritage of these lost tribes from generation to generation.

The king of Eboru's palace was a decrepit building because it was said to be the first shelter built by the Orisha, according to the official griot of these lost tribes. This palace was a gigantic, puddled, laterite mud structure supported by various sculptured stones and carved wooden pillars that were allegedly made by their progenitors. Though decrepit by age, yet the palace was as strong a structure, as when it was actually built. A massive three stories building into the underground, with above the ground structure *that was* constructed into a sweeping roofs and supported strategically on clusters of huge, extraordinarily tall, carved timbers and gigantic sculptured rocks. There were carved wooden posts and giant, immovable stone sculptures everywhere and around to buttress this stupendous mud structure. The palace's walls were decorated with animal trophies and sculptural monuments were erected breathtakingly that any sight of them would definitely facilitate a memory push to imagine the ancient generations romanticising the mythological interactions of Eboru and her history. Outside this palace was an aged tree, standing mightily heavenward, spreading its boughs widely and under this tree were oval pit sculptured Precambrian outcrop of different stones slabs that covered a large area for the tribespeople awaiting the king's audience to sit or recline.

Inside this decrepit palace of Eboru was a big hall of gathering for the king, his chiefs, the elders and the emissaries from other tribal settlements to congregate and deliberate. This huge hall was also full of carved stone stools that were arranged in amphitheater setting, facing the sacred throne of Eboru, a throne covered all over with zebra skin and according to tradition, it was a taboo to uncover or even move the throne itself. In fact, no one knew what this throne *of Eboru* was made of because no one had ever seen it with their naked eyes, except the generations of Babalawo, *the possessor of secret ancient knowledge and wisdom,* who were saddled with the divine responsibility of maintaining and making sure the throne was intact. Albeit, not even the king of Eboru himself knew what his throne looked like. The zebra skin covering the throne was loved by these tribespeople, as a reminder that the king of Eboru was the supreme king of these lost tribes. The king of Eboru's regalia were a mystic scepter and another long scepter, a white fly whisk and a round, black, beaded, shaggy leather crown. The black, beaded, shaggy hair of this leather crown was extended lightly to cover the king's face, as a reverence to the belief that the king's face was too sacred to be fully bared before the public. The king's sandals were made of cheetah's skin and of leopard's skin. Traditionally, these connoted the king's trusted adjudicative position and his believed impartial and infallible swiftness in solely administering justice. The king's apron was made of tiger's skin and extended up to the king's knees and at the back the king had a colourful, *rare* boa's leather, so long it dragged on the ground as he walked. It was traditional that at its length of forty-one feet was where anyone should stop coming closer to the king of Eboru whenever he wore this leather, except if the king would summon anyone to come closer, no one dared violate this custom. The boa's leather was so girthed the king could conveniently truss himself up in it. This beautiful boa's leather *colour* was *rich* cream base, patterned with green sparsely, but with more reddish brown saddles that became pronounced towards the tail. Its arrow-head shape had distinctive green and reddish brown stripes on it. The reddish brown ran dorsally from the snout to the back of the head and then from the snout to the eyes and the green from the eyes to the jaw. The boa's mouth was wide opened with all its fangs well displayed so that the king's face could be within the dropped jaw, as a reminder to the king of Eboru that the whole tribespeople deserved his protection and care at all times. Around the king of Eboru's throne were *live* wild animals: lions, tigers, jaguars, leopards, hyenas and cheetahs and these were said to be tamed by the progenitors of these lost tribes for the protection of the sacred throne of Eboru from the greedy ones, who were foretold to be organised thieves *of soul and property,* robbers and marauders according to the supreme griot of these lost tribes. It was predicted by their ancestors that at the advent of the forbidden soul, these animals of the throne - *lions, tigers, jaguars, leopards, hyenas and cheetahs* - would abandon their positions and then these organised greedy ones would have their opportunity to perpetrate the unknown evil.

The king's mystic scepter was about two feet long, made of pure gold and carved into a hooded cobra with seven heads around the top. This sinuous scepter was to be in the king's left hand at all times. This mysterious object would vanish at the demise of the king to reappear at the coronation of the next king and therefore crucial to the king's installation event. As it was believed that without its appearance, the newly chosen king of Eboru wasn't from the gods, *a fortiori, the mystic scepter wasn't released by the ancestors and the gods.* No one else could touch this scepter except the chosen king of Eboru alone and by this scepter alone the king could promulgate any order without being challenged. This mysterious scepter was the only extant gold amongst these lost tribes and therefore, it was significant and highly venerated.

Another longer scepter of about six and a half feet long, made of iron, but wrought sinuously into the arrow-head shaped of a boa with wide opened mouth, *just like the head on the king's boa leather covering.* This scepter was decorated with tiny and colourful beads that drooped around the head to a length of about two feet. This was a form of staff of office that could be sent with the *official* bearer to convey the king's presence or order *anywhere* and would attract the reverence of these tribespeople, as the king himself *would in person.* The staff's presence was as revered and authoritative as the king in person and it stood as the regent at the demise of the king, if the gods hadn't preternaturally chosen any human regent.

Certainly, by tradition and unlike other tribes of these uncontacted people, only the gods could choose human regent for Eboru via the sacred revelation of what these tribespeople called fire of the gods.

Iron was sacred to these tribespeople and even venerated. The Orisha, *primordial being,* who these lost tribes claimed taught them mining and smelting was Ogun, whom they referred to as the god of iron. Their mythology credited Ogun as expert in smelting, hunting, politics and war, according to the supreme griot. Therefore, Ogun's simulacrum could only be made of iron and could also be sacrificed to through any makeshift of iron representation.

It was only in Eboru palace from time immemorial that the whole of these lost tribes depended for the supply of iron tools and weapons for hunting, because *according to tradition* only in Eboru alone should they rely for the supply of iron works, not only as symbol of the king of Eboru's paramountcy, but also as the land of ascendancy of all these tribespeople worthy of such sacred importance and pioneering.

The beads of these untouched tribes were of materials like ivory, horns, shells, bones, scales, quills *of porcupine* and seeds, made into different shapes and sizes. The use of ivory beads was a matter of shapes and sizes. Thereupon, round and big ivory beads were reserved for the adornment of the king and his wives alone. Flat, big or small shaped ivory beads and white beads were used by the Babalawo, *the possessor of secret ancient knowledge and wisdom –* the official Ifa oracle custodian of Eboru, who also according to tradition was the royal priest of Eboru and the chief priest of the whole tribes. Only the small and round shaped ivory beads could be worn *at ceremonies* by anyone who could afford them, especially the wealthy. However, these are rarely seen on people because they were too costly to barter.

These tribespeople also wore tattoos, but their tattoo culture ranged from tribal, family, animal representation, objects of the celestial sphere and even the depiction of the images of their gods and so on. These tattoos were made by grounding the leaves of mucuna pruriens with that of a cashew seeds, mixed with content of charcoal and *sometimes* colouring matter, then, applied to the part of the skin pierced to shape by a sharp, long thorn that had been washed with black soap and soaked in special sterilising herbs before use.

Though the king was believed to be chosen by the gods, but his coronation had to be performed by five top chiefs and two elders, whose titles also traditionally occupied the kingmaker's post. However, without the help of Ifa oracle by the Babalawo, *the possessor of secret ancient knowledge and wisdom,* the king wouldn't be accepted by tradition and the whole tribespeople. Even after all these traditional observances, it was believed the *preternatural* mystic scepter would have to be sent by the gods to crown the effort of these kingmakers or refused to appear, signifying malpractices, thereby, annulling such chosen king.

These seven kingmakers were saddled with the responsibility of investigating, scrutinising and presenting before the Babalawo, *the possessor of secret ancient knowledge and wisdom,* the names of potential occupiers *of the throne* from the ascendant families. The Babalawo would then consult Ifa oracle to reveal the mind of the gods and the ancestors on the right choice. However, if possible that none of these prospective names submitted for vetting process by Ifa oracle were chosen, then, the Babalawo, *the possessor of secret ancient knowledge and wisdom,* was saddled with the onus of divining by Ifa to pinpoint the right choice to the throne.

The king of Eboru was hailed thus;

> King indomitable
> Son of the guardian of the heavens
> Commander of thunder
> Ruler beyond the seas
> Inhabiter of the sun and the moon
> The sole protector of the stars
> Because serenity in Eboru
> Is serenity of the closed calabash *the Earth*;
> Far be thought of chaos in Eboru
> Or else the closed calabash would crack
> *(Disaster in the world),*
> Even beyond the unknown
> You're the protector of Eboru
> The vicar of the gods
> Chosen by the true Ifa oracle
> Kabiyesi O!
> *Your majesty, O king!*

Undoubtedly, one could imagine the unmitigated, brazen presumptions and distasteful, crude experience awaiting Mother Endor's protégés – *Shea O' Shepherd and Pott Carver.*

Chapter Two

URPRISINGLY, Shea O'Shepherd and Pott found themselves imprisoned in a filthy, stinking and *seemingly* endless dungeon with many different vast underground chambers. This woebegone subterranean domain was a massive rock-cut dungeon that went seemingly endlessly into the core of the Earth. Shea was the first to be let down into the dark, filthy and stinking cell and it was like hell instantly she got in. Immediately she got into this dungeon, she knew she indeed would need brightness to move around and her mind went to her solar-powered mobile's LCD, *Liquid-crystal display*, but before she could put this on, Pott was let down into the dark cell too. While Shea was still trying to get her mobile's LCD on, Pott had got hold of his explorer's kit from his rucksack and switched on the handy torchlight he took *out* from inside it.

None the less, this cell seemed empty, as Pott's beam of torchlight was traveling around through the darkness in the dungeon. Though, one thing made them suspicious that it wasn't indeed void and that was because it stank of rottenness. They both wondered what could be stinking so horribly in this dungeon and this charnel smell further strengthened their curiosity to find out. Shea was moving cautiously behind Pott, who was searching through the dark cell's chambers with the beam of his tiny, bright torchlight. Surprisingly to them, the horrible cell seemed endless and empty, as it took them from one underground to another. Certainly, they did never expect it would be so vast, therefore, fear gripped both of them when suddenly they heard the sound of movement.

"What was that?" whispered Shea.

"Someone moved?" she added, before Pott could say a word.

"I'm not sure what that could be, Snow!" muttered Pott.

They talked to one another quietly, as if they didn't want someone else to hear their voices. Pott continued to move quietly towards the direction of the sound *of this movement* they heard, until the beam of his torchlight fell on a thin, malnourished little girl with

13

her eyes sunk deep into her head. She was trying to hide from them in a corner and they were so aghast to find her alone in this darkness, also at the condition in which they found her.

"Are you okay, lovely?" asked Shea quickly, with a grin that easily assured this girl that she was a friend. She still continued to shy away from them, turning her face away from the beam of Pott's torchlight and at a point, she tried to bury her bony head with her shriveled, shaking hands, spying at them through in-between her fingers.

"She isn't only perishing from hunger, she's also starving from affection." whispered Pott.

Shea quickly took out of her rucksack a piece of biscuit and moved closer to this hunger perishing girl. She bit the biscuit gently to exhibit her intention to this innocent girl and pointed the rest to her with a friendly smile. Immediately, she turned to Shea, stretching her weak hand to reach for the biscuit. She took the biscuit from her gently and slowly aimed for her mouth. This malnourished girl gave the energy-giving biscuit a weak bite, looking at Shea as she squatted beside her, holding her hand softly and caringly. She rested her head on Shea's arms, biting weakly and gently into this piece of biscuit. Pott came closer and handed to Shea a bottle of mineral water, which Shea poured into her palms and gave the girl to drink. Though, she did only have a taste of the water, it was so relieving for her that in a short while she already began to fondly look at Shea and Pott. Shea drew her closer again and rest her head on her chest, while she continued to manducate the piece of biscuit in her hand and Shea's eyes began to trickle with tears, but she persevered not to distract this fragile girl with her emotions.

Subsequently, the girl continued to look straight into the beam of Pott's torchlight as she stood *weakly* before them on her feet. Though, nearly all her skeletal system was obvious through her skin, yet, she seemed spirited by her visitors. She began to walk away, beckoning to them to follow her. Shea and Pott were concerned and somehow scared of whatever might lie ahead. However, they followed her as she took them through the dark cell's chambers and passages, until they came to a small opening that led further underground. The girl entered into the opening straightaway and descended further into the darker underground of the dungeon. Pott aimed the beam of his torchlight into the opening and saw no one, only the stairs that this girl dismounted.

"Where's she?" asked Pott, as he used the beam of his torch to search the domain, as far as he could see from his position, yet saw no one.

"She's somewhere down there!" whispered Shea.

"Be careful, Snow." warned Pott, as Shea too was dismounting the stairway.

He dropped the torch into Shea's hands before he followed her into this dungeon's darker underground. The chamber they descended into was empty as their torch's beams unveiled, but immediately they walked into another passage, the beam of their torch fell on the unfortunate little girl, standing in the thick darkness of the dungeon and beckoning to them again to come after her. Nevertheless, her creepy behaviour began to be *seemingly* scary to Shea and Pott. Though, they both understood she wasn't a menace to them in anyway after all, they knew *perhaps* she had something to show them.

As Shea and Pott continued to walk after this girl, they began to perceive the smell of strong stench again, so heavy that they had to cover their nostrils with their hands this time. Eventually, the girl led them to a big chamber, full of impoverished, naked, hunger beaten children. Some were so weak, they couldn't even stand on their feet and on their bodies were visible marks of serious torture, mutilations, cuts, burns and whiplashes. These marks were still fresh on few of them.

"Oh, my Gosh!" gasped Shea, at the sight of these severely impoverished children.

Pott's eyes immediately went through these children quickly, Shea started to check the breathing and heartbeat of the dying ones and painfully for her, she found some of them cold dead already. She quickly began to revive the ones that were still breathing. Afterwards, she managed to put some biscuit crumbs into the mouths of the ones she could revive and sprinkled water on the faces. They licked the water drips, tripping on their faces down to their lips. Afterwards, some opened their eyes and looked at their new visitors. One crawled to touch Shea for more crumbles of biscuit and taste of water. He opened his palm and Shea poured the last crumbs she was sharing into his hand. He gave Shea a stifled smile, as he looked preciously at the biscuit dust on his palm.

However, while Shea was on her life saving sorting out on these hunger perishing children, Pott had gone *on the lookout* into the chambers of this horrible *seemingly* endless dungeon, using the bright light on his mobile after he had helped in reviving the dying children. In some of these chambers he found skeletons of children and in some decaying bodies, all of children of course.

"Pott!" called Shea repeatedly, when there was no sign of him.

She got hold of the torchlight Pott hung *by the door* on a post and beamed its rays around the dark dungeon, yet, there was no sign of Pott. She looked at these children and found out that all she could do was to move them to the upper floor of the dungeon. She beckoned to them to follow her and some of them, who hadn't recovered fully from their exhaustion, still they managed their strength to crawl after Shea while some walked on all fours. At the sight of these children clinging to life, Shea was deeply moved to tears by their endurance, perseverance and determination, but tried as much as possible to bury her emotions within her.

She helped them to climb up the stairs to the upper floor of the dungeon and led them to the *previous* place, where they met the first girl. She sat them down on the ground and from her rucksack brought out some more biscuits, canned foods, chocolates and everything edible. She made tiny meals on their palms and every one of the children ate *gently*.

Though, unknown to Shea and Pott, these hunger perishing children's spirit were uplifted by their outlandish visitors, even more than the food given them. Anyway, they continued to awe *within themselves* at the torchlight and the mobiles' LCDs.

"There's only one way out of this hell of a place, as far as I could find." said Pott, as he was walking towards Shea, out of the dungeon's darkness.

"Where have you been?" asked Shea, but before Pott could answer.

"You've got me worried." she added.

"Sorry, Snow." apologised Pott.

"Got to find a way out of this damn place, but I think there is ain't no other way than the only way we came in." declared Pott.

"It's really horrible out there and fucking down there!" said Pott ruefully, as he was pointing his hand to demonstrate his words.

"Really, really, really disgusting, Snow." drawled Pott.

"These are the lucky ones." he hinted and Shea understood what he was trying to say, as she could imagine what terrible dehumanisation these children had been enduring *all along*.

"You mean more dead ones down there?" responded Shea.

"What the hell's going on?" asked Shea, looking quite woebegone.

"This place had been for ages, I guess, and I'd think it's kept as traditional, eternal separation. There are age long skeletal remains out there. Though, all of children." muttered Pott sadly.

"Why'd anyone do this to children?" she queried.

"Look at all the children and find out." said Pott.

Shea looked at the children and noticed that one thing was common to them, they were all tortured, with the marks of these still fresh on the bodies of some of them. Instantaneously, the okapi riding lad came into Shea's thought with his unusual eyes and inability to hear or talk.

"This place's kept for accused children." she said. She sadly turned to Pott.

"C'mon, Snow! Wake up! They aren't only kept here, they were abandoned here without mercy to die of hunger and disease. This place is their some kind of hell." mouthed Pott.

"They are condemned as castaway to rot in this hell." he groaned sadly.

"Condemned?" retorted Shea.

"These are the newly condemned ones and that's why we meet some of them alive." said Pott to Shea, who was looking at the children sympathetically.

"What'd these innocent children have done?" asked Shea.

"What'd they have been accused of, Pott?" asked Shea further with puzzled mien.

"I ain't sure, Snow." answered Pott.

"This is total cruelty against these innocent children." cried Shea.

"What're you talking about, Snow?" queried Pott.

"Among primitive people you're talking of children's right!" snorted Pott.

"Or the fucking human right we don't even have in our own so called civilised world?" remarked Pott.

"Oh, c'mon Pott, save me this primitive bullshit." said Shea.

"Primitive or not, they've got senses!" snarled Shea.

"Eh, relax." said Pott with hand gestures.

"Yeah, in our own modern world where we've got good social structure and children's right, yet, greed, wickedness, sadism and corporate dominance are causing even the most noble ones to perpetrate worst and most heinous crimes than this." commented Pott.

"Are you justifying what is going on here?" queried Shea.

"No, don't get me wrong, au contraire, I'm only saying, don't compare our world with theirs." replied Pott.

"No matter what, I see them as victim of ignorance." remarked Pott.

"But in our civilised world, would you infer our hegemonies are suffering from ignorance?" asked Pott.

"I guess you're right." said Shea lugubriously.

Shea looked at the children again and her eyes screened over the cuts on them and also the deformity on some of them. She found it hard to understand why they were abandoned. However, she thought, perhaps it was for cultural reasons.

"I'd think the beast riding lad we saw is a fugitive, already." guessed Shea.

"I'd think so, too!" murmured Pott.

"But why are they so panicky of him?" muttered Shea to herself.

Shea and Pott slept in the dungeon that very day, however, what was worrying them most wasn't their captivity and the whiff in the air. Their main worry was how they could keep the children alive. They rationed the little food they had among these children, while they themselves went on without eating.

They also tried to reach Mother Endor on their mobiles, but where they were was obstructive to GSM, *Global System for Mobile Communications*. Nevertheless, Shea took the pictures of the bodies and skeletons in the chambers on her phone, while Pott videoed the dark cell's scenes on his mobile with its superb video light that fascinated these children so much.

Shea began to teach the children some of the functions on her mobile, indeed, the moving pictures made their hearts jumped and they were amazed at the cartoons they were watching, with an amused expression written all over their faces. Even, these spirited them more than food, as they happily watched, laughed and loved what they were seeing.

In fact, it was torturing for Shea and Pott to witness such a deliberate abuse of children. On their life they didn't expect such an encounter in this mission, therefore, Shea's mind echoed one of Mother Endor's lessons.

"She was right." she said.

"Who was right, Snow?" asked Pott.

"Mother, of course!" said Shea excitedly.

"Inkling me, Snow." said Pott.

"'Lesson Three: Don't be a witch at all times, live as one of them and you never know what experience might await you.'" quoted Shea.

"If we hadn't been here or had resorted to use of psychic means to escape from the hands of our captors, we wouldn't ever have known about these innocent children. Perhaps, their plight would entirely elude our knowledge." she reasoned.

"No one could easily discover the entrance of these dungeon, it was cleverly hidden and if we hadn't been sent here we wouldn't have been aware it existed. I'd agree with you that she was indeed right." replied Pott.

"I do think we'd try our best possible to liberate these kids, but what are the chances and how are we to continue to feed them here?" suggested Pott, while Shea brightened up her mobile's LCD light, as she was looking for a place to hang it for brightness in the dungeon. She found a crack in the wall that was suitable. The children were fascinated by this *LCD* light of Shea's mobile, as they mused their eyes on it, and by Pott's torchlight, too, every time he switched it on and off. They all gasped at these lights with amazement every time their musing eyes were interrupted by their going on and off. They took Pott's torchlight and examined the object with reverence of sort, as if it was magic.

None the less, Pott couldn't help spraying his fragrance into the air because of the malodour in the dark cell and these children also couldn't help but breathe deeply the scented air of Pott's fragrance with all delight.

Finally, the early morning sun dazzled narrowly into this dark dungeon when the hunters came – *led by the 'OluOde'*. They lifted the small, disguised wooden door of the hidden entrance into the dungeon and let down the long, bamboo made ladder for their strange captives to come out, which Pott quickly helped Shea to climb.

"Egbin, *untouchable strangers!*" cried the 'OluOde', *the generalissimo of hunters.*

"We have to get in touch with Mother!" shouted Pott to Shea, as he was climbing this ladder after her, some of the children who dared to climb after them with the eagerness to get out were shook off the ladder mercilessly by the hunters.

"Eewo, *taboo!*" cried 'OluOde' repeatedly, as he got hold of this ladder and shook off these unfortunate children.

Shea and Pott were led to the palace's hall of gathering under guard by these hunters and as they approached, they began to hear voices and one unfamiliar voice particularly sounded different.

"'At the advent of the forbidden soul, the beast of the gods and the ancestors will depart from the palace,' says our ancient oral prophecy." Shea and Pott were within earshot of this quote by the supreme griot of this lost tribes, as they approached. This didn't make meaning to them because they had no idea of the local language of these lost tribes and whatever they were discussing. It was their first full sight of Eboru's palace since they were sent to the dungeon directly from the market centre.

Entering the hall of gathering, Shea and Pott found the chiefs and elders of Eboru gathered *traditionally*, but unknown to them were the wild live, *animals, – that adorned the throne of Eboru* – which had fled the palace to Igbo with Ajala on the day he came to rescue his mother. Therefore, they called for the supreme griot of these lost tribes to interpret this dire occurrence.

As soon as they entered the hall of gathering, almost all the faces they met there were familiar to them because they had cognizance of many of these faces from their hiding position, that very first day the 'eternal bird' led them to the lapidation ceremony of Ajala's mother.

The hunters who tracked the footprint of Ajala's okapi that very day, in order to find out the exact direction Ajala went, confirmed they discovered the prints of lions, jaguars, tigers, leopards and cheetahs exiting the palace and traveling with Ajala's hoof footed beast. They affirmed that no doubt these were the tracks of Eboru's palace animals being taken away by Ajala and the tribespeople dwelled on this to further buttress that Ajala was the predicted forbidden soul.

However, Eboru's throne was naked without its wild life adornment and hence the chiefs and elders of Eboru sent for this supreme griot to inkling them, if this phenomenon had any connotation in their oral prophecies and histories. Indeed, it did, as spoken by the supreme griot and in turn overheard by Shea and Pott, as they were being led to the palace, under the guard of these towering hunters.

Immediately Shea and Pott entered the hall of gathering, they saw a man standing in the middle of the gathering, full of grey hairs and beard, his face was radiating wisdom and his eyes shining with insight, as he gently turned to them. Instantly, Shea and Pott knew this was the voice they heard, as they drew near to this palace hall. He was staring at them while their eyes were wandering round the gathering, scanning through all the inimical faces they did saw at the rally of final judgment against Ajala's mother. They forthwith noticed that the man sitting on the throne of Eboru was the same person on whom the fire *of the gods* fell the previous day.

Pott reminisced his face vividly in his memory, as he saw the fire fell on him. Shea and Pott turned to look at one another and cued for capturing the scenes on their mobiles. Shea's eyes caught some baskets full of different fruits in a corner, she pointed and gestured she was hungry. The 'OluOde' signaled to one of the hunters to fetch Shea and Pott some fruits from the basket to eat, but the man on the throne quickly forbade him.

"The regent of the great throne of Eboru speaks, there shall be no food for these intruders." he said.

"Egbin ni won, *they're untouchable strangers,* and they must be starved to death." he added. This seemed shocking to all that were present, as they looked with surprise and disapproval into one another's eyes, but the supreme griot of oral history and prophecies of these lost tribes remained calmed and quiet, with his wooden staff in his hands. Then, he raised his face up, towards the regent.

"'No accused stranger in Eboru shall be neither starved deliberately nor maltreated until tried, judged and condemned by the gods', says the tradition." quoted the supreme griot ad lib, facing the regent, as he related from the stupendous volumes of poetic history and prophecies, which were stored in his memory about these lost tribes.

"Who're you to dictate to me?" shouted angrily the regent of Eboru at supreme griot and the whole gathering fell into prostration before him.

"Kabiyesi, *your majesty!*" cried the gathering.

The regent turned his glower at Shea and Pott, as they and the supreme griot were the only ones remaining to prostrate and until after Shea and Pott went flat on their bellies like lizard as the others did he reclined back on his throne.

Afterwards, an elder from the gathering came forward, stood in front of the regent, before he turned his eyes on Shea and Pott.

"Perhaps they haven't eating since we incarcerated them in the dungeon among the untouchables. They are strangers on our land and it's forbidden to starve strangers, whom the gods hadn't tried, judged and condemned, according to the mores of the land." affirmed the elder.

"Kabiyesi, *your majesty*!" he said and prostrated.

The regent looked at the elder and his eyes went through the gathering and found out everyone were in support of what the elder had just said to buttress the saying of the supreme griot. He motioned reluctantly that Shea and Pott be allowed to eat.

A basket full of exotic fruits was brought before Shea and another one for Pott, the hunters made them sit on the ground and they were provided each with a calabash bowl of water to drink. Seeing the water, Shea and Pott looked at one another, as they knew they wouldn't drink from this muddy and dirty water. While they were eating, the whole gathering's eyes were on them, which made them really uncomfortable despite the bit of hospitality they were having *from their captors*. When they had had their stomach full, Shea took a huge coconut from the basket of fruits, smashed it on one of the carved stone stool beside her and the chief sitting on it quickly moved aside and frowned at Shea's lackadaisicalness, as she was drinking water from the coconut.

"So – sorry, sir!" she said with a chuckle to the chief and she again smashed one for Pott *on the same stone stool,* to the consternation of this chief. The whole gathering sat with their eyes, examining Shea and Pott and every move they made. Indeed, they waited for them to finish eating, but Pott realised the regent was looking at them suspiciously and inauspiciously.

"Now, it's cleared that the forbidden soul, Ajala, is cursed by the gods and rejected by the ancestors, he must be doomed before he desecrates this land." boomed the regent.

"I, as the regent of the great throne of Eboru, do hereby demand, with no further delay, the immediate execution of the child called Ajala, henceforth." he pronounced.

"Kabiyesi, *your majesty!*" cried the whole gathering with the usual prostration that should go along with his reverence. Only the supreme griot tilted a bow, instead of prostration, due to his old age that didn't allow him such mobility.

"It isn't in the mores of Eboru, for anyone accused of any crime to be executed at sight by fellow mortals, without the trial and condemnation of such accused by the gods. The accused is to be arrested and questioned by the chiefs and the elders, then, condemned in the presence of the gods, if found guilty as charged. However, if all known man to man means to get him or her arrested fails, then, this council may resort to any metaphysical means possible for the arrest or execution of such alleged offender." buttressed an elder.

Of course, the mystical scepter, with which he could pronounce judgment without being challenged wasn't available for a regent. The use of this authority was reserved for the chosen king of Eboru alone. The whole gathering murmured support for this objection and obviously the regent was indeed uncomfortable. He wasn't satisfied and his hatred of the enfant terrible *Ajala* was burning wild the more inside him. Shea and Pott, hearing the name, Ajala, since they came into the hall of gathering, had perceived the name to be that of the okapi riding lad that came for the naked woman at the market centre.

"But it's in the mores of the land that whoever dare venture into Igbo – *the land of the gods or the evil forest* – and came out alive, be executed at sight!" cried the regent angrily, as he suddenly stood up, and the whole gathering fell once again on the floor with the usual hail of him, in reverence of his abruptly getting up the throne.

"Yes, my lord!" cried the supreme griot.

"Kabiyesi!" he added.

"But before this child Ajala is executed for wandering into Igbo, which is a sacrilege according to the mores of Eboru and the tribes. Firstly, he'd have to confess or defend himself against the crime of witchcraft of which he's been accused and for obstructing the traditional public execution of his mother and most notably, for stealing the animals of the throne." he added.

"Kabiyesi!" he revered.

"It isn't certain the child Ajala wandered into Igbo, only the tracks of animals were seen, but neither that of Ajala himself nor of any human that may suggest Ajala went into or out of Igbo – *the land of the gods or the evil forest* – and no one, hitherto, had witnessed Ajala entering Igbo. In a nutshell, all this gathering wants is caution on these looming issues, so that we do not violate the same tradition we're gathering here every day to protect." remarked the supreme griot and everyone murmured support for him.

Nevertheless, the regent remained unsatisfied, but he had nothing to hold on to for his ambition to get Ajala exterminated on sight from defiling the tradition. He knew the chiefs and elders of Eboru were also trying to curb his powers and he was right, because these chiefs and elders believed if they allowed him free pass on everything for the main reason that they wanted Ajala dead, he *perhaps* might get power drunk after all and thereby constitute a terrible obstacle for them in choosing a new king. The regent turned his attention on Shea and Pott instead with a daring look.

"What does the tradition reveal we'd do with these 'egbin', *untouchable strangers*?" he asked, with his hand towards Shea and Pott.

The supreme griot of Eboru turned calmly to Shea and Pott, walked closer to them and Pott got on his legs. He stood in front of Pott closely, his eyes were right before Pott's eyes. He stared into Pott's eyes deeply and turned to Shea too, did the same thing and then walked back before the regent's throne.

"'The arrival of 'egbin', *untouchable strangers*, is a portent of defeat for the forbidden soul, but the gods and the ancestors will resolve their fate.' says the tradition." he related from the oral prophecies of these tribespeople.

"Then, let the official mediums be summoned to the next gathering of this council concerning their fate." ordered the regent. His thought went back to Ajala's issue again and another chance to get at the child erupted in his mind.

"Now, how do we get Ajala here and if we do, how would Ajala, a deaf and dumb child defend himself before us?" asked the regent.

"In my opinion this child was doomed *to die* by the gods,

even before his birth and he has nothing to confess or defend, but only to die!" asserted the regent.

"Yes, we'd also think of this fact that only his mother can communicate with him effectively and perhaps she's dead ...." reasoned a chief.

"We aren't sure his mother's dead, and for him to have stood on the way of justice of the gods against his mother was another sacrilege he committed. I'm sure his mother's alive with him wherever he's now." interrupted another chief of Eboru and this delighted the regent that another glaring offence was being counted on Ajala.

"Let there be bonfire near Igbo at midnight by the renowned members of our hunters and let them ambush and capture Ajala, whom, probably would be attracted by this fire." suggested the supreme griot.

This idea sounded really nice to the gathering, most especially the regent, who wanted no delay in getting Ajala executed. The gathering was relieved, as they muttered to one another about this issue. In fact, this suggestion made sense to them all, although, the Convener, who had remained silent all the while, wasn't convinced yet.

"Kabiyesi!" said the Convener, with prostration before the regent.

"Have we forgotten we sent the great combatant of the gods, the invincible Shigidi against this evil child called Ajala and nothing came off it?" he asked, reminding the gathering of this remarkable fact.

"You're right, but the mistake was ours and not because Ajala's some sort of powerful demigod or in any way protected by the gods. Of course, we offered the invincible Shigidi the wrong sacrifice for the boy's soul. His mother got caught by the same Shigidi because we offered the right sacrifice." said the regent.

"Ajala isn't a boy as we all thought, Ajala's a girl." revealed the regent.

The whole gathering was jaw dropped at this bombshell, as they gently rose to their feet, looking at one another in utter disbelief and many were wondering how their regent came to know this fact. However, they somewhat knew their regent was passionate to protect and preserve the tradition, therefore, he must have been investigating and doing everything possible to achieve this, as expected of him. Anyway, they were all aware of the equivocalness of Ajala's sex, hitherto, they indeed all experienced that sometimes no one could say for sure, if he was a boy or a girl. As no one asked the regent the whys and wherefores of this bombshell about Ajala's real sex, he assumed his hegemony was beginning to earn their trust.

"Indeed, Ajala's nature's a kind of enigma that has given rise to speculations amongst our people." muttered the Convener.

"Let the 'OluOde' of Eboru see to this suggestion of ambushing and make sure that tonight Ajala's caught and presented before this council at our next meeting." pronounced the regent.

"Return these ones to the dungeon of the untouchables, until the next meeting of the council." ordered the regent, and the hunters got hold of Shea and Pott and led them back to the dungeon, but unaware by the gathering, Shea and Pott had sent to Mother Endor texts messages, pictures and video messages they recorded all along, even from the market centre and this council's deliberations *to which they were summoned.*

Fortunately, before they were dropped into the horrible dungeon *again*, Mother Endor's reply was received by both Shea and Pott instantly, in just few words, *focus, courage, endurance, vigilance, and perseverance.* However, they already put their mobiles on silence mode, so that the hunters wouldn't be attracted unnecessarily, when reply would come in from Mother Endor. Albeit, they were surprised the old lady didn't mention anything witchcraft.

The *untouchable* children were happy to see Shea and Pott back, they met them with smiles and excitement, as they came down the ladder into the dark dungeon.

"What are we going to do, now?" asked Shea. She looked at these children, as they crouched around her, starring at her as their light at the end of the tunnel.

"Snow, one thing's sure, we ain't going to leave without them. It's either we die here with them or we liberate them." answered Pott.

"How do we liberate them, Pott?" queried Shea. The beam of the torchlight in her hand was pointing here and there, as if searching for a way out, while Shea stood environed by these children.

Pott took the bright torchlight from Shea and continued to wander around the chambers and passages of this dark, filthy, and vast subterranean dungeon, looking for a *possible* way out. However, the more he moved around in these subterraneous rock-cut, the more he discovered its *seemingly* endlessness and piles of children's skeletons that were evident of the long existence of this child cruelty tradition.

Chapter Three

THE media had taken over the sudden and mysterious disappearance of Erin Eyers and the justified publicity that followed was massive. It was rolled out in the dailies almost every day as front covers, and on the television and radio, no news was complete without reporting Erin's disturbing and bamboozling disappearance.

On the streets and all over central London there were solidarity marches to intensify the search, which created strong awareness of this strange incidence. Erin's posters were everywhere, in the airports and in the planes, train stations and in every train, metros, bus stops, on taxis and in fact everywhere one looked or walked into in the United Kingdom. Erin's poster had the beautiful, innocent face *of this missing girl* that greeted everyone. The Metropolitan police kept briefing and appealing to the public relentlessly for information, though without any substantial tip off that could facilitate a major lead *in the investigation.*

It was during one of these extensive publicity that Mother Endor had a glimpse of Erin parent's interview on one BBC morning show. When the handwriting *borne* of Erin's dream was presented for the public to see, along with the composite photograph of her oneiric African friend, – *created by a sketch artist of law enforcement agent* – who inscribed this handwriting in her dream, Mother Endor was stunned by this sketch artist's near perfect image. She slowly reclined on her chair with rapt attention, eyes fixed on her television screen, listening to Erin's mother as she was narrating how Erin told them about her dream that borne this striking, scattered, mysterious inscription.

On the instant, Mother Endor realised that this composite photograph bore stunning resemblance to the African lad she saw in the pictures and video messages sent to her by Shea and Pott. She took her mobile, played the video messages again, and also viewed the pictures. While doing this repeatedly, she slipped to her text messages and her eyes suddenly caught the word, *hajahlah*. This word Pott managed to write for the okapi riding lad's name, as his ears heard it pronounced when they were taken to the hall of gathering, during the leaders of Eboru's traditional session.

"Eureka?" drawled Mother Endor *ad-libbed*. She covered her mouth with her palms in astonishment.

She also discovered the exactitude of this name Pott sent her, lo and behold, with the one borne out of Erin's dream that was shown on television. She remained mused awhile, pondering if there could be connection between Erin's dream, her sudden disappearance and her psychic generations' prophecy.

Mother Endor's eyes went goggled, as her suspicion was further excited when another identikit image of the African lad of Erin's dream – *made by another artist who neither knew the first sketch artist nor was aware of the image he created* – was shown on television screen during this BBC interview of Erin's parents. In fact, she was able to observe the two images for a considerable amount of time. She compared the two images with her eyes and she could see how no one in his or her rightful mind would deny these two images weren't a true resemblance of the okapi riding lad that Pott and Shea forwarded to her mobile.

However, she got the hunch that if she had to find out anything about these perplexing issues, it would be by having a personal contact with this paper containing the handwriting borne out of Erin's *paranormal* dream, written by the oneiric African lad. Immediately, she picked her phone and dialed the show number that was displayed on the television screen for whoever had information about Erin's disappearance.

"Hello!" she got accosted by a correspondent.

"I'm Mother Endor and I'm watching your interview of Erin's parents about the disappearance of their daughter..." she detoured.

"Do you have any information regarding the girl's disappearance?" asked the correspondent before Mother Endor could make her request. The correspondent in anticipation cut in and Mother Endor took a deep breath that was audible at the other side *of the phone call*.

"My dear, to be candid, I just want a personal contact with the handwriting borne of Erin's dream." confessed Mother Endor.

"Guess you're a psychic?" replied the correspondent bluntly.

"Yeah." responded Mother Endor sharply.

"Since you're trying to help, I'd try to help you also. Nevertheless, I think the girl's parents would have to decide if they do want to involve a psychic in the search for their daughter." said the correspondent.

"Kindly leave your phone contact with me and as soon as we establish an approval with Erin's parents, we'll call you to let you know. Are you alright with that, ma'am?" asked the correspondent.

"Brilliant!" confirmed Mother Endor and immediately dictated her phone contact.

"Thank you very much." expressed Mother Endor.

"No worries!" mouthed the correspondent.

"Bye!" they both finished the word together.

Mother Endor placed the phone handset in its fix and reclined again on her chair, musing about this whole confounding scenario. Suddenly, she sat up to browse through the pictures and video messages again and as she continued to do this repeatedly with keen interest, she realised she had to run these shots on her computer for better viewing. She went to her desktop and downloaded these pictures and video messages and she continued to watch them in different resolutions. Then, she copied Ajala's video on a disc, but she left the other videos and the text messages on her mobile's memory. While she was still doing this, her phone rang and she quickly, as fast as she could, got up from her computer desk and picked the call.

"Hello! Am I talking to Mother Endor?" asked the erstwhile correspondent from the BBC.

Instantly, she recognised her voice but at the same time remembered she didn't ask for her name during their previous discussion.

"Yes, sweetheart!" confirmed Mother Endor.

"Good, the girl's parents aren't willing for a psychic's interference." said the correspondent.

"Sorry about that, ma'am!" said the correspondent *politely*.

"Thanks for your help, darling!" replied Mother Endor.

"If I may ask, who am I speaking with?" she asked *quickly*.

"My name's Lucy Kickstone!"

"I'm grateful for your help, Lucy." said Mother Endor.

"That's alright, ma'am."

Instantly the voice cut off. However, Mother Endor was still holding the handset to her ears, as if still receiving the call because her mind had wandered deeply within her, thinking of what to do next. While she was entirely lost in her own thought, the handset slipped from her ear, down to her chest before she shuddered out of her absentmindedness and realised she was still holding the piece. She looked at the handset and smiled briefly before placing it right in its fix. While she rested her hand on the piece, she continued to gaze at it until her mind geared her up to an idea of what she would have to do. She mused over this idea for a while before she went to her computer and ejected the last disc she copied Shea and Pott's video messages of Ajala and kept it safe in its cover.

Straightaway, she headed to the borough of the Eyers family to browse through the voter's register, peradventure, she could come across their home address and post code. She did recollect that the family's GP, who was also with the Eyers at the interview, mentioned Covent Garden when she was talking about Erin and her parents' visit to her surgery.

When she got to this borough, luck did smile on her when she met a fellow-witch, who was a staff at the borough's offfice. She raised her eyeballs from the desktop before her forthwith she was hit by Mother Endor's *psychic* aura as she entered. She cued invisible, mystic sparks from her eyes directly into Mother Endor's eyes with no one suspecting their psychic transmission. When Mother Endor received the psychic signal, she turned to behold where this mystic signal was projected and her eyes fell on this benign fellow witch, whose mien immediately overwhelmed Mother Endor with friendly disposition. Mother Endor raised her left eyebrow and her left eye glowed brightly in acceptance and as she walked to take a seat before her *fellow-witch*, their astral selves emanated from their bodies and these walked into a big room, while their physical-selves continued to exchange pleasantries without the people around suspecting they knew each other.

"What does a witch of Avalon seek in this place?" asked the staff's astral self.

"Er, – er, a witch of Endor." she replied with a make-believe frown.

"On a personal investigation." added Mother Endor's astral self.

"About the missing girl?" queried the witch staff.

31

"I can perceive your thought, O hag of Aval ... Endor!" said the staff and they laughed together.

Then, Mother Endor remained silent looking at her, not willing to go into details. The staff quickly realised the import of Mother Endor's silence and she immediately offered her a seat and placed before her the register she quested.

"I know what you're seeking, but I don't know why this concerns you so much." said the witch staff.

"I can see that an ancient secret burns deeply in your psyche, old witch." she commented.

Mother Endor wasted no time talking, as she wouldn't let out to any fellow-witch the details of her mission. She was already flipping through the register's pages, as soon as it was placed before her and suddenly her eyes hunted out the Eyers name, address and post code. She looked at this find with a deep smile all over her wrinkled face and her scattered plaque teeth exhibited towards her helper. She closed the register and gave it back to this witch staff.

"Thank you!" she said.

"I'll never forget this kindness!" she mouthed, as she walked straight to the door, looked back at her, tilted a bow and to which she returned the same. She walked out of the room and straightaway her astral-self entered back into her mortal body, as she was discussing with the mortal body of the witch staff.

"You're welcome!" whispered the witch staff.

Immediately Mother Endor's astral-self arrived into her mortal self, her fellow-witch's astral-self came into her body, too.

"Thanks a lot for your help!" said Mother Endor. Then, she got up and left, but before she exited she looked back at her and tilted a bow again.

On getting home, she took the disc, where she copied Shea and Pott's video messages about Ajala *fortuitously* coming to their rescue, enveloped it and addressed it to Eyers mother. At the other side of the envelope she wrote her own address. She walked to the post office, bought stamp for the envelope and posted this clip to them.

Then, she went home calmly with *the* firm hope that very soon she would hear from Erin's parents, except if they wouldn't get her parcel.

Chapter Four

ON the seventh day of Shea and Pott's incarceration, the bamboo made ladder was coming down *once again* through the small opening into the dungeon. The ladder touched the floor of the dungeon before Pott opened his eyes and saw rays of light from above, as it shown into this dark subsurface. He quickly put off Shea's mobile LCD light and woke her up. They were indeed both weak from hunger, as the food and water that they had with them ran out some days ago. Though, the hope of getting out to daylight once more strengthened them a bit.

"Egbin, *untouchable strangers!*" cried one of the hunters, looking down through the small opening. Shea and Pott climbed out of the dungeon by this ladder into the hands of the hunters.

The children were asleep around Shea and they slept deeply because they were so comforted by their presence. They weren't in anyway bothered by the husky voice of the hunter. They all slept and didn't wake up to see Shea and Pott climbing out of the dungeon with their rucksacks on their backs, as usual. On getting out, they saw that the sun was just surfacing and while Shea was looking at this *emerging* twilight, her mind was musing over the hardship and endurance of these innocent children incarcerated in total darkness.

They were *once more* led to the hall of gathering where they met the regent and the chiefs and elders of Eboru already seated. Shea and Pott were made to sit on the ground. Now, getting out of the dungeon was another opportunity for them to communicate with Mother Endor. While Shea and Pott were cautiously trying to text Mother Endor, there came into the hall of gathering a dwarf woman surrounded by seven naked hunchback men. Their bodies were pierced from head to toe and also heavily festooned with all sorts of charms. These hunchback men were without covering, but their pubic hair had grown into long locks that shielded their manhood properly. Their protruded back was also festooned with different kind of fetishes and on their heads were weird dreadlocks, dangling with cowries and shells of different types and shapes.

The dwarf woman was having human skull dangling on her

neck and round her waist were bones of human hands, arranged to detail in their skeletal form and fitted together on a bottom length black leather loincloth. She held big scapulae in her hands, with which she slowly beat through the air from time to time, one after the other.

Immediately she entered the hall of gathering, she walked before the throne and tilted a bow before the regent, together with her hunchback men.

"You're welcome!" greeted the regent.

"The people of Eboru welcome you." he added, shaking his white fly-whisk towards them.

"Who're these 'egbin', *untouchable strangers,* and what shall we do with them?" asked the regent without wasting time, pointing his white regalia fly-whisk to Shea and Pott.

"I want to know everything about them, why they're here and where they come from?" added the regent.

The dwarf woman didn't say a word. After bowing down again, she turned her back on the regent and walked few steps to her hunchback team. The men in a slowed motion movement, as if under spell, formed a circle around her and while these seven hunchback men slowly moved clockwise around her, the dwarf woman was turning anticlockwise on the spot where she stood, with open arms, holding out sideways the big human scapulae in her hands. Shea and Pott watched as they began to murmured, groaned and hummed incomprehensible incantations and spells.

"They're shamans." said Pott.

"Shamans?" retorted Shea.

Shea wondered why the regent, chiefs and elders of Eboru involved shamans and invited them to witness their conjuration.

"They aren't just shamans, they're dangerous necromancers." hinted Pott.

"They can manipulate the living through the dead." he added.

"The circle made by the hunchback men is the world of the living and the contrary motion they started is to psychically usher in the world of the dead into the world of the living," explained Pott.

"You mean to manipulate us?" whispered Shea.

"Ay, us, the living in question." replied Pott.

"They want to manipulate us to confess by ourselves why we're here?" asked Shea.

Suddenly, under the watchful eyes of everyone in the

gathering, the ground within the circle that was formed by these seven hunchback men opened into an abyss. The dwarf woman at the centre and her seven hunchback team were now standing on an empty space, – *on the surface of this abyss* – but they continued their magical counter circumgyration movement, as if they weren't aware there was a bottomless pit opened underneath their feet.

However, dark clouds of horror started rushing out of this abyss underneath the dwarf woman and her hunchback team. These dark clouds spread all over the roof of the hall of gathering like a smoke and formed a mushroom shape, as they continued to ascend and descend nonstop. The dwarf woman and her seven hunchback team were soon covered from the sight of everyone by these horror clouds.

Consequently, as these terrifying, mushroom shaped clouds continued to flutter up and down, their umbrella top began to circumrotate both clockwise and anticlockwise. Then, scary voices, horror cries, terrifying shrieks and dashing movements – *as if closing in from all sides* – were audible from these clouds. Many that were present saw the faces of their dead loved ones in this strange phenomenon and some heard messages whispered to them directly by their dead loved ones. Even Shea heard the voice of her late grandmother speaking to her.

"Oh, Shea, this is a daunting lifetime mission you took on yourself." said her grandmother.

"Granny!" cried Shea.

"My little flower!" she called.

Shea was stone-stunned because she knew only her grandmother called her by this sobriquet. She bursted into tears when she saw her in these clouds coming towards her. At a stone throw distance, she threw to her an ornamented, heart-shaped golden locket, having a red gemstone on one side and a blue gemstone on the other side. Inside the red gemstone was written the message, '*I love you granny*' and inside the blue gemstone on the other side was another message, '*From your little flower*'. When Shea de facto caught this apport in her fingers and read these messages, she couldn't get her head around this occurrence. None the less, she knew where this apport came from and the sentimental value behind it.

"Wear it, my little flower, right now." said her grandmother.

Shea was dumbfounded, as tears continued to stream down

her cheeks.

"I love you, my little flower." said Shea's grandmother and turned her back, after waving her goodbye.

"Oh, granny!" she groaned, as the old lady continued to walk away.

Pott was trying to calm Shea, who was shaking out of her innermost feeling, as she opened the locket and saw her baby photograph on one side and her grandmother's ninetieth birthday photograph on the other. In a flash she remembered those happy days behind the locket. She remembered the moment she dropped this significant locket into her granny's grave during burial. While Pott was calming her, he also suddenly heard the voice of someone dear to him.

"Hey, asshole!" heard Pott.

Instantly, he knew it was the voice of his most intimate *late* teenage friend and when he looked up to the clouds' mushroom roof, there he saw him in the circumrotating, umbrella-shaped cap of these dreadful phenomenon.

"What the hell are you doing up there, John?" asked Pott out of speechlessness.

"It's John!" said Pott to Shea with agitated excitement and Shea knew he was probably having his own episode of what did just happen to her.

"Calm down!" said Shea, trying to encourage him, as she was putting on the apport she received from her grandmother.

"I'd be the one asking you that fucking question, man!" responded John, as Pott was staring at him absentmindedly.

"Miss ya lot, asshole." said John. Pott instantly bursted into tears.

"Calm down, please!" encouraged Shea.

"You've got to be focused." advised Shea.

"I can't calm down, he was my best friend and he died protecting me!" he hinted Shea with a heavy heart that was entirely immersed in profuse tears and running nose.

"These primitive guys are no joke, jackass. What the fucking heaven are you doing putting your badass on the line!" said John to Pott.

"Oh, Jesus f-u-c-k-i-n-g Christ!" grumbled Pott, as he drawled the word fucking.

He was deeply heavy at heart that John was still out there, trying to alert him of danger.

"I've got to go, Pott, it's kind of weird here, too. There ain't no beer, no fag and no sex." complained John.

"You know my stuff, man." added John.

Pott nodded his head in acknowledgement to the fact that he did never forget John and his indulgences.

"Gotta go, pal!" he said.

"M-I-S-S Y-A!" drawled John's voice and gradually grew to faint, out of Pott's hearing.

"W-E-I-R-D-O!" cried Pott *furiously*.

"I miss you too, John!" he whispered tearfully, Shea was mopping his tears.

It was a magical moment that astounded everyone because there was no one *who was* present without a message from the dead. However, all this while, either Shea or Pott, one after the other, managed to capture *clandestinely* all scenes on their mobile camera, since they entered the hall of gathering.

All of a sudden, as Pott was still mourning and at the same time trying his best to capture on his camera what was occurring, a portion of the horror clouds fell, hit Pott on his head and instantly vanishing into him. Concurrently, Pott slumped, his mobile fell off his neck as his body hit the ground and the device landed beside Shea. Shea quickly fell on the mobile with the pretence that she was trying to help Pott. She hid it in her pocket but unbeknownst to her, these lost tribes wouldn't even touch anything that belonged to them deliberately, as they were classified untouchables items too, therefore, no one would dare deprive them of their property.

"Pott, are you okay?" asked Shea.

I'm okay, Snow. Replied Pott within him, as he gently rose to his feet.

"We're witches from the other side of the sea, we were led here by the 'eternal bird' and we're here by destiny to help doom the forbidden soul." confessed Pott.

Shea was amazed to find Pott speaking fluently the dialect of these lost tribes, though, she couldn't understand what he was saying, yet the response of the gathering made her aware she was the only one missing out of Pott's speech. However, she later found out that she wasn't so much as stunned as the gathering, when Pott stood before the throne and forcefully opened wide his eyes that were shut immediately the cloud portion hit him.

"You're the forbidden soul!" cried Pott, as he pointed at the regent and the whole gathering was enraged. Though, like a possessed soul, Pott pointed still at the regent, he managed to force his eyes wide open, as he was struggling to resist the power that took control of him. He was stretched on his toes and his eyeballs started to sink into his head as he was doing his damnedest to resist. The regent looked at Pott and at once bursted into a heavy laughter.

"Kabiyesi, y*our majesty!*" cried the gathering, as they prostrated to show their reverence for him in rejection of Pott's insult.

Only Pott was left standing and his finger still pointed at the regent. After a while of him staring at Pott, as he was standing still, pointing accusing finger at him. He shook his white fly-whisk towards his people and they all got back on their seats.

"This 'egbin', *untouchable stranger,* had confessed they're witches, why'd we be enraged by his words, even by his accusation? Hmm, the words of his mouth are as untouchable as his being." ridiculed the regent.

"The conjuration of the shamans had run him mad, kabiyesi!" said the Convener.

"Nevertheless, his insult shouldn't go unpunished." added a Chief.

"Let him be damned, who insulted the soul and sanctity of Eboru by calling me the forbidden soul!" raged the regent.

"I, the regent of the great Eboru, who was chosen in the presence of the whole tribes by the fire of the gods!" he boasted in anger to the quiet gathering, rising to his feet.

"Kabiyesi, *your majesty!*" hailed the gathering in his reverence.

"As the regent of Eboru, chosen by the gods in the presence of all my people, I condemn you to be sacrificed immediately to Ogun, *the god of iron.*" pronounced the regent, standing on his feet, pointing his white fly-whisk at Pott.

"Kabiyesi, *your majesty!*" cried the gathering again.

They remained prostrated in acknowledgement of his verdict of death on Pott. Until he would shake his fly-whisk at them, they didn't dare get up.

Shea, who didn't understand what they were saying, watched

ignorantly as the preparation to behead Pott was going on forthwith the regent pronounced it.

"Do you have anything to say for yourself?" asked the dwarf woman, after she dashed out of her conjuring cloud like a spirit, standing right before Pott.

"I've spoken." answered Pott *sharply*.

Instantly, she dashed back into her enshrouding, conjuring cloud circle, after starring at Shea, who was struggling at the hands of two hefty hunters that held her back from perturbing Pott. All she could do was shouting his name and still making sure her mobile was positioned properly on her neck to capture the scenes. In fact, Pott seemed possessed beyond this world and was totally unresponsive to Shea's voice.

The preparation to behead Pott was on ground at the pronouncement of the regent. A big, flat, table height slab, covered with leather was unveiled in the hall of gathering by two hefty hunters. The two hunters were helped by four other hefty hunters to remove the cover of the blood stained, table height slab. On both sides, inside of the stone's flat surface were carved out perfectly the shape of human figure to fit in into the space, so that only the neck and the head of the condemned would be visible and the other parts of the body entirely trapped within the slab.

Immediately, Shea knew that the inside of this stone, *the human figure shaped spaces,* were carved for beheading purpose and she could perceive from time immemorial the age long existence of this ritual stone of doom and the souls it had consumed. Pott was quickly prepared to fit into the space in-between these heavy slabs and only his neck and head were poking out for severing.

When the hunters finished this preparation, they took their positions and one of them went straight into the inner chamber of the palace, with the eyes of the chiefs and elders of Eboru *village* awaiting his arrival, as they focused their attention on the door he went through. After a while, he came out and following him was a stout, middle-aged, gor-bellied giant of a man. Human bones were laced in exoskeletal pattern along his body as covering, his head within the skull-mask of these bones. In his hand was a unique, big, sharp, flat headed cutlass, designed to *be in* arch-shape at the flat end that was finely sharpened for beheading. Shea's eyes popped up at the sight of this terrible head chopper and his freaky cutlass. Of course, she has never seen anything of such a scary killing implement before and instantly realised there was no saving Pott from this ritual killer.

When the chiefs and elders of Eboru saw this head chopper, they breathed a sigh of satisfaction and smiled to one another. This stolid head chopper *in waiting* quickly took his position beside the slab with his unique, flat headed cutlass raised, ready for the signal from the regent to chop off Pott's head at one stroke. It was a dreadful moment for Shea, as Pott seemed possessed and entirely unaware of what was going on around him.

While the preparation for the beheading of Pott was in progress, the enchantment of the dwarf woman and her hunchback team continued. None the less, as the head chopper lifted up his cutlass, waiting for the regent's signal to chop off Pott's head in honour of Ogun, *the god of iron*. There was a sudden, massive, gruesome stampede that heavily rocked the earth, terrorising the gathering to a standstill.

Apart from the fact that this terrible stampede was unthinkable for the gathering, the thought of how to respond to this happening, too, caught them napping. The villagers ran into their houses and hid themselves from being trampled underfoot or crushed by this gruesome onrush. The more this large-scale stampede got closer to the palace, the more everyone got terrified. When this stampede seemed at the doorsteps of the palace, it abruptly stopped and it was like waking up from a nightmare for the regent and the chiefs and elders of Eboru *village,* as they all heaved a sigh of relief.

Then, through the door of the hall of gathering slowly emerged Ajala on a magnificent zebra, with sun rays shown behind him as he came in. There was confusion in the gathering, everyone panicked and many clung to one another out of fear because the name Ajala in itself had been tied to unspeakable evil in their minds and in the mind of every one of these tribespeople – *though unwitting by the lad.*

However, the necromancers and Pott were indifferent to what was happening around them and the head chopper also – *who held his position still to chop off Pott's head* – was more focused on carrying out his duties, despite the pandemonium around him.

As soon as Ajala's zebra stood before the gathering, the hunters seemed to await order from the regent to attack him, but after him gently walked in seven lions, tigers, leopards, hyenas, jaguars, giant gorillas, huge rhinos and boa constrictors, all in a stalking move, followed by myriads of different types of venomous snakes. These swarmed into the hall of gathering *en masse* and crawled on everyone, even under their covering, holding them into transfixion. The robust ones reared up around Ajala, charging against everyone, as they safeguarded him. The hunters, seeing these animals, immediately withdrew from their *potential* action. Some of these animals came into the hall of gathering with fierceness that threatened everyone into subjection.

Ajala on his zebra was looking at the gathering with confidence and effrontery none of them had seen in a child before, albeit, all potential threats to his person were being warded off by his animal friends. Everyone had snake's fang displayed around them and these threats were indeed ubiquitous. The hunters holding Shea let go of her, as these animals were coming in and Shea herself was surrounded by seven reared up cobras.

These animals demonstrated their readiness to strike if anyone would attack Ajala. They held their position against the gathering with much precision that there was neither room for movement, nor escape for anyone. Then Ajala shifted his attention on the necromancers, who were still chanting inside the conjured, dark mushroom-like shape clouds that enshrouded them. He was really surprised at their magic, when his psyche heard voices whispering to him, particularly, calling on his name.

"Ajala, my son," he heard a female voice.

"Worship none, spirit or flesh or whoever or whatever, but love everyone, spirit or flesh or whoever or whatever." said the female voice.

"Please, my son, stand up for yourself in every way, do not be controlled by whatever or whoever, but always remember that love, empathy, sympathy, reason and justice are your foremost tradition and belief. Remember, these are inseparable." she added.

"Don't forget everything I told you." she cautioned.

Ajala was astounded to perceive these voices whispering to him.

"Ajala, my son!" cried a male voice.

"You aren't the Babalawo, the official Ifa oracle custodian of Eboru, the royal priest of Eboru and the chief priest of the whole tribes and you'll never be, O my son!" said the male voice. Ajala was wondering in his mind who this male voice was.

"The great Babalawo hath spoken, I'm your father and you're Ajala my son." claimed the voice. Ajala was bamboozled by this male voice he perceived.

"Yes, Ajala, your father, the great Babalawo of the tribes speaks." said the female voice that previously spoke to Ajala, confirming the male voice.

Ajala looked and inside the clouds there was his mother walking towards him.

"Do not believe in the gods, let the gods believe in you." said Ajala's mother and he realised the female voice he has been hearing was his mother.

"The powers of incarceration and death of the innocents are the cowardice and ultimate doom of rulers, O Ajala!" she remarked.

The gathering in their uneasy position were wondering in their minds what was happening to him, as he focused his attention on the conjuring cloud, shuddering from time to time out of amazement.

While Ajala's mother began to walk away, out of deep-seated passion for his mother, Ajala's unwonted eyes spontaneously went goggled on the dark clouds and instantly shut *back* in reflex. Of course, he couldn't just believe what was going on about these perceptions he was experiencing. Responding to Ajala's unintentional eye movement, the abyss under the dwarf woman and her hunchback team closed up and the part of the mushroom-shaped dark clouds above the ground got trapped, whistling and hustling around agitatedly.

Shea, whose eyes were on Ajala since he came into the gathering, was astonished to see what his eye movement did, but Ajala himself wasn't aware. *As soon as the dwarf woman and her seven hunchback men fell to the ground, the abyss closed up instantly.* The trapped clouds *above the ground* eventually rushed into the dwarf woman and her seven hunchback men, also the portion that fell on Pott came out of him through the *ritual stone* slab and violently rushed into the necromancers. Nevertheless, Ajala himself wasn't aware of what had happened through his fatefully flinched eye contact.

Pott regained his total consciousness and began to struggle to free himself from the slabs immediately the cloud came out of him, as a result of Ajala's unintentional eye movement, which derailed the invocation session of the dwarf woman. While Pott continued to *vainly* in-between these ritual slabs, Shea was still making sure she got all the scenes on her mobile video recording. Pott looked and saw the grotesque head chopper ready to cut off his head and he became deeply terrified.

"What the hell's going on?" he cried.

Of course, the head chopper couldn't lower his cutlass because he had a fierce hyena in-between his legs, clinging to his manhood, while a lion was standing in front of him with a frightening look.

Ajala sat on his zebra bemused of all that was happening, while his infrahuman friends scared, captured and secured unto utter subjection the gathering for him.

Then the dwarf woman rose to her feet and her seven hunchback men sat on the ground around her.

"My name's Ajala, son of the late Babalawo of the tribes. I'm free from your customs, your traditions, your villages and your people. I've nothing to do with you, O Eboru! All I want is peace and this is why I have come here today." the dwarf woman spoke and it dawned on the gathering that the deaf and dumb Ajala was speaking through her. Ajala himself was amazed that his thoughts were being made known by this woman, most especially his reason for coming to the palace. Therefore, he realised he could communicate through her.

Fortuitously, Ajala discovered he could somehow speak through the woman and he was really satisfied, as he continued to communicate through her. The chief and elders of Eboru were stunned, but too scared to utter a word. However, within them they were convinced all the evil they heard and experienced about Ajala were true and he actually was unveiling these maleficence right before their own eyes.

"There'll be no more bonfires to disturb me, O Eboru!" she added *from Ajala.*

"You're the forbidden soul and your place should be with the untouchables or rather, you should be in the grave." answered the regent boldly.

"Moreover, how dare you invade my palace?" shouted the regent.

This prompted the lion, tiger, jaguar, hyena, cheetah and the leopard *some of the former animals of the throne which kept guard around the regent* to rumble at him and, at the sound of these fierce animals, he shivered and reclined on his throne. When the gathering recognised that these animals among the ones that came with Ajala, they were convinced the more that there was no gainsaying that every evil thing they heard about this child was true.

"This is why I have come, let there be no struggle between me and Eboru and the entire tribes." said Ajala through the dwarf woman.

"My late father did laudable services to this land and there's no gain saying he was my father, even if he wasn't my father, I think no one would deny the fact that my mother was my mother and she was born of this land. Therefore, I'm an indigene and a direct link of the ancestors of this land, so I've rights in this land and to this land like anyone here, even, if not more than you all." declared Ajala.

He paused to stare at everyone present, while the gathering was still subdued to him by his animal friends, nobody neither dared move against him, nor say a word, except the bold regent.

"There are allegations against you of which, according to tradition, you must present yourself before this council for your defence." said the regent.

Ajala rode closer to him and continued to look at him straight in the eyes and for these lost tribes this was an affront against the throne.

"You stole the animals of the throne which our ancestors tamed to protect the palace, as evidence of their presence and that of the gods in Eboru." the regent began his allegations against him.

"You violated the ancient tradition of the land of Eboru by stepping into Igbo – *the evil forest and the land of the gods* – which from time immemorial it was forbidden to enter because only the gods can survive living there." the regent continued, as Ajala was still staring into his eyes.

"You attacked the ritual men of the League of Priests and eventually killed a paramount member of the League in the presence of everyone here." he said and Ajala flinched his eyes briskly at these accusation.

"You also revealed the witchcraft and the diabolical tendencies in you when you vanished some nights ago after being caught by the bonfire hunters, who laid ambush to catch you." he alleged, pointing to the hunters that laid ambush for Ajala with a bonfire that night.

These hunters later reported that Ajala vanished after being caught, therefore, they couldn't present him to the gathering as ordered. None the less, under the fierce guard of the wild animals keeping watch over them, the hunters managed to nod their heads in agreement with the regent's words.

Ajala's eyes scrolled through all the hunters, allegedly by the regent to witness his disappearance after being caught on the night of their bonfire ambush.

"And finally we saw what you're doing right now in our presence, by using your tabooed magic to halt official, traditional invocation proceeding and you even took over the mind of our necromancers." alleged the regent further.

Ajala was confused and nonplussed. The regent realised his confusion and he buttressed his allegations against him.

"The same act of witchcraft you're exhibiting now because you're deaf and dumb, yet you're speaking through our official medium." he continued.

"You also obstructed the lapidation of your mother by snatching her away from facing her fatal penalty to the end. Thereby, you prevented her head being stuck to her mud shack, according to tradition and that's a crime punishable in itself by death ..." he accused.

"Let my mother alone!" interrupted Ajala angrily *through the dwarf woman.*

He seemed awakened by the regent's mentioning his mother. This alarmed the gathering, as they remained calmed under the guard of the wild animals around them. Ajala's zebra walked round the gathering while his eyes were examining everyone. Suddenly, his zebra stood on hind legs and whinnied. Ajala patted the animal *with his palm* to calm it down and the animal walked around gently, while Ajala talked through the dwarf woman again.

"Yes, I indeed saw the bonfire that night, but I got the feeling it's a decoy, so I did never approach it. Instead I went further into the forest where I hid myself till morning." said Ajala.

"I neither saw any of your hunters, nor did anyone capture me. I'm neither a witch, nor diabolical and I do not vanish from the hands of anyone, as you alleged." added Ajala.

"Immediately I saw the bonfire I retreated into a cave where I slept that night, because I felt protected there, and for the reason of this bonfire threat I became bold to visit you today to implore you to leave me alone." pleaded Ajala *through the dwarf woman*.

"You're a liar, a coward and the forbidden soul of our ancient prophecy. How could a kid like you vanish, if you aren't a witch?" queried the regent.

"We also heard of your diabolical appearance and disappearance when the League of Priests came for propitiation rituals to purge Eboru and the tribes of your evil fate." the regent further attacked him with allegations.

"You stampeded all these animals and manipulated them to molest us and subdue us to your tabooed wizardry and still you're denying all these glaring allegations?" cried the regent.

"You killed Oleobugije …"

"I didn't kill anyone!" interrupted Ajala *through the dwarf woman*.

"I did never attack the ritual men!" cried Ajala.

"I'm not a murderer, O Eboru!" he cried.

"I didn't kill any member of the League. I'm not a murderer, please! All my life I have neither kill a chicken, nor shed human blood. I've said it, O Eboru! I've nothing to do with you and I have always got nothing to do with you." he added.

As Ajala continued to speak through the dwarf woman, her voice gradually continued to change from that of a matured woman into a girl's voice.

"You've nothing to do with Eboru, but you encroached at Igbo – *the evil forest and the land of the gods* ..." replied the regent.

"I'm the son of the Babalawo, the chief priest of the whole tribe." shouted Ajala on top of his voice through the dwarf woman, interrupting the regent once again and the whole gathering could realise Ajala's passion in the message.

"You're an untouchable and the forbidden soul of our ancient prophecy. You're a taboo to the gods. As the regent of the great and sacred throne of Eboru, I henceforth banish you from Eboru and the tribes if you refuse to give yourself up for the judgment of the gods and the ancestors." pronounced the regent.

Ajala stared daringly at the regent awhile, then, he shifted his unwonted eyes on the chiefs and elders of Eboru and on the hefty hunters around. He looked at Shea where she stood surrounded by snakes, watching the whole scenario and he had a flashback of her on the day he came for his mother. He looked at Pott, who was still trapped within the slabs. The words he heard from his mother and father echoed through his mind and his eyes fell on the regent with a frown.

"I've said it all that I've nothing to do with you, O Eboru! Your traditions, your customs and any of your mores are none of my concern. I'm a denizen of the great Igbo, the evil forest …"

"And Igbo belong to Eboru!" cut in the regent on Ajala with an outburst of anger, as he suddenly rose to his feet.

As usual of the gathering to prostrate in reverence, but when the animals on guard around them murmured back at their intention, they all remained transfixed, calm and quiet from doing any obeisance. The regent looked around to hear his reverence observed, but found his subjects totally overwhelmed. He slowly reclined on his throne, looking at Ajala desperately.

"'The evil forest may belong to Eboru before you were born, but now it belongs to you. I can see you're safe here my son.' said my mother to me before she died." revealed Ajala.

"'You're an illustrious son of these tribes, but do not believe in their gods, let their gods believe in you,' so my mother admonished me and I'm standing up for myself now, until I breathe my last." declared Ajala.

"Moreover, Igbo is called the evil forest because none of you could dare enter, owing to your evil deeds and it's called the land of the gods because only the innocents can live in there and survive. Judge for yourselves, O Eboru! It's my home now." declared Ajala.

"Even, the animals of the throne left you because of your evil deeds, look into your prophecies deeply, O Eboru!" said Ajala through the dwarf woman, as he fixed his conspicuous, unusual eyes on the regent.

"If the gods are so pleased that I'm evil, let the gods themselves vomit me out of their land, but no human has the right to banish me from Igbo, save the gods themselves." shouted Ajala at the regent.

"Not even you!" he drawled with impudence, pointing to the regent. This act of defiance flabbergasted the chiefs and elders of

Eboru.

"Now, I take my leave." uttered Ajala when he found out the regent wasn't willing to say a word to him again because he has made mockery of him by defying his order.

As Ajala turned to exit the gathering, his animal friends still held their positions against everyone. Shea was absorbed in clandestinely capturing the happenings on her mobile *video* that was hung around her neck.

"What're you doing, little flower? He's your lifeline to get out of this condemnation!" Shea perceived her grandmother's voice from the locket *apport* she threw to her. Instantaneously, she was able to perceive everybody's thought and could commune with them, including Ajala.

"Right, now!" cried Pott.

Pott too realised the locket *apport* imparted to Shea the ability to reach Ajala's mind.

"Hey, mister!" shouted Shea.

Ajala was at the doorway, about to totally exit the hall of gathering and he was stunned when Shea's voice hit his psyche. He was spellbound, but after a while he turned his zebra around and his strange eyes straightaway fell on Shea.

"My name's Ajala, son of Ifaloba, the son of the late Babalawo of the tribes." telepathised Ajala with Shea *directly*, which was also perceived by Pott and everyone in the gathering too by the psychic transmission of the apport.

"Lady, who're you?"

"I'm Shea O'Sheperd."

"What happened to him?" asked Ajala quickly, referring to Pott.

"He's to be beheaded for being a witch and for calling him the forbidden soul." replied Shea, referring to the regent. Ajala was delighted at this report.

"Is he the forbidden soul?" he asked Pott, pointing to the regent.

"He already committed the sacrilege of insulting the sanctity of Eboru *village* by calling me the forbidden soul," the regent said to Ajala.

"He's a witch, anyway." he hinted, but Ajala waited for Pott to speak to him by himself.

"What the hell are you guys talking about?" responded Pott.

"I knew nothing about this forbidden soul or whatever you goddamn call it!" added Pott.

Ajala was disappointed he didn't get the answer exactly as Shea informed him.

"Are you a witch?" asked Ajala before Shea could utter another word.

"Yes, I'm a witch." answered Shea.

Instantly, Ajala went goggled-eyed at the pointblank confession from Shea. He knew it was baneful for anyone to confess he or she was a witch, according to the mores of his tribespeople, therefore, he found it strange someone could open up the way Shea just did.

"Is he a witch, too?" he asked, pointing to Pott.

"Yes!" answered Shea. Ajala turned to Pott for confirmation and he nodded agreement in favour of Shea's confession.

"I'm a witch." he added.

Ajala was perplexed someone could just confess to being a witch.

"What's going on here?" he cried.

"Did you realise what you just did to yourselves?" he asked with a frown.

"You're a witch also, Ajala." said Shea.

Ajala was daunted by Shea's *seemingly* accusation, covering his mouth with his hand and his eyes opened wide out of confusion. He turned to Pott with his hand still on his mouth and Pott nodded agreement again for Shea's stance.

"Why is everybody calling me a witch?"

"I'm not a witch!" exclaimed Ajala on Shea with anger.

"I'm Ajala Ifa!" he added, with a direct glower on Shea.

"Since you're witches, I've nothing to do with witches." said Ajala, with a gentle voice, staring at Shea.

Immediately, he turned his zebra towards the exit, Shea realised he wouldn't consent to being called a witch, as this was a crime amongst these lost tribes.

"Please Ajala, take us with you!" requested Shea, as he rode towards the door, but Ajala refused to care. He rode on towards the door, while his animal friends still held their positions against the gathering.

"They'll kill us, Ajala!" shouted Shea.

"See, if you leave us here, they'll kill us." added Shea, pointing to Pott's position and Ajala looked back straight to where Shea pointed her hand and his eyes caught the head chopper, as he remained motionless with his big cutlass raised against Pott's head. He was sweating profusely from the uneasy position the wild animals put him, as also everyone in the gathering weren't at ease either.

Shea knew she still hadn't convinced Ajala to see reason for saving them from the hands of the regent, as he turned towards the exit.

"They'll kill us as they killed your innocent mother." said Shea, as soon as Ajala got to the doorway *once again* to exit the hall of gathering.

She reminded Ajala of his mother's death and as Ajala heard this, he got transfixed *again* at the doorway and somehow seemed confused on whether to respond or not. However, the day he went to rescue his mother flashed back into his senses and he remembered Shea and Pott helping him.

"... but always remember that love, empathy, sympathy, reason and justice are your tradition ..." his mother's words flashed into his mind.

"Do you really want us to die? Do you want these people to kill us as they killed your innocent mother, whom they probably accused of witchcraft, too?" Shea quickly buttressed her argument with reason she perceived would hit Ajala's heart.

Suddenly, Ajala alighted from his zebra, left the beast at the doorway and walked to Shea. His pointed, long gourd penis sheath popped Shea's eyes, as it was directly towards her as he was walking closer. Shea dodged aside slightly, in order to avoid Ajala's long gourd penis sheath, but Ajala ignorantly followed her movement. When she found there was no way out of Ajala's remarkable gourd penis sheath, she knelt on the ground. While Ajala was absorbed with trying to feast his bizarre eyes on her before responding to her request, yet Shea found this pointed thing was directly on her face. Therefore, she recollected that the first time she saw Ajala *on the day he came to rescue his mother,* he wore a different gourd penis sheath that arched towards his navel, ornately engraved, with the groove coloured in reddish ochre.

"You won't die!" cried Ajala to Shea.

"You're a good person." he added. As he continued to look at Shea cap-a-pie with screening eyes, the regent immediately reacted.

"She's evil, they are evil, Ajala!" claimed the regent

"And moreover, she's Eboru's affair." added the regent.

Ajala turned his attention to him, looking at the regent and at the same time shifting his eyes on Shea and Pott at their different positions.

"You gave your words never to interfere in Eboru's affairs, they're out of your reach Ajala and I know you won't go back on your words." the regent reminded Ajala and, as soon as he heard what the regent said, he walked back to his zebra penitently and mounted it. *But always remember that love, empathy, sympathy, reason and justice are your tradition.* Mused Ajala on his mother's words for a while, trying to understand them in reference to Shea's plea, as he was sitting still on his zebra facing the exit.

"Yes, I'll take you with me." said Ajala, as he was sitting still on his beast of burden. He turned his zebra around towards Shea.

"You're my benefactor, lady. No one, except my mother, – whom you alone ever pronounced innocent – since I was born, has ever shown me sympathy, but you did on the day I came for her rescue at the market centre. I'll take you with me." said Ajala *to Shea.*

Shea breathed a sigh of relieve and she smiled to Pott, who nodded his head to her for her well done persuasion.

Ajala took his flute and blew his usual dirge his late mother taught him in a dream, which all the tribespeople knew belonged to him alone. As he continued to sing this song with his flute, two huge gorillas rushed into the hall of gathering and Ajala pointed to Pott. These gorillas went and removed the heavy slab off his body.

"You can't take them away, they're untouchables." argued the regent.

"Today, love begets love, empathy begets empathy, sympathy begets sympathy and reason begets reason. Am I not pronounced untouchable and forbidden by you? Obviously, the same hatred you nurture for me, you also nurture for these strangers too and it'd be a mistake if I let you deal with them, according to the way you dealt with me and my mother" continued Ajala through the dwarf woman.

"By the way, why do you call strangers untouchables?" queried Ajala.

"It doesn't matter if they are strangers or not, we have a tradition here and they are on Eboru's land." argued the regent.

"Can't you see they're different?" he added. Ajala looked at Shea and Pott keenly.

"Yes, they don't look like us, but different or not, I don't care. They showed my mother, who you tortured to death, sympathy and love, even though, you my own people showed us no such kindness." replied Ajala, as he was still looking at them.

"Ajala, your handshake has exceeded Eboru's elbow already. These people confessed to being witches and you did just say you've nothing to do with witches." said Ajala.

"He's to be sacrificed to Ogun, *the god of iron,* for insulting the great throne of Eboru." added the regent, pointing to Pott.

Worship none, spirit or flesh or whoever or whatever, but love everyone, spirit or flesh or whoever or whatever ... do not be controlled by whatever or whoever, but always remember that love, empathy, sympathy, reason and justice are your tradition ... do not believe in the gods, let the gods believe in you. Mused Ajala over *some of* his mother's words that came to his mind again.

"As I live, no harm shall come on any of them and I don't care if you accused them of witchcraft as you did allege I am or you pronounced them untouchables like you *all* dubbed me or forbidden or whatever!" responded Ajala, turning to the regent.

"As for Ogun, your god of iron, let Ogun himself ask me for his sacrifice." challenged Ajala.

"Far be the thought, Ajala!" shouted the regent.

"You dare challenge Ogun, our great god?" cried the regent.

"Yes, but let Ogun be the judge and not you!" cried Ajala at the regent and instantaneously clapped to the gorillas and these beasts led Shea and Pott out of the hall of gathering, while Ajala mounted his zebra and rode around the gathering subdued to him by his animal friends.

"I'm Ajala!" he cried.

"I take my leave, now!" he proclaimed gently, turned to the doorway calmly and confidently exited the hall of gathering.

As soon as he exited the hall, his animal friends began to withdraw after him without hurting anyone. The gathering breathed air of freedom, as Ajala and his friends lifted their burden off them.

Immediately Ajala and his animal friends left the gathering, the regent walked to the door to have a look of what was going on outside and the chiefs and elders of Eboru were jittering after him. The hunters rushed carefully ahead of the regent to protect him, but when they had a view of what was outside, they were all dumbfounded, jaw dropped and many went popeyed out of astonishment and fright.

Actually, they found the whole of Eboru *village* and its skies full of Ajala's friends. Trees, roof-tops, everywhere and also on the horns and bodies of big animals were perched birds of all types. Amidst all these hordes of wild animals were Ajala *on his zebra*, Shea was sitting on a sturdy rhino and Pott on a giraffe and many buffalos, elephants, boas and robust pythons surrounded them.

"Did you see his penis sheath?" alarmed the regent, out of sheer flabbergastation of Ajala's gourd penis sheath.

"It's stupendous!" remarked an elder.

"Deplorable." snorted a chief.

"It's a declaration of defiance." added the official griot and the supreme griot, who was standing beside the regent, nodded his head in agreement when the regent descended his eyes on him for confirmation.

"This evil lad already defied us by his birth." squeaked the regent.

"Kabiyesi, *your majesty!*" responded the griot.

"It's more than that, now." he remarked.

The whole gathering turned their grim look from Ajala *and his friends* towards the griot, because they understood he had a mythicised connotation for what Ajala's gourd penis sheath denoted. Though, unknown to them, Ajala only donned this *symbolic* gourd penis sheath by somnambulation. However, he was entirely ignorant of the traditional affront behind its connotation.

"Kabiyesi, *your majesty,* this is a knotted penis sheath and it's esoteric." revealed the griot.

"Wise one, what did you mean by that?" queried the regent.

"Kabiyesi, *your majesty!*" responded the griot.

"In primordial times, this is the penis sheath the gods called, 'waka', *knotted penis sheath.*" continued the griot.

"Literally, it means, f-u-c-k y-o-u-r m-o-t-h-e-r!" he drawled with a bow.

"What? Our mothers?" the chiefs and elders retorted in shock all together. They were all nonplussed, as they fastened their glare at Ajala.

"And its riddle goes thus," continued the griot, "If a man is married to one's mother, then, he is one's father also, even if he were to be younger and as the Babalawo, *the possessor of secret ancient knowledge and wisdom,* is culturally believed to be the husband of all women and thereby the father *paternal carer* of *all* mankind. In essence, the child is protesting against *our* hegemonic hardheartedness and at the same time laying claim to his late father's position as Babalawo." explained the griot with a side glance to see the regent's reaction.

"In a nutshell, this is totally intolerable defiance." complained another chief.

"This is the way of protest for the gods in primordial times, kabiyesi." postulated the griot.

"But the gods don't have penis, O wise one!" raved the regent.

"Kabiyesi, *your majesty!*" they all cried in reverence of the regent's ireful remark.

"Kabiyesi, you have said well." said the griot.

He moved closer to the regent and whispered into his ears and the regent's eyes went goggled - *in total shock with disbelief –* by what he heard from him. The aged griot nodded his head couple of times to let him know he was sure of the secret he shared with him.

"That's the hidden meaning of Ajala's bizarre 'gourd-knot' penis sheath." added the griot.

"This enfant terrible does not even believe in the gods, does he?" complained the regent.

"How does a child born yesterday know such allegory of which we are ignorant?" snarled another chief.

"This penis sheath also bespeaks willingness to die for the truth, kabiyesi." the griot further interpreted.

"Even so, this tabooed child must die!" mused the regent.

"Amin, *so be it!*" responded the chiefs and elders.

"But how do I know what you muttered into my ear is true?" asked the regent.

"Do as I'll do, kabiyesi." responded the supreme griot.

The aged griot immediately pointed his arm forward and flashed open his palm towards Ajala and everyone present did the same, but Ajala, Shea and Pott were surprised, wondering what they were doing.

"What on earth are they doing?" asked Pott.

"I don't know." answered Ajala.

"Kabiyesi, *your majesty,* you aren't with us?" snorted the supreme griot, when he noticed that the regent was just staring at Ajala without pointing his opened palm towards him like the rest of them. They all shuddered when Ajala also retaliated with his palms flashed open at them instantly he found the regent's palm towards him.

"Do you think they want to attack us?" asked Pott.

"I don't know." replied Ajala.

"This is 'waka', kabiyesi." unraveled the supreme griot.

"Why would he respond to you, if he didn't understand the signification of the suspended gourd on his penis sheath?" he remarked.

"He understood perfectly the legend behind this 'gourd knot' and that the wide opened palm is practically the spectacle for 'waka', t-h-e f-u-c-k y-o-u-r m-o-t-h-e-r conundrum." buttressed the supreme griot drawlingly.

Nathless, Ajala was all smiles when he found Shea and Pott beside him with their palms also flashed wide open towards the regent and the chiefs and elders of Eboru. The lad seemed to be enjoying this make-believe show.

"These 'egbin', *untouchable strangers,* understand 'waka' too." asked the Convener, when he saw Shea and Pott flashed open their palms.

"No, they don't, birds of a feather flock together." responded the regent.

When the regent withdrew his 'waka' observance, Ajala, Shea and Pott also lowered theirs.

"When we opened our palms towards him, we were saying, 'f-u-c-k y-o-u-r m-o-t-h-e-r, too'. Therefore, he responded with his own palms to reinforce the connotation of his gourd penis sheath." the griot explained and they were all bedazzled.

"The suspended, small, cowry lined gourd and the three feathers you see on this penis sheath is the brand." verified the griot, and they all nodded agreement in reference to his observations, as they listen attentively.

"This is called, 'AdoIsura'." he revealed.

"And what does that mean, wise one?" asked the regent.

"Celestial blessings, esoteric blessings, blessings of the gods …"

"O wise one, save me those cock and bull story!" interrupted the regent.

"Kabiyesi, where 'AdoIsura' is suspended matters to its connotation, if it's at the tip of 'waka', it means the child isn't only peacefully protesting for freedom, but also seeking an end of your hegemony, kabiyesi." interpreted the griot.

"If it's at the base of 'waka', it means the child is protesting for a violent end to your hegemony, if you wouldn't abdicate peacefully. That is to say, the child's ready to lock horns with you, kabiyesi." he said with a bow.

"However, where we see the suspension now, somewhere in-between the base and the tip, meant that Ajala is only and humbly protesting for freedom or at least, laissez faire." literalised the griot.

"Anyhow, 'waka' is all about protest *for freedom*, kabiyesi." asserted the supreme griot.

"And the 'f-u-c-k y-o-u-r m-o-t-h-e-r' legend behind 'waka' goes thus…"

"Enough of this canard, wise one!" cut in the regent.

"You'll speak to me in camera about the rest of the matter." he ordered, when he realised that Ajala's 'knotted gourd penis sheath' – *allegorical gourd penis sheath* – was a threat to his hegemony by connotation.

"Kabiyesi, *your majesty*!" cried the griot.

"What the heck's that, Ajala?" asked Pott psychically, pointing to his fascinating penis sheath. Ajala looked at his gourd penis sheath.

"My dignity." he answered.

"It's cool, man!" remarked Pott.

"Thanks!"

"Can I have one?" requested Pott.

"Why not?" responded Ajala, and Shea looked at Pott with a side glance to signal her suspicion for his cynical request.

"Who's a witch, anyway?" Ajala turned to Shea and asked, as they all were looking at the gathering from afar and the gathering's glare deepened into an obvious glower of resentment for Ajala.

However, before Shea could open her mouth in response to Ajala's curiosity, a white owl hooted from afar and flew towards Ajala. He raised up his right arm to receive this owl and it landed on his hand. On the instant the owl flew off his hand towards Igbo, the horde of animals that came with Ajala began their stampede blitz towards Igbo *after the owl*.

Amidst them, Ajala was sitting on his zebra, Shea on a rhino and Pott on a giraffe, striding side by side speedily, as birds were flying above them and monkeys jumping from one height to the other. That very day, Eboru was full of rampaging animals, even to the least of squirrels and mice and the dust raised by this romping drove of wild animals nearly blackout Eboru. The regent, the chiefs and elders of Eboru watched in awe of this incredible stampeding spectacle that challenged their hegemony in every way and *thereby* tremor deeply their innermost being.

"A witch's someone who has extra sensory potentials and can use them at will." shouted Shea to Ajala, as they continued their romping blitz towards Igbo.

"Is a witch evil?" asked Ajala inquisitively.

"Evil or good is by choice. Even someone who isn't a witch could be evil." replied Shea.

Ajala was so impressed at the boldness, clarity and sincerity in Shea's response.

"Why being a witch?" he asked.

"Maybe ..."

"What does a witch do?" he cut in out of excitement before Shea could respond.

"You just did one of those things a good witch does!"

"What?"

"Standing up for the good of others."

Ajala looked at Shea and they smiled to one another. Tiny, beautiful and colourful birds were swarming around them joyously, as they saddled into Igbo their different beast of burden amongst the roisterously stampeding animals.

> "How I ululate into your ears,
> With the strength of Jakuta,
> That the gods are dead, O Eboru!
> Your ears you blocked with corncobs,

But the corncobs Ajala took off today,
Peradventure, you'd hear me now,
That the gods are dead,
And all your sacrifices in vain.
Your Sun is scorching you,
O, tribes of the dead gods!
The mouth of your Sun
Runs like rivers in the forest,
Yet their tears like dew.
Their moon is without husband.
O, Ajala the forbidden soul must die!
The conqueror of the dead gods must die,
Ajala, the forbidden child!
Ajala, the forbidden child!
Ajala, the forbidden child!
O, Ajala my child!"

Yawa, *the mad woman,* emerged from her hiding place the very moment Ajala departed and began singing, giggling and dancing all around Eboru, shaking her rotund bum and virgin boobs at everyone.

Chapter Five

*U*NTOUCHABLE, *untouchable, untouchable and outrightly detestable! A forbidden child and an outcast cursed by the gods. Why am I so held abhorrent by my own people? I'm like a toddler, starved half dead and surrounded by myriads of vultures. O what a helpless state! The sun neither shines pity on me, nor the moon smiles empathy. They went about their ordinances without any regard for my plight. Though, I looked up to the clouds for help, yet none showers on me. The rivers continued their courses without washing off my moaning and when the heavens did weep, I found no sympathy for my unfortunate fate in her tears. How thou art mute, O gods! I'm turned to a child that only a mother could love.* There was a pause.

Everywhere I pined for hope, care, peace and security due to me as a child, like any other child, I was irrationally shunned by the very people who were supposed to love me and safeguard me from abuse. Therefore, breathe itself became a thorn in my flesh. Why was I born into this misery? Am I so different to my peers? There was a deep sigh. *But, am I really a different child in any way that'd make my own people detest me so much? I can't understand these things.* A brief pause again, with eyes gently closed and head lowered down to the chest, as if dozing off. Then, slowly he raised his head up.

I did call for friendship, but my peers turned their backs and passed aside. To my song they refused neither to dance nor to listen. The tone of my flute to them was like hooting of a familiar owl. Why me? Oh, why me? He cried inside him. *O Eboru! Why my mother, too? Was it just because she gave birth to a child like me that she suffered so much? O mother! In another life a child like me you'd prefer not to bring forth I guess, however, now I'm convinced and confident you were the only one left for me and had you been against me or my birth, I'd be long dead, O mother!* He snarled deeply within him.

Motherhood should be worshipped in this world rather than the gods! Anyway, who're the gods? They've voices, but can't be heard? They've hearts, but empty of love? They've eyes, yet can't see a thing? They've feelings, but don't care? They've emotions, but neither do they sympathise nor empathise? They've power, but can't move anything? Why are they hiding themselves and who're they hiding from? Every god we worship under the sun, why're you hiding? As for me, hitherto, you're all laid-back cowards! He breathed deeply.

Do these gods have children at all and bothered about their welfare like my mother does? Oh, no! I don't think so! If they do, they'd have come to my aid in this wretched fate I'm immersed by my own people. Of course, they're not by birth, so they knew nothing of birth, zounds! What're they waiting for, anyhow, until I die? Why did these gods we venerated everyday hide their faces, when they were so much sought after by the innocent? They sit back and watched, as those oppressed were shamefaced and perished. Behold, every god we worship on this earth are laid-back cowards! There was a brief silence. *Peradventure, they have their own ups and downs also, yet, why do they remain the vacuum we can't fill, however, we can feel. Whatsoever, they're just vacuums.* There was utter quietude, so deep Ajala himself could feel his heart beating.

I'm quite sure this isn't right. Why won't anyone see me a child like any other? Even if they won't accept me, they'd leave me alone to my fate. None the less, it could be too late for me, as it did happen to my mother. She was left ostracised, dejected and a lonely widow. Oh, dear mother! How your miseries touched my soul unto death. I'm grateful that you did never allow your fortitude to be broken, you stood firm for me, even in the throes of lapidation. He mused with deep seated grief.

Hey, come to think of it, what have we done? Yea, I did ask myself lot of times, but no real answer came. Of course, who in his or her right mind could fathom how the mores of the land should be exalted over the life of an innocent child. What'd be more precious, a child's life or the mores of the land? What a catastrophic shame! O crepuscule, you shouldn't have helped my mother on the day of her woes in blood and water, perhaps, I'd have been with the ancestors, free of all these stigmatisation, segregation, castigation and rejection. He began to weep, but struggled to stop his tears with his palms.

My late father was said to be the hierarch of the tribes, yet, I was made untouchable, so as to make me unworthy of succeeding him. O Mother Earth, open up and swallow my being because I'm a stigma to my kindred and a taboo to the mores of the land! What am I living for anymore? What's my pride before my mother that she has a son? A son who's the cradle of her abjectness? A deplorable villain in a miserable existence, at the heart of her motherhood I'm made to become by their so called tradition. He continued to wipe his tears across his face with his palms and the back of his hand, his eyes wandered around, before he gazed the unveiling starry night sky.

Oh, the eyes of the hiding deities are gathering once more to my hatred! Oh, what a vicious wheel I'm in! Well, another night of horror to unveil another day of anguish and a new threat of imminently offering my soul as a propitious omen. Perhaps, I'd escape from this land before it's too late. However, should I flee to a strange land that is void of my mother's grave? She remained my cradle and the only one I knew as my bona-fide friend and trusted carer, and she was indeed perpetual. Despite all the imminent dangers to her life, she stood by me all the way while other parents gave up their children to the mores of the land. I won't leave you, even though you are dead, O mother! If the heavens should rain blood as water and the sky send forth fire as sunlight, O mother, together we shall be to the very end and in death or in afterlife, nothing shall separate us. He continued to gaze the sky *still*, as his imagination wandered around Igbo and this sparked a brief smile on his face.

Igbo, the evil forest and the land of the gods, I'm here with my mother and I'll always be here. I know my fate in this land is a foregone conclusion. Oh, how I wish that I had never been born! None the less, this is insufferable for me any longer. These thoughts were raging through the confused and gloomy mind of the rejected child, Ajala, as he was musing in deep somnambulation and at the same time, he was ignorantly and unwittingly dressing up himself in 'waka', – *a long and straight gourd penis sheath, with a small cowry decorated gourd suspended at the middle.* This 'waka' of a gourd penis sheath of Ajala was fastened in place by a thin strip of cowry lined leather that he strapped around his waist and this was extended from the gourd penis sheath to hold a *symbolic* cowry decorated small gourd in suspension. At the base of this 'waka' was a drooping, bundle of hay-like material – *which Ajala ignorantly coloured white*

61

this time – and atop this were three *symbolic* feathers of green, yellow and red. At the upper part of his arms and shanks he fastened cowry lined leather that held in place different colourful feathers and on his ears he wore earrings of beautiful feathers, suspended respectively by *joined* three cowries. On his head he strapped cowry lined leather, embedded with colourful feathers, cowries, and mollusk. On his neck he wore the necklace he made from lion, tiger, leopard, cheetah and jaguar's teeth. These he collected from the carcasses of these animals that he came across during his wandering around Igbo.

In this remarkable somnambulation, he was dreaming of himself sitting on a stump, motionless, staring the sky absent-mindedly, his unwonted eyeballs dripping with tears one after the other, as the sky gradually continued to spread its darkness over the sun. "Ajala, you're as defenceless as an infant tethered in the middle of the jungle invested by hyenas and wild dogs. Don't be afraid, my son, don't be afraid because death or life makes no difference, the difference you make in life is what really matters." he heard his mother's voice during this somnambulation. Immediately, he got up the stump and began to dress himself up in 'waka'.

He actuated his okapi, instead, a zebra responded and many of the animals in Igbo approached him. Ajala mounted the zebra with the cowry lined rope he made to control his beast of burden in his hand. Immediately, this zebra began to stride rapidly towards Eboru and Ajala descended on the village with these hordes of rampaging wild animals. However, Ajala didn't get out of this bizarre somnambulation, until his eyes hit the necromancers. Yet, he took over from where his somnambulation stopped, as if nothing unusual had happened.

Chapter Six

MOTHER ENDOR was still asleep when she was suddenly athrilled by her mobile phone *ringing* and she eagerly picked the call with the very thought that Shea and Pott were calling, but she was indeed frustrated when she couldn't hear a thing on her phone. Actually, Shea was trying to reach her *but the network was bad*. Mother Endor seemed frustrated with the bad network, because she was indeed getting worried about these two protégés – *whom she sent to the unknown* – most especially, at times like this when she couldn't reach them on their mobile and vice versa. However, she continued to perceive that a remarkable call would hit her mobile that very day. While Pott was trying on himself some of Ajala's gourd penis sheath, which indeed fascinated him much, Shea was asking him to use his mobile. However, Pott was so enthralled in these penis sheath he didn't hear her on time. Even when Shea walked to him and touched him, he quickly pointed to where his mobile was and continued modelling in these gourd penis sheaths to Shea's amusement. Shea wagged her head as she was looking at him.

"Hello, good morning!" a call came in from the United States.

"Hello!" responded *a* BBC correspondent.

"My name's Tisseewoonatis Twitters, I'm a paranormal journalist involved majorly in the investigation of off-the-wall activities."

"My Gosh, I've watched some of your documentaries on paranormal themes." answered the BBC correspondent.

"You're fantastic!" she commended with excitement.

"Thanks!" replied Tisseewoonatis.

"Thanks a lot!" she added.

"My name's Lucy Kickstone"

"Nice to meet you, Lucy!" said Tisseewoonatis.

"What can I do for you, today?" queried Lucy *quickly*.

"I watched your BBC show on the puzzling disappearance of Erin Eyers and the unusual dreams she had before this mysterious disappearance. I wanna be involved in the investigation, at least, in my own way …"

"Hang on Tissee, while I get in touch with Erin's parents if they'd cooperate or want a paranormal investigator involved in the search for their daughter at this stage." responded Lucy.

"Are you okay with that?" asked Lucy.

"That's fine!" responded Tisseewoonatis. She hanged on the phone, while Lucy dialed Erin's parents. Though, no doubt Tisseewoonatis' professional touch on paranormal investigative journalism wasn't hidden from Erin's parents too, but they were reluctant to cooperate with her in the investigation she craved. In fact, they wouldn't want any interference or distraction of some sort with the thoroughgoing police investigation. Erin's parents finally refused to accept her involvement without thinking twice.

"Tissee, are you there?"

"Yes, Lucy!"

"Erin's parents wouldn't want any distraction from the ongoing police investigation. Sorry about that!" relayed Lucy.

"That's alright!" responded Tisseewoonatis.

"Thanks Lucy!" she added.

"If there's any relevant information that'd be of help, please give me a call." requested Tisseewoonatis.

"I don't think so at the moment, except a psychic who called to request having contact with the letters borne of Erin's dream." hinted Lucy.

"A psychic?" retorted Tisseewoonatis. Of course, with her thoroughbred experience, she knew every clue accessible to her off-the-wall scientific scrutiny shouldn't be left out.

"Yes, Tissee!"

"Could you link me with this psychic, please?"

"Of course, but the only information we know of her is her phone contact." hinted Lucy.

"Oh great! Can I've it?"

"Sure, Tissee!" Immediately, Lucy dictated Mother Endor's phone contact to Tisseewoonatis. She scribbled it on a paper with the pen she picked from her table, holding the handset against her shoulder with her chin

"I'm so grateful for your effort." said Tisseewoonatis.

"No worries!"

"Kindly forgive me that I rounded up your name to Tissee."

apologized Lucy.

"The very first time I watched one of your documentary and I saw your name, I got this candid snapshot straightaway." said Lucy with humour and they both cackled with laughter over it.

"Bye Tissee and good luck!"

"Thanks!" answer Tisseewoonatis risibly.

The metropolitan police had gone thoroughly through all the CCTV footages of the area where Erin disappeared. The NHS Hospital indoor CCTV cameras where Erin vanished, captured Erin going into the lavatory, but didn't capture her coming out, but the same footage showed that her mother went into the same lavatory after her at exactly ten minutes after Erin went in, and came out at exactly sixty seconds after. And to further bamboozled the investigating team, the outdoor CCTV footages of the hospital showed a tiny, beautiful bird flying into the same loo through the window at exactly the same time Erin entered and this bird, too, like Erin, was never seen flying out of the loo, either through the door or the window.

"We saw them entering but none came out, except her mother, this is bizarre." complained one of the investigating officers, as they were viewing and reviewing the volumes of footages collected for their investigation.

"Where are they?" queried another in confusion.

Detective Chief Inspector Briggs came in, clapping his hands couple of times to get the attention of his investigating team.

"We're gonna damn fucking split up into three teams." informed Briggs.

"Right now, I want the first team to mount a road block on the roads leading to the crime area and try to talk to everyone driving in and out of the area, perhaps they have any information about Erin or if they saw anything suspicious on that day she vanished. The second team should convey the technical investigation into the possibility of all the damn Close Circuit Television (CCTV) in the area being diverted or somehow tampered with. And the third team is to convey a door to door interview with the residence around the crime area, and I'll carry out further interview with the security officers and the front desk staff of the hospital that were on duty and off duty that day." instructed Briggs.

"Let get the damn thing moving, pending the outcome of the

in depth forensic analysis going on." he added, clapping his hands again to urge them on.

"There ain't no bullshitting any clue, no matter how trivial!" he said.

"Sir, it seems you've got only this fucking, b-u-l-l-s-h-i-t thing?" drawled Jade, and the whole team turned to her with a suspicious look *to hear what she was about to insinuate.*

"What the fucking hell did you mean by that, badass?" asked Briggs.

"Sir, I mean, why not some p-i-g-s-h-i-t, d-o-g-s-h-i-t, h-o-r-s-e-s-h-i-t, m-o-n-k-e-y-s-h-i-t, c-a-t-s-h-i-t, c-h-i-c-k-e-n-s-h-i-t, or even manshit, sometimes." japed Jade, drawling these as everyone cackled along with laugher.

"What?" guffawed Briggs.

"What of Jadeshit?" amused another gumshoe, and the whole team continued to entertain themselves with detective Chief Inspector Briggs' platitudes.

"Thanks for the jokes and laughter, guys!" appreciated Briggs.

"I maybe swearing, at least I'm not fucking katagelophobic." joked Brigss.

"However, there ain't no Jadeshiting me, guys!" amused Briggs, as he was laughing.

Somewhat, this humour lightened the squad's mood, as they walked out for further investigation, according to Briggs' directives.

Either we guffaw at this in bona fides or we'll all go mad. This investigation is indeed nerve-wracking. Mused Briggs.

Of course, the lavatory where Erin went missing could be described as securely built for children's safety, because the only way in was in fact the only way out and the option of any other outlet of exit was impossible. So, the question of what happened to Erin, was a daunting task indeed, most especially with the CCTV footages yielding no clues.

On detective Chief Inspector Briggs' mind was the niggling suspicion that the young lady was probably kidnapped, but by whom and why, were the boggling questions he had no answer for. Though, he nurtured some thoughts that he wouldn't share with anyone, until the investigation would confirm the direction the case was heading. Everyone involved in this investigation knew that at the moment there was no lead to follow and the fact that this dead end in itself remained unexplainable was undermining the credibility of the British policing system.

Detective Chief Inspector Briggs went back into the hospital and conducted further *one on one* interview with every staff to ascertain no one, at least, came across anything suspicious and also that everyone was clean. However, none of the staff could vouchsafe they heard or saw anything that would be of help to the investigation and as Briggs continued to eliminate suspects, the perplexity surrounding the occurrence mounted. It was indeed frustrating for him, but the more the investigation got dicier for his carrier, the more he got enthused with getting to the bottom of whatever happened to Erin.

Inspector Briggs was advised by his doctor to opt out of the investigation because one of the factors helping his condition was severely perturbed. In fact, he lost his sleep and couple with his special condition, matters could only get worse for his wellbeing. The other factor left to help him was beginning to be spurned by himself, due to its offensive nature before his audience, who weren't aware of his helpless condition. Therefore, to the risk of his health, he tried *in vain* not to use expletives when talking to people.

However, he knew within him that he wouldn't let go of the investigation because of his unique medical condition, no matter what. After all, he also felt personally attached to this case for the stronger reason that his daughter, though younger than Erin, shared the same forename with her. This brilliant, quiet and taciturn daughter of Briggs, started to be more talkative with him about Erin and the investigation surrounding her disappearance. He could understand that her daughter was also somehow emotionally attached to the puzzling issues surrounding Erin, as the young lady would comb through newspapers about the search for her and the progress of the investigation. As soon as her father arrived from work, she would waste no time confronting him with what she read and how she felt about it. Nevertheless, detective Chief Inspector Briggs always took her concerns with a grain of salt and was cautious of whatever he shared with her and at the same time realised she was just a child, who felt Erin had to be found at all cost.

"Dad, perhaps someone invisible took her." she did suggest.

"Like alien adoption?" teased Inspector Briggs.

"Yep, something like that, dad!" she reply excitedly.

"But aliens aren't invisible, are they?"

"They could choose to be, I guess!"

None the less, detective Briggs compensated for his inability to sleep properly, since this investigation began, with laughing up his sleeve by his daughter's *deemed* childish suggestions.

"Perhaps, you'd involve in the investigation a psychic or a priest or a magician or whoever could find her!" suggested the young lady *to him one day*.

"Erin, that isn't empirical." he said *to her*.

"I've been searching the internet for information and I found out that psychics could indeed be of help." said Erin.

"You watched too much of news, read much of newspapers and surfed lot the internet these days." he chirked up his daughter.

"My super sleuth you are, aren't you?" he added.

He carried her on his shoulder, tickling her to a heavy laughter just to take her mind off the *missing* Erin's issue. He would often engage her in roughhousing, but he found out that the favourite she would want to play was *mocking up* the search and finding Erin.

However, after the family had amused themselves, day in day out, with many playful activities together, bothering mainly on search and finding Erin as initiated by Briggs' daughter. One day, this young lady, in her infantile mind thought out a play, where she played an investigative psychic, who worked with a psychic composite sketch artist, played by her father – *Detective Chief Inspector Briggs* – and she chose her mother to play the role of a metropolitan police detective in charge of the investigation – *of Erin Eyers*.

"Are we ready, guys?" she asked, after she had placed the drawing materials on her father's hands and positioned her mother for observation.

"But I don't know how to etch a thing!" complained Briggs.

"You've got to try, dad!" she said.

"Okay, but it might not look like whatever you wanted me to draw." insisted Briggs and the family descended into laughter awhile.

"Dad, I know, but you can still try." she said, and went into a feigned meditating mood. Detective Chief Inspector Briggs looked at his wife, as their young daughter closed her eyes and drew a veil over her head.

"I saw a tiny, colourful bird coming through the window."

she said.

"What species of bird is it, lady?" asked detective Chief Inspector Briggs, with a chuckle.

"Don't laugh, dad." she said, as she maintained her cogitative mood.

"Just sketch a tiny bird, please!" she drawled.

"I'm trying to imagine through the evidence in the CCTV footages." she added.

"Now, Erin's coming into the loo." she continued, while detective Chief Inspector Briggs was struggling with the sketching. As his daughter innocently played her role, his wife was glancing from time to time at his risible sketches.

"What causes your laughter?" he asked his wife, without the resonance of his vocal cord, as she quietly pointed to his laughable caricature-like drawing, in order not to disturb their daughter. *What are you drawing, a toad or an ostrich?* She demonstrated to him with her hands.

"So, what!" he said audibly.

"So, what?" retorted Briggs' daughter.

"Yes, Erin's in the loo." she responded, with the mind that her father was talking to her.

"Sketch it, I'm still thinking." she added *quickly*.

Then her mind opened up to a possibility she thought might have happened to Erin on that fateful day she disappeared.

"Erin loved this tiny, beautiful bird immediately she saw it and the bird flew into her hands." she envisioned.

"Erin, the bird is beautiful, but its evil. Be careful, please!" the young lady put up a drama that her parents were indeed enamoured to hear the outcome.

"Erin was playing with this bird and of a sudden, when she found out the bird was disguised, it was too late." she said, and went silent awhile, her parents waited in earnest expectation of the outcome.

"Too late for what?" asked Briggs, earnestly.

"What happened next?" asked, her mother.

"I'm thinking, mum!" she replied.

As she remained mused, she was pondering where next to direct her feigned psychic investigation and in her infantile mind she remembered that only an ostrich would be a bird big enough to describe what struck her mind.

"Of a sudden, this tiny, beautiful bird turned to an ostrich." she posited.

"And what happen?" inquired her mother.

"Erin was so scared, she tried to scream, but this evil ostrich overwhelmed her and it snatched her away." she concluded. Her parents looked at one another soberly and, after a while of silence, her father cleared his throat, as he was struggling to sketch her daughter's imagination.

"Can I ask a question?" he said.

"Yes, daddy!" she replied.

"Ostriches don't have hands, right?" he asked.

"How did this ostrich carry Erin and how did this bird and Erin exit the crime scene without being caught by the CCTV cameras or anyone?" he queried, teasing his daughter.

"Let me think, dad!" she cried.

"Give the bird a hand, one human hand to snatch Erin and the other to cover her mouth." she suggested, and at her repartee they all cackled with laughter.

"Okay, but how did they leave the scene unnoticed?" asked Chief Inspector Briggs.

"They both vanished, dad!" she said. She removed the veil off her head and breathed deeply.

"Now, dad, you have to discuss with detective mum on what to do." she instructed. Her parents laughed for calling her mother detective mum.

"My part's done." she added.

Detective Chief Inspector Briggs continued to laugh together with his wife and she went into laughter with them.

"Detective mum?" called Briggs on his wife with a side glance.

"This is your suspect on this case." he said.

"It may not look like anything you did ever seen before, because I'm not a good artist, but I can assure you our psychic here divine it's an ostrich." explained Briggs.

"Thank you, sir!" she replied, but when they took a look at what he sketched, they all descended into a brouhaha of laughter for a while *on Briggs caricature*.

"But I'd need advice on where to find this bizarre ostrich of a culprit?" she inquired, as they were still laughing.

"I'd think our little psychic had an answer to that!" said Briggs and she found her parents focused their eyes on her for a response.

"I guess you'll have to go into the jungle to find one!" she suggested and the family laughter went on.

As they weltered in this laughter, detective Briggs' mobile rang and when he looked at the display, he saw that the call was coming from Jade Knight, *one of the lady officers in his investigative squad.*

"You've got to see this, sir!" said Jade.

"What?" he asked.

"I don't know how to explain this, you've got to see it yourself." coughed Jade.

"Okay, see you in the office." said Briggs.

"I'll be waiting, sir." said Jade.

In a rush, Briggs dashed for his coat, put it on and got hold of his muffler too, flipped it round his neck and put on his gloves.

"Is everything okay, darling?" asked Briggs' wife.

"All's fine, I can assure you." he replied, as he quickly gave his daughter a kiss in the heard.

"My greatest psychic!" he commented.

"We'll continue when I come back, okay!" he said. He walked to his wife in haste for a kiss, before he dashed out of the house.

He jumped into his car and broke the speed limit for a while, in total anticipation of what Jade might have for him that she couldn't even explain on phone. Moreover, on getting to the police station, he jumped out of the car almost before it halted and hasted into the office, leaving the ignition key on and also the driver's door opened.

"Jade, I'm here!" he announced, as soon as he entered the office.

"Welcome, sir!" responded Jade.

"I want you to meet Omorisha, he's from Cuba." introduced Jade, as she spread her hand politely towards the afrocuban bloke sitting in front of her. He got up on his feet too, as soon as Jade stood up to welcome her boss.

"I'm detective Briggs Blues!" said Briggs, his eyes browsed briefly the heavy, well-kept afro on Omorisha's head and his bushy beard and moustache that *almost* hid his mouth.

"Omorisha Babalu-Aye, id est., child of the Orisha called Babalu-Aye." said the afrocuban, with his lung powered *deep* voice, as he shook hands with Briggs.

"Nice to meet you." he added.

"The pleasure's mine." responded Briggs. He was wondering what sort of urgency brought a guy with a strange name before him.

Jade pulled out her desk's drawer and brought out a cartridge, A4 size bound book and placed it on the table before Chief Inspector Briggs. As he laid his hand on the book, his eyes moved back and forth on Jade and Omorisha. Instantly his hand lifted the cover of the book, his eyes struck the bizarre drawing on it. Detective Briggs straight off knew what the import of the drawing was, but found it infra dig to his profession to embrace such notion.

"What the mother fucker damn hell's this bloody cocksucking bullshit?" he inveighed with expletives *spontaneously*.

"Those are strong invectives, sir." responded Omorisha.

"My grandfather is 116 years old and all his life was devoted to the worship of Babalu-Aye. So is his father and his grandfather and his great grandfather and his great great grandfather and his great, great, great grandfather and his g-r-e-a-t, g-r-e-a-t, g-r-e-a-t, g-r-e-a-t grandfather before they were misappropriated from their ancestral land of West Africa into a foreign land of slavery by the criminal act of accessary and murderous violence by Europeans." said Omorisha to Chief Inspector Briggs, who still seemed bemused by whatever would come out of this meeting.

"Despite the Spanish colonial authorities, colonial in quote," he said, as he demonstrated with his fingers.

"I called it criminal authorities by every standard, and despite their brutal effort to impose Catholicism on Yoruba slaves that were taken in great number from Nigeria to Cuba, they managed to keep their Orisha hallowed in their hearts by syncretising them with Catholicism and hiding each Orisha under the disguise of a catholic saint." hinted Omorisha. Detective Briggs relaxed himself with a sigh, as Omorisha words began to interest him. Though, he still couldn't understand what this has to do with his investigation or the disappearance of Erin.

"For example, Chango, *the god of fire, thunder and lightning,* was worshipped in the form of Santa Barbara and Babalu-Aye, *father and lord in the Earth or spirit of the Earth,* under the guise of san Lazaro." continued Omorisha.

"Er, man! I'm talking here about the criminally premeditated and calculated abuse, displaced, marooned and massacred of my forefathers." remarked Omorisha.

"I think I understand." answered detective Briggs, looking at Omorisha with a suspicious glance.

"But what the hell's this Orisha stuff got to do with my investigation?" he asked, with his eyes back and forth on Jade and Omorisha.

"Orisha are primordial intelligence from the heavens, who visited the Yoruba people in ancient time ..." explained Omorisha.

"Thanks!" interposed Briggs *sarcastically.*

"My grandfather called me from Cuba a week before Erin disappeared to let me know what remarkable revelation he had from the great Babalu-Aye. He wanted me to sketch it because he knew I had this artistic talent from childhood and that's why I'm in the United Kingdom to further my studies in the arts." continued Omorisha.

"In short, he dictated to me on phone this revelation from Babalu-Aye and I sketched it out, even before it happen." he said.

"You can take a look at the date on my sketch, please!" he affirmed.

"I haven't show it to anyone, until Jade came to my door for information on the missing girl." he inkling.

Detective Chief Inspector Briggs was dumbfounded for a while, staring at Omorisha, before his eyes went back on the perfect drawing.

"Excuse me!" said Briggs. He got hold of Jade's arms, dragged her into a separate room and pushed her against the wall.

"What the hell's that goddamm fucking drawing all about?" he shouted.

"I just wanted you to see it, sir!" responded Jade fearfully

"See what, Jade?" he asked.

"See a black ostrich with human hands and head, snatching Erin away?" he asked angrily.

"Is that what you want me to announce to the whole of the world?" he said.

"And get arrested, indicted and try in the court of law and

eventually send a fucking weird goddamn ostrich to prison?" he shouted to her face in anger.

Jade was indeed scared by Briggs' rage. She didn't expect it would enrage him the way it did, anyway, her aim was to gather whatever intelligence that would probably give some lead to the investigation.

"But you said, 'There ain't no bullshiting any clue, no matter how trivial'"

"Yes, I also said, 'there ain't no Jadeshiting me' too, goddammit!" cried Briggs.

"Now, you're Jadeshiting me, gal and this sucks." he added.

"I'm so – sorry!" uttered Jade, with panicky and deep remorse on her face. Briggs realised he hadn't handled her gentlemanly.

"I'm the one to apologise, Jade." he said, as he calmed his nerves.

"You scared the shit out of me, sir!" said Jade.

"Sorry!" he apologised and they stared one another's puzzled countenance awhile.

"F-u-c-k t-h-a-t s-h-i-t, Jade!" he drawled.

Detective Chief Inspector Briggs casually instructed Jade in his cussing manner, and she immediately understood he meant she should dismiss Omorisha instantly. In fact, she didn't seem surprise, as she walked towards the door straight away without uttering objection or raising any suggestion.

"When you're done with him, gather all my squad for a briefing on the forensic investigation." said Briggs to Jade, as she was about to exit the room.

"Jade!" he called, and she turned to look back at him.

"I don't want any more of this Jadeshit distraction in my investigation." he warned.

"Yes, sir!" responded Jade.

"Will you do me a favour?" said Omorisha, as Jade was approaching him.

"Tell him I was dedicated to the great Babalu-Aye the very day I was born." he said. He got up on his feet. Jade nodded acceptance gently as Omorisha turned his back to leave.

"Sir!" called Jade.

"Your drawing!" she said to Omorisha.

"You keep it, lady." he replied.

"I have Babalu-Aye." he added, as he was about to exit the police station. He walked out of the station and Jade placed the cartridge book properly on her table, after looking at the drawing again.

Jade was somehow pensive about Omorisha Babalu-Aye's drawing, but didn't know what to make of it. Anyway, she convened the squad and came back to contemplate on this perfect drawing from Omorisha Babalu-Aye. Afterwards, she walked to the briefing room to join her other members of investigative squad, yet within her she resolved to know more about how this drawing of Omorisha came to be. Notwithstanding, without detective Briggs knowledge.

Jade was the last member of the squad to come in into the briefing room and as she entered, she saw top detective, Chief Superintendent Carl DeJesus standing beside detective Chief Inspector Briggs.

"Have your seat, Jade." said detective Chief Superintendent Carl.

"Thank you, sir!" she replied, as she took her seat with the squad.

"Right now, we're in a mess." informed detective Chief Superintendent Carl.

"And if this squad messed up, the whole of United Kingdom Police's in a mess, too." he added, and mood turned to be one of wistfulness among the squad.

"As far as I'm concerned now, with all the reports from your investigative effort and the forensic analysis, we're in a limbo." he announced, as he walked left and right, looking at the forensic bulletin in his left hand with his thumb and index finger under his jaw, his eyes went on the squad again.

"I know we can do this, we can find this innocent girl no matter how mysteriously daunting her disappearance seems to be. I do believe some criminals were somehow a step ahead of us and we indeed do have to catch up with them." he encouraged.

Detective Chief Inspector Briggs' eyes and Jade Knight's unexpectedly met and they both seemed to know what was going on in their individual minds.

You didn't even ask me how I came across Omorisha. Jade thought in her mind towards Briggs.

I don't wanna know anything about that weird goddamn

Babalu-Aye paranormal bullshit! Mused Briggs in his heart towards Jade.

We could at least verify his claims or interview him for information's sake. Jade's thought.

I won't tolerate such goddam untenable distraction, Jade. He mused *in response.*

I'm gonna find out more about this, anyway. Jade's thought, as they both were staring one another from their sitting position.

"We've also looked into the possibility of paedophiliacs at work and all forms of paraphilia had been investigated and all alibis corroborated, yet, we ain't got any lead. I'm quite sure something will come up and I want us to step up the good work and make sure we find Erin Eyers." said Carl, and was quiet for some time.

"Ladies and gentlemen, presently, both the investigative and the forensic opportunities had yielded no lead in this case." concluded detective Chief Superintendent Carl DeJesus.

"Your squad leader would brief you on one possibility we've to consider, while we continue to further scrutinise every suspicion surrounding this case." said top detective Chief Superintendent Carl DeJesus.

"Thank you, sir!" said Chief Inspector Briggs to his boss, and walked before the squad to address them.

"I know your pain and frustrations on this case, but that shouldn't discourage us. Now, we're gonna be investigating all the known rogue scientists and researchers because we are having the suspicion Erin could be their target, because of her unique genetical make up. We are going to start from the victim analysis. Thank you, guys!" summed up detective Briggs. Immediately the squad dispersed for further investigation.

"Ladies and gentlemen, I want answers." added top detective Carl.

The squad all together looked back, as they heard top detective Chief Superintendent Carl's voice and they saw him discussing with detective Chief Inspector Briggs without his attention towards them.

"If any of you'd require help, let me know." said detective Chief Inspector Briggs, as he looked to them briefly, turning his face back to his boss to continue his discussion with him. Suddenly, something struck his mind.

"Excuse me, sir!" he said, as he snapped towards the exit, dashing out of the briefing room through the squad.

Everyone looked at one another, wondering what did just snap in Briggs. However, her daughter's puerile thought out home-play that very day hit his mind and he remembered that the afrocuban's sketches expressed the same idea to what his daughter suggested during their feigned family-play before Jade called him. He rushed to Jade's table to take a look at the diagram again. He wondered if his daughter had been chatting online on this issue, as he couldn't get his head around it. He ran to his car to find out from his daughter how this coincidence came to happen.

"Holy shit!" he howled, when he saw that he left his car door opened.

When he began to search for the ignition key, and later found out he left it on, too.

"Fuck you, Briggs!" he muttered *to himself.*

Chapter Seven

T HE day broke on Ajala, Shea and Pott, while they were still sleeping inside a huge cavern that hollowed in a rock, when Mother Endor's call came in and surprisingly to Shea and Pott – *who knew Ajala was deaf and dumb* – the mobile's ringing tone also woke up the lad.

"What was that?" he communed with Shea.

"Sorry, it's my mobile." she replied.

"What sort of witchcraft's that?" he asked.

Ajala, who was frightened out of his sleep by the ringing tone of Shea's mobile, communicated with his new friends in the usual extra sensory manner *the apport from Shea's grandmother facilitated among them.* Pott grimaced to Shea, with the surprise that the boy could hear the ringing tone of the phone.

"It isn't witchcraft, Ajala." said Shea.

As Ajala was still awed, he retreated himself a bit away from Shea, looking at the ringing mobile she held in her hand with fright.

"Then, what's it that shocked my being so much?" he queried. While Shea was receiving Mother Endor's call, Pott, who had adopted the culture of wearing gourd penis sheath *with Ajala,* took on the explanation with him.

"It's a mobile phone." said Pott.

"A mobile phone?" retorted Ajala with pulled eyebrows that was expressive of the awe he felt.

"This is witchcraft, for sure!" he said.

"It isn't witchcraft." replied Pott.

"But you said you are witches?"

"Yes, we are, Ajala, but this isn't witchcraft." said Pott.

"It's a mobile phone."

"What's a mobile phone?" he asked *quickly* with raised eyebrows.

"It's a technological device designed to talk to someone not within your reach." cried Pott. Ajala remained quiet, as he rested his back on a stone, staring at Shea with awe as she was talking with

Mother Endor, before his attention came back on Pott.

"What sort of witchcraft's technology?" he asked *again.*

"I guess you're practicing super witchcraft!" he added.

The apport continued to work for Ajala and his visitors, so that they could hear and communicate together effectively. Though, the gems on the apport glows as it attuned them together, but none of them could see or perceive this happening.

"Hello, hello, Mother."

"I was worried about you, guys."

"Oh, Mother, we're fine!"

"Pott's okay?"

"Yes, Mother. He's okay."

"We know you must have been trying to reach us and as you should expect, lot of trouble here." hinted Shea.

"Pott's head almost got chopped off, but the lad named Ajala saved us." she added.

"A- j- l- a." stammered Mother Endor with the name on her lips. Her mind at once flashed the letters borne of Erin's dream that she saw on BBC and also the name Pott managed to write in the text he sent her. She was wondering, if there could be any coincidence or connection between her psychic generations' prophecy and this lad called Ajala and the mysterious disappearance of Erin Eyers.

"Yes, Mother, the same lad on the strange animal in the video messages we sent to you." Immediately Mother Endor heard this, she went silent because the thought of these two kids – *Ajala and Erin* – being the reason for Shea and Pott's mission boggled her mind and how this drama was to play out *in toto* eluded her psychic dexterity. The connection between these two enigmatic kids being the reason for her age long psychic generations' prophecy was totally unknown to her, and psychically unfathomable and unsearchable *by her sixth sense.*

"Hello, hello, Mother!" called Shea repeatedly, when she couldn't hear Mother Endor saying a word again.

She looked at her mobile to see if the signal was affected. She rushed out of the cavern and quickly climbed a tree with the hope of increasing the signal strength of her mobile, pointing the device towards the sky in anticipation and it did work for her. Instantaneously, Ajala ran after her to see what she was trying to do with the device, his eyes were awfully fixed towards Shea *on the tree.*

"I'd think there's something strange about that lad in relation to a missing girl."

Finally, Shea heard Mother Endor's voice again.

"A missing girl!" retorted Shea.

"What missing girl?" asked Shea.

"Okay, girl, I'm glad you're both fine, but stay close to this lad and try to understand him because I do think he's vital to your mission. Yet, I can't understand why and how." said Mother Endor. She wouldn't want to confuse issues further.

"Got the message, Mother. I'll send you the video messages of our ordeal and the eventual interference of Ajala."

"Please, do now!" said Mother Endor, and Shea, without tarrying, scrolled her mobile down to video messages and send their recorded nightmare before the regent and the chiefs and elders of Eboru *village,* and the eventual interference of Ajala to Mother Endor.

"Is she talking to the gods?" asked Ajala, when he saw Shea pointing the mobile device towards the sky. He was holding Pott's hand, who *also* came out of the cavern to hand over his own mobile to Shea.

"No, she's talking to a friend." answered Pott.

All along, Ajala's bizarre eyes were on Shea as she was speaking to Mother Endor on her mobile. After Shea had sent the video messages on her mobile and on Pott's to Mother Endor, she came down from the tree, moved closer to Ajala and hand over her device to him and the other to Pott.

Ajala was examining this mobile, when Shea winked to Pott to dial her number. Pott took his mobile, making sure Ajala wasn't aware. He dialed Shea's number and of a sudden the mobile rang and vibrated in Ajala's hands. He got scared and panicked, as the mobile agitated his being. Immediately, he let go of the device, while Shea and Pott bursted into laughter, but when Pott pointed his mobile to Ajala, he *at once* understood their pranks and joined them in this boisterous laughter. Ajala cracked up so much as if he was having the first excitement of his life and Shea and Pott indeed perceived his loneliness in this *simple* occurrence. Eventually, Pott had to shake him up to stop him from wallowing in his laughter.

"It's okay, now." he said to him and Ajala gradually simmered down.

"That's what I called, abderian." said Pott to Shea.

Forthwith, he put on a somber hue because he couldn't believe he laughed so much. He stared Pott in the eyes, as if he was asking him if he did laugh so much, and the day he cackled in laughter together with his late mother and the river goddess worshippers came to his mind.

"This is my second time of experiencing the power of deep-seated laughter, indeed, I never knew it could be this uplifting." he communed.

He got up the ground and walked towards Shea's mobile, which he threw away out of panicky, picked it up and gave it to her. Shea took Ajala into her arms and hugged him tightly. He was indeed comforted as he rested his head on Shea's body with the memory of his mother running through his mind.

Afterwards, Ajala happily snapped from Shea's arms towards the huge cavern's entrance and there he stood, looked back at Shea and Pott with a friendly smile and beckoned to them to follow him. He led them to a compartment, where he kept gourds of different shapes, small and big, cut out for different utilitarian purposes and well designed, with marks of fine artwork by himself. He took one calabash bowl, with a rope handle that was lined with cowries attached to it, he gave it to Shea and he took one for himself and cued Pott to have one too. Shea looked at this well-crafted calabash bowl Ajala handed over to her and the delicate design of mysterious artwork he inscribed on it.

"I made them myself." communed Ajala, as he led them into the jungle.

"You made this yourself?" asked Pott, who was also examining the splendid artwork on the good canteen he picked up.

"You'll see more, my friends!" he said to them, when he saw they were indeed absorbed in his intricate designs, but before they could reply, Ajala had climbed up a tree with his calabash hung on his shoulder. While Shea was wondering where he had gone, Pott pointed her to the top of this leafy tree. This tree was so leafy Shea and Pott couldn't see Ajala on it and while searching with their eyes for him, they found some red, pod-like fruits, raining on the ground as Ajala was shaking the branches of this tree. Pott picked one and looked at it carefully.

"Exotic." he said. He was examining this fruit, which its pod opened into three parts at the sides. However, some of these fruits were yet to open unlike the rest.

Ajala came down with his calabash bowl almost full of these fruits and met Shea and Pott examining them. He jumped down the few distance remaining for him to come down the tree and placed his calabash on the ground. He took Shea's calabash from her and began to pick up these fruits that fell on the ground and filled Shea's calabash container. Shea and Pott noticed he avoided picking the ones that their pods were yet to split open. He gave Shea's calabash container to her and took Pott's from him and filled it up too with these exotic fruits and at the same time made sure he only picked the ones with opened pods.

"Those were not tasty." he communed to them of those fruits which pods were yet to open.

He took one of these fruits from his container, splat *opened* the pod into its three parts with his hands and plucked out one of the three small fruits inside, stalked on a black nut. He plucked the fruit off the nut with his teeth and chewed it, passed it to Shea and Pott *too,* to have their own taste of it.

"So creamy." said Shea.

Ajala led them to pick up more of exotic fruits. They loved the taste of these *exotic* fruits and Shea continued to go for more.

Then, the lad walked towards a slender and tall palm tree, placed his calabash container, *full of these fruits he gathered,* at the foot of the palm tree and without wasting time, climbed up the extremely tall and thin palm tree, with his bare hands and legs.

When Shea and Pott looked up, they saw a big gourd bottle tied to the neck of this palm tree. Ajala climbed to this bottle, took it and hanged it across his shoulder and began to dismount the palm tree. Immediately, on touching the ground, Ajala walked away while Shea and Pott looked on and after some minutes he came back with another bigger gourd bottle. He climbed up this tall palm tree again and tied it in place of the one he brought down *from the palm tree.* Shea looked into the gourd bottle he brought down and found it full of whitish liquid with dead bees on its surface. Ajala came down and balanced the gourd bottle he brought down from the palm tree on his head and the one full of fruits he carried with his two hands. Shea and Pott followed him as he headed back to the cavern.

Ajala sat in a corner of their cavern abode, eating these fruits, while Shea and Pott were also trying to eat the ones he gathered for them. When Ajala was satisfied, he got up, went out of the cave and came back with three worked gourd cups in his hands. He poured the whitish liquid from the gourd bottle into the three cups and served Shea and Pott, before he started to drank his own. The work on these gourd cups won Pott's attention and he began to wonder, as he was looking at it, contemplating how on Earth Ajala was able to design almost every gourd his hands touched.

"It is alcoholic." said Shea to Pott, after she drank the liquid. Pott took his own cup and drank too.

"So naturally tasty." he remarked.

"Could be intoxicating, if you drink it lot." added Shea.

"I was amazed he could hear the mobile ringing." remarked Shea, and Pott looked at Ajala, who also was looking at his art design that he made on the gourd cup he did just drink from.

"The fruit we just ate is called, 'ushin' and this liquid we are drinking is known as 'emu', palm wine." he communed to them, as he absentmindedly was observing his markings on the gourd cup.

Meanwhile, his eyes caught the drawing of the sun he made on the gourd cup and his mind reminisced flashes of his dreamy experiences, most especially, the outlandish girl he saw in his keen imagination, about the happenings in the vision of the priestess and was sure this girl had the same appearance as Shea and Pott. When Ajala noticed Shea and Pott were staring at him, he threw the gourd cup in his hands to Pott and got up the ground.

"Follow me, friends, I will show you something." said Ajala to them, as he walked out of the cavern.

He led them into the jungle and showed them an extraordinary huge gourd, outstandingly decorated by him with expressive artwork of his dreams and imaginations. What indeed struck Shea's attention was the inscription Ajala made on this gourd about the strange girl *he saw in the sun of his imagination*. The mention of a missing girl by Mother Endor came back to Shea's senses and Mother Endor's attitude about the name Ajala, when she mentioned it *to her*, also surfaced in her mind.

She began to examine carefully all the markings Ajala made *all over* this huge gourd and found the drawing of bizarre creatures like ostrich with human head, humans with animal bodies and various weird artworks. Shea and Pott also saw the markings of two similar phantoms with many, but different binary eye patterns and also a depiction of a pot, covered with cowries and these stuffs indeed stunned them. They thought there must be secret meanings to these depictions.

"What're these things?" asked Shea.

"And how did you make them?" added Pott.

"I don't know, friends."

"You mean you just did them out of mere imagination?"

"I mean, I don't know how and when I did them." confessed Ajala.

"You're kidding me?" gruffed Pott.

"This is amazing." remarked Shea.

"All these must have some sort of meaning." whispered Shea to Pott.

"Anyway, you're a master gourd worker, Ajala." commended Shea.

"Not only that, Snow. All my life I've never seen so much a huge bushel gourd."

"He's a master gourd worker, too!" said Ajala, pointing to the gourd penis sheath Pott was wearing. He actually taught Pott how to make this gourd penis sheath with arched groove that hung around Pott's neck.

"There are more!" he communed.

"You mean there are more?" retorted Shea.

"Come with me!" communed Ajala.

Ajala led them to his exhibition field of gourd carving, crafting, painting, decorating, cutting and gourd art posters. In fact, Shea and Pott were enthralled, nonplussed and totally agape at the *sight of* myriads of breathtaking masterpieces of his gourd artistic dexterity. But by the time Shea and Pott looked back to talk to him, they found he wasn't there with them and they wondered where he was gone. Though, Shea tried to commune with him, she couldn't reach him and she started to look around *for him*, while Pott was absorbed, observing the massive forest of beautiful gourd works before him.

"We've to find him." cried Shea to Pott.

Suddenly, Ajala's flute filtered into Shea and Pott's ears with the same usual note he sang on the day he went to rescue his mother during her public execution. They saw that all the animals and the birds in the jungle were converging towards the sound of the flute and this prompted them, too, to follow these wild creatures to be part of the assembly.

Finally, Shea and Pott found Ajala crouching on the ground, sitting on his heels and his flute in his mouth as all the animals gathered around, looking at him. Shea and Pott, hitherto, hadn't seen many hoards of animals since they came into Igbo – *the evil forest and the land of the gods*.

That very first day they rode into Igbo with Ajala, all the animals dispersed to their different abode instantly, as if marshaled by Ajala's actuation. Only the zebra, the rhino and the giraffe they saddled took them to the entrance of the cave before they dispersed too. Ajala immediately offered them kola nuts, bitter kola and water to drink, according to the custom of these lost tribes, in entertaining visitors *prima facie*.

Shea looked around and once again found everywhere full of Ajala's friends, as they gathered for this solemnity. However, seeing the mounded ground before Ajala, on which he focused his tearful eyes, Shea and Pott knew this must be where he buried his mother.

"This must be some sort of tribute." said Shea.

"Perhaps to his mother?" suggested Pott.

"I guess, but who else could it be, anyway?" concluded Shea and walked to a nearby, wild blossom. She plucked a flower from it, walked to the mound before Ajala, and they stared one another, as she placed it on the demarcated ground. Pott came with his stalk of flower also and like Shea, placed it on this mounded ground.

The animals and birds around them uttered their various cries and Ajala looked at Shea and Pott, while they were prowling their eyes over the animals and birds on every side. Then, they both crouched beside Ajala in sympathy and solidarity, as these empathetic animal hoards continued to utter their different whacking cries.

Chapter Eight

ERIN'S parents got Mother Endor's parcel, though, it was muddled together with the other mails somewhere in the living room, in desperation of holding press conference that day with the Metropolitan police to further appeal to anyone who might have information about the disappearance of their daughter *to come forward*. Hurriedly, the couple left for this conference with family and friends, all together donning on 'Search for Erin T-shirt'.

On the morning of the day after the conference, it started to rain very early and Mother Endor had woken up to a steamy cup coffee. While drinking the coffee, her mind went to the video messages received from Shea, of which she downloaded on her computer for a more conspicuous viewing and careful examination. As soon as she laid her hands on the mouse to click for a reviewing *again* of these video messages, there was a knock on her door. Mother Endor's hand rested motionless on the mouse and she did pull a face, wondering who could be knocking at her door before six o' clock in the morning.

As she got up from her computer desk to spy through her peephole, she heard unfamiliar voices at her doorstep. She watched through the peephole and her eyes caught a beautiful lady, talking with a couple. Instantly, she conjectured in her mind that these must be Erin's parents, but as for the other lady, she wasn't sure who she was and why she came to her door. Mother Endor peeped properly on her person cap-à-pie, yet, she couldn't recollect ever seeing her before.

"Okay, let's find out." she said to herself, as she threw her door open to them, standing right in the middle of her doorway, beaming her almost toothless, dingy smile towards them.

These three strangers seemed dumbfounded at the sight of Mother Endor and she at once perceived their stone-dead attitude.

"None of you expected to see this wrinkled face, plaque teeth, squint eyed and squeaking voiced old Scottish hag, standing right before you?" said Mother Endor gently to them and immediately she careened into her house, leaving the door opened for them to enter.

"No, ma'am, it's just that we felt sorry to have perturbed you so early in the morning." responded Tisseewoonatis politely, as she entered after Mother Endor.

Erin's parents were still confused, looking at one another and wondering if they were at the right door. Erin's mother swooped her eyes again on the house name and the flat number, she dipped her hands into her handbag hastily and brought out the parcel they received some days ago from Mother Endor – *which Erin's father accidentally discovered this morning* – to double check if the address they approached was right. After her verification of the return address, she put the parcel back into her handbag as her eyes briefly prowled over the milieu once more. She nodded to her husband that they were indeed at the right house.

"Are you the only resident in this address, ma'am?" queried Erin's mother, as she entered the house of Mother Endor.

"Yes, my dear and you two must be the parents of the missing girl?" replied Mother Endor, as she turned her attention to Erin's parents. The couple looked at one another, when Mother Endor's words showed that she seemed to be waiting for them. *What a sheer stroke of good luck!* Tisseewoonatis echoed within her about this coincidental meeting with Erin's parents, whom she in fact had on her agenda to visit.

"Ma'am, you're right, we're Erin's parents, but if I may ask you, did you send us this?" asked Erin's mother, as she held the *opened* parcel out towards Mother Endor. She took the parcel, checked *out* its content, and returned it into the envelope.

"I did send it, some of days ago." she answered, as she handed the parcel back to the couple.

"We'd like to have a word with you, please!" opened up Erin's father, but before Mother Endor could reply.

"My name's Twitters." interrupted Tisseewoonatis, as she introduced herself to everyone.

"Tissewoonatis Twitters." she added.

"I called you couple of days ago, remember?" she said.

"Yes, I do." replied Mother Endor.

"I'm pleased to meet you." said Tisseewoonatis.

"Me, too!" said Mother Endor. She shook hands with the

American journalist and paranormal investigator.

"Hi!" gruffed Erin's father briefly, while his wife was too worried to respond to respond to Tisseewoonatis.

"Please, have your seats ladies and gentleman." Mother Endor *finally* welcomed her guests, after they all got to know themselves.

"Cup of coffee?" asked the old lady. However, while Erin's parents weren't in the mood for coffee *out of anticipation,* Tisseewoonatis wouldn't mind.

"Excuse me, please!" said the old lady. She careened into her kitchen to make a cup of coffee for Tisseewoonatis, with the eyes of her guests following her weak frame.

Tisseewoonatis looked at the couple and they chuckled briefly to her. She knew it was plain good luck to have met her prime interviewees, whom she intended visiting before she kicked off her investigations on the mysterious disappearance of their daughter. None-the-less, experience inkling her to keep her cool, until the atmosphere would unveil the right moment.

The gaunt Mother Endor, in her senectitude, careened back into the living room from her kitchen with a cup of steamy coffee in her hands and as soon as Tisseewoonatis saw her coming, she got up to receive the coffee from her.

"Thanks!" appreciated Tisseewoonatis.

"The pleasure's mine, darling!" responded Mother Endor to Tisseewoonatis, as she sat on the armchair opposite her visitors.

While Tisseewoonatis was having sips of her steamy coffee, Mother Endor's eyes were on her splendid Native American jacket. She scrolled her eyes all over Tisseewoonatis' contemporary shining black coat with hand-appliquéd Native American artwork wool and sterling silver moon buttons, fully lined and at each lower side of these silver moon faced button coat was embroidered colourfully, adjacent to each another, the porcupine headdresses of Native Americans. A white turtleneck T-shirt brighten up this coat on red trouser jeans that stood straight into her pointed toe, long leg white boot with medium stack effect heel that set her directly above six feet *height.* A buffalo skin hat delicately graced atop her neatly packed hair.

"Ti-ss-ee-wee-nat-in?" stammered Mother Endor, trying to pronounce her unique name.

"Ti-ss-ee-woo-na-tis." she drawled, helping Mother Endor through her name.

"I'm so – sorry about that!" apologised Mother Endor, for pronouncing her name improperly.

"Oh, Mother, that's fine!" responded Tisseewoonatis.

"What a nice, long name you've got, darling." commented Mother Endor.

"Thanks!" replied Tisseewoonatis.

"I'd take this as a remarkable compliment." she added.

"It's a Native American name meaning 'she who baths with her knees'." explained Tisseewoonatis, as she grasped her cup of coffee again to have another sip.

"An outstanding name, for an outstanding lady, from outstanding people!" remarked Mother Endor.

"Thanks for your comment!" responded Tisseewoonatis.

Erin's parents were sitting, holding hands and looking at Mother Endor, who sat confidently, talking to Tisseewoonatis. As Erin's mother was staring Mother Endor's eye-catching face, she could somehow imagine it radiating mystical insight into the unknown. Instantaneously, she was contemplating a new dimension in her mind about this boggling whodunit that was surrounding her daughter's disappearance. Erin's mother was beginning to think that the disappearance of her daughter might not be ordinary after all. However, skepticism struck her mind with the foolishness of such self-assuredness. Of a sudden, she became deeply worried and panicky about the whole issue.

"Where's my daughter, old lady?" cried Erin's mother and everyone went quiet, looking at each other. Mother Endor herself remained quiet, looking at the couple. Erin's father was holding his shivering wife cozily.

"What on earth's this?" cried Erin's mother, breaking the utter silence and holding out the disc containing the video messages of Shea and Pott, which Mother Endor mailed to them. Mother Endor remained silent, still looking at the couple, while Tisseewoonatis put her voice recorder into action. Mother Endor's eyes swayed on the recorder as she placed it on the stool beside her. She looked at Tisseewoonatis and gave her a friendly smile. She turned to Erin's parents again, but before she could utter a word, Erin's mother lost her cool.

"Where's this boy, in Hollywood?" exclaimed Erin's mother in tears. She dropped the disc on the floor before Mother Endor.

"What can I say, ma'am?" said Erin's father. He held his wife closer to his chest, patting her hair with the palm of his hand.

"Please, something in me tells me you'd be of help!" pleaded Erin's father, as he was still comforting his wife. Mother Endor shuffled herself properly on her chair.

"I'm Mother Endor." she introduced and at this point, Tisseewoonatis began snapping pictures.

"Now, let's talk about why we're here this morning." said Mother Endor.

"She's a freelance paranormal journalist involved in the investigation of weird events, hunted places and even UFOS. We spoke at length couple of weeks ago before we met this morning and I believe you're also meeting her for the first time." said Mother Endor about Tisseewoonatis.

"I do think we both should approve of her involvement in this issue, right?" said Mother Endor and Erin's father nodded agreement. He seemed more prepared to hear Mother Endor, speaking about his daughter's disappearance than her preamble about Tisseewoonatis.

"After I saw you on BBC, with the paper containing the handwriting borne of your daughter's dream and the composite image of the African lad of your daughter's dream, I tried to contact you for a possible access to this strange piece, so that I can psychically examine it, but you declined. None-the-less, the same BBC correspondent connected Tisseewoonatis to me. When she called me couple of days ago and introduced herself, I welcomed her straightaway into the preternatural search for your daughter." explained Mother Endor, while Erin's parents seemed puzzled the more by her calling the search for Erin a supernatural one. Certainly, Tisseewoonatis busied herself capturing every scene of this encounter on her superb camera and at the same time, her camera was *capable of* videoing the scenario. Also she was following the discussions keenly.

"When I saw the broadcast of your daughter's disappearance in the United States, with the experience I've had on the unusual and unpredictable realm of supernatural, I knew it wasn't an ordinary phenomenon." said Tisseewoonatis, as she continued to click her camera on every move being made.

"I've been involved in several paranormal phenomena activities like ECETI, the UFOS, appearance and disappearance of aliens, alien adoptions, the issues of ghosts and demons, angels, cemetery investigation, witchcraft and paranormal dreams." added Tisseewoonatis.

Immediately she mentioned paranormal dreams, Erin mother's memory flashed back to her daughter's weird dreams and she hurriedly dipped her hands into her handbag to bring out the paper containing the oneiric handwriting that was borne out of her daughter's dream. She pointed the piece to Mother Endor, but Tisseewoonatis, after snapshots of Erin's mother with the paper in her hand, got hold of it and took it to Mother Endor. As Tisseewoonatis got hold of the paper from Erin's mother, Mother Endor leaned forward, picked the disc Erin's mother dropped on the floor and gave it to Tisseewoonatis, as she was receiving the paper from her.

"You'd watch this." said Mother Endor to her. Tisseewoonatis quickly brought out her super-slim, extra-small, rugged and waterproof, OmniTouch *model* notebook of 10GB DDR and 10000 T*erabite* HDD, known for its state of the art software *programs*, effectiveness, efficiency and durability. She inserted the disc and was watching, while Erin's parents sat quietly as Mother Endor was examining the oneiric handwriting.

"Is this Hollywood clip?" asked Tisseewoonatis, as she was watching the clip on her notebook. Of course, the clip made no sense to her too because like Erin's parents, she had no prior knowledge of the whole events behind it, as Mother Endor indeed had.

Unbeknownst to this *seemingly* secret gathering, the met squad of detective Chief Inspector Briggs had put the Eyers on surveillance, since Erin's mother had been tagged a possible suspect in the disappearance of her daughter. She had been placed on a twenty-four-seven surveillance and the officers on the watch over her were baffled what this secret meeting was all about.

"As I said previously, I'm Mother Endor and my psychic generations had been the custodian of the Temple of Endor for aeon, an otherworld Temple of which every current custodian, in every generation, had to keep vigil on a secret, prehistoric, psychic prophecy." continued Mother Endor.

"My psychic generations had done this for many millennia." confessed Mother Endor.

"Millennia." she retorted, looking at everyone in the eye, as she knew they seemed puzzled by what they were hearing.

"Millennia?" repeated Tisseewoonatis with astonishment as she clicked on her camera, capturing these unveiling moments she patiently anticipated.

"Yes, millennia!" affirmed Mother Endor.

"Though, you may not understand fully what I'm trying to say. Therefore, I believe we'd concentrate on the nitty-gritty of this matter, that's Erin's puzzling disappearance." she opined and continued, as everyone remained attentive to listen to her.

"I was so lucky for the advent of the 'eternal bird', which is a crucial phenomenon to the occurrence of this prophecy and I still couldn't believe that this age long, prehistoric psychic prophecy's about to be fulfilled in my lifetime." said Mother Endor with some strange reverence on her face.

"I was in the otherworld Temple of Endor, giving the necessary psychic training to my two protégés, when the 'eternal bird' appeared. Its bigger than the Temple, flickering body dazzled through the training chamber and instantly I remembered it was written in my psychic generations' prophecy that, '... at the coming of the eternal bird, one of the two fateful shall be sent to behold its mystique ...' Forthwith, I sent one of my trainee protégés to look out through the window and she saw a sparkling, tiny bird, perching on a tree branch and with this portent I knew the threshold of my protégés' mission had just begun. Instantly, I sent them home to prepare to follow the mystique of the 'eternal bird' whenever it's on flight and to wherever it might lead. When they got to their different homes, they communicated on phone and realised this bird was with both of them at their respective locations. When its mystique flashed on them, they prepared themselves in a hurry and on their bikes they rushed after the ethereal bird, which led them to the airport and perched on an airplane. They found out the destination of this particular airplane and they applied for their relevant travelling documents. Some days later, they boarded this plane on which the benign fey avian perched to show them where fate's leading them. Eventually, with the help of this phenomenal, foretold sacred bird, I sent my two psychic protégés to an unknown land and also after an unspecified mission, guided by the 'eternal bird' as my prehistoric prophecy portended." continued Mother Endor. Though, none of her listeners could comprehend the in depth of her discussion, yet they listened with rapt attention.

"From this part of the world, the 'eternal bird' led them to a remote location somewhere amongst a lost tribe in West Africa, where the video messages you watched on the disc came from and I'm indeed sure that where this 'eternal bird' led them is of remarkable focus in the affairs about to be fulfilled in my psychic generations' prehistoric prophecy." concluded Mother Endor. But Erin's parents were somewhat hurt, when they couldn't figure out how the disappearance and finding their daughter fitted into all Mother Endor enumerated.

"Everything's out of context here." said Erin's mother with a discontented voice.

"What concerns my daughter with your psychic omens of 'eternal bird' or whatever it is you call it?" she asked.

"Would you mind telling me where my daughter's right now, if you know?" exclaimed Erin's mother on top of her voice. However, her husband was still holding her closer to his chest.

"We'd all calm down for a good analysis of the whole issue and with my experiences, I know nothing's impossible in this life, when it comes to paranormal world. Though, I wouldn't pretend I'm not somewhat confused too, Mother?" confessed Tisseewoonatis, as she walked to face the old lady and before she could reply, Tisseewoonatis cut in again.

"I'd like to ask you few questions, Mother." said Tisseewoonatis.

Mother Endor looked at her and she could see on the old lady's countenance that she was more than ready to give answers to her questions.

"What does the phenomenon you called 'eternal bird' meant?"

"It's the balance of dominion between good and evil, the ultimate arch-power and authority anyone could ever possess, but in human history only one prehistoric person had had the privilege of possessing it, and that was in the beginning."

"It could be called arch-witchcraft." she added.

"What did you mean by psychic generations?"

"Psychic DNA flows from one particular psychic generation to the other or from one psychic person to another. Psychic generation has nothing to do with blood ties, race or nationality, but when one inherited a particular psychic aptitude that conveys with it distinctive, metaphysically coded messages that I called psychic genome, of which such heir would therefore be responsible. When this particular sequence of psychic nucleotides involved many generations, as it's been in my case, then we have psychic generations."

"These metaphysically coded psychic messages or rather psychic genomes embody *part of* what you meant by psychic generations' prophecy?"

"Brilliant." answered Mother Endor with a smile.

"It could be either forth-telling or foretelling psychic genome, but in my case, I guess it's both!" added Mother Endor.

"However, I still don't grasp fully what you're saying, ma'am?" confessed Tisseewoonatis.

"How did our daughter got involved in all these strange things we couldn't even comprehend?" interrupted Erin's father.

"This puzzled me, too." responded Mother Endor.

"Of course, it isn't known to me the relevance of your daughter in this whole issue and concerning her disappearance, even the prophecy didn't stipulate anything I could relate to her. What, where, how and who my prophecy is or will be all about, I don't know, but I'm quite sure things will take shape, as I continue to forth-tell the prophecy." said Mother Endor, looking at everyone.

"My psychic generations' prophecy stopped at the advent of the 'eternal bird', '... when the 'eternal bird' shall pass through the Temple of Endor upon the two protégés, under the tutelage of the fateful psychic, it shall guide them to fulfill the age long prophecy.' Nothing more was said of the prophecy again or what it's set to fulfill" explained Mother Endor.

"I'm only trying to see how I can safeguard this prophecy to the right path." she commented.

"However, the whole issue became more arresting when I heard of Erin's dream from you on TV." continued Mother Endor, referring to Erin's mother.

"You gave a vivid description of the African boy of your daughter's dream and also you presented the oneiric handwriting that was borne out of her dream – *hajahlah*. When I saw the name of the African lad borne out of her dream and his identikit image, I noticed that he was as much alike as the West African lad in the video messages my protégés sent to me from somewhere in West Africa."

said Mother Endor, with her attention towards Erin's parents.

"No doubt, the name of the African lad of Erin's dream, his description, compared with the name of the African lad texted to me and his look, though intricate, but at the same time striking. In fact, the identikit image was amazingly true of the look of this African lad my protégés sent me in their video messages." related Mother Endor.

"And this was my main aim of wanting to contact you personally, so that I can make psychic connection with this paper containing the handwriting borne out of your daughter's dream."

"Please, do now!" said Erin's father, pointing to the paper of Erin's dream that Mother Endor was still holding in her hand.

"Thank you." said Mother Endor, who did almost forget the paper was still in her hands, therefore, she at once looked at the paper painstakingly.

"First of all, this handwriting's psychically bona-fide." confirmed Mother Endor, as she was staring at the paper.

"Through this phenomenal handwriting borne of your daughter's dream and by the residual psychic energy on it, I can reach her wherever she's now. If she's alive, my psychic clinamen will find her, she'll respond and you'll even hear her voice." she claimed and Erin's mother began to show more interest, when she heard she would possibly hear her daughter's voice.

"But if she's dead, she'll be silent, I'll be the only person to hear her voice or perhaps see her. If you'd like me to conduct this transcendental search is up to you." explained Mother Endor and Erin's mother looked at her husband in the face, with fear and devastation of the unthinkable possible outcome written all over her. She was visibly shaking out of anxiety that suddenly took over her.

"I'm scared." she whispered to her husband.

"It's alright, darling." he encouraged *his wife.*

"If you don't want this, I don't want it either." he muttered into her ear.

"I know you're stronger than you did ever think, my dear." encouraged Tisseewoonatis. Mother Endor sat with the strange paper of Erin's dream in her hands, waiting for Erin's parents to give her permission to contact their missing daughter psychically.

"Let's give it a try." said Erin's father finally, on behalf of his wife, who was too numbed to give the permission.

"Sometimes dreams are one of the keys to our subconscious

and no doubt your daughter's dream showed me that she's a unique subconscious mind and her fate is intertwined with the fate of whoever wrote this word." remarked Mother Endor.

She placed the paper of Erin's dream on her laps, placed her arms gently on the chair's arms support and stared intently on this strange handwriting *borne of Erin's dream.*

"I can perceive that the handwriting on this paper is full of complicated mystique." she said.

She closed her eyes slowly in a trance-like gesture and at this point, Tisseewoonatis made sure her camera was on video for the action and at the same time she continued her photographing the meeting. There was utter silence in the room, except the clicking of her camera, one after the other and after a while of cogitation into the subconscious state *on this unusual handwriting* by Mother Endor.

"Let the girl's mother invoke her daughter's name, now!" she pronounced gently in a shrilling voice that sounded androglossia and Tisseewoonatis knew she was probably speaking out of her subliminal self. Erin's mother stared at her husband, who nodded her to go ahead, as Mother Endor had said and as soon as Erin's mother called her daughter's name.

"Yes, mum, I'm here mum, help me!" responded Erin.

Erin's voice was heard from no particular direction by all present, as if Erin's voice was from within them. However, Erin's mother thought her daughter should be somewhere in the house

Tisseewoonatis' camera caught a strange image as she snapped pictures concurrently with the sound of Erin's voice. She was shocked by this image's psychic stream and the camera fell off her hands. Couple with the sudden apprehension from Erin's mother, who snapped to attention and rushed higgledy-piggledy against Tisseewoonatis, the furniture and doors of the house, thinking her daughter was somewhere in the rooms.

"Holy cow!" cried Tisseewoonatis.

"Simmer down!" shouted Mother Endor, who, on the instant of the panic-stricken Erin's mother, woke from her psychic brown study.

"Please, ask her where she's." requested *the confused* Erin's mother.

"Help us, please!" pleaded Erin's father *passionately.* Of course, they heard their daughter's voice.

"Calm down!" responded Mother Endor, pointing Erin's parents to their seat.

"I saw something." said Tisseewoonatis.

"What, where?" asked *all together* Erin's parents and Mother Endor. Tisseewoonatis from her standing position, pointed her finger to her camera on the floor.

"I think, it's dead." said Mother Endor, as she picked it up, looking at it.

"Hope I haven't damaged the stuff!" she said.

She took the device from Mother Endor and while she was examining it, the camera came up again.

"My goodness!" she exclaimed, as she saw a strange object she snapped incidentally on the camera's screen, when Erin's voice was heard.

She showed the strange object to Mother Endor, who suggested a playback from the moment she started the invocation process. Tisseewoonatis played the invocation scene again and Mother Endor discovered that the object appeared in lieu of Erin's voice, which was not audible on the camera's video. Tisseewoonatis connect her camera to her notebook immediately and downloaded the image, printed it on her mobile printer for Mother Endor to see clearly. Mother Endor stared at the odd black pot, adorned with cowries in a well arranged form and from the top of this pot, down to below its bottom, were drooping cowries like curtains round its brim.

"What the hell's this?" asked Erin's mother. She was looking at the picture in Mother Endor's hands.

"It's so strange, Mother." said Tisseewoonatis, but Mother Endor was silent, staring at the strange object intently.

"Mother, can you understand why this strange thing appeared on the camera?" asked Erin's father, but she gave no reply.

She sat, musing on *the picture of* this odd object and her bemused countenance was obvious. Everyone went back to their seat, awaiting Mother Endor to say something about this strange pot. Though, they knew she was also somehow bewildered by the object.

"Could you be so kind to ask our daughter where she was taken and who took her and why?" asked Erin's mother, interrupting Mother Endor's silence out of anticipation.

"No, my dear, I can't."

"Of course, you spoke to her just now!" shouted Erin's

mother at Mother Endor in desperation.

"No, I didn't speak to her, you did!" cried Mother Endor *angrily*.

Erin's mother broke down in her husband's arms and Mother Endor instantly felt pity for her. She apologised for being harsh on her and explained to the couple how the issue of Erin's disappearance was one of pain for her too. She made them understand that if the child was indeed part of her psychic generations' prophecy, then, she had to find her quickly because if anything happens to her, this could also mean the bane of her lasting prophecy. She made the couple realise that the residual psychic energy of the handwriting could only be exploited once and that it was impossible to use again any sixth sense effectively on the handwriting to reach Erin.

"You shouldn't have interrupted the session the way you did. Perhaps, we'd have got whatever information you crave from your missing daughter through your voice." said Mother Endor to Erin's mother and she apologised for her lack of equanimity.

"Notwithstanding, my dear, I have a hunch the disappearance of your daughter has to do with this strange pot in the picture, and if I must put things together, I noticed the pot appeared on the camera, when your daughter answered your voice. There's a psychic attraction in this, I mean, between the strange pot and your daughter. Also, since cowries were predominantly used from olden days in West Africa for juju purposes and cultic decorations, I presume your daughter is somewhere unknown to any of us in that region." conjectured Mother Endor.

"You meant our daughter was kidnapped by Africans?" asked Erin's father.

"Why would they abduct my daughter?" queried Erin's mother *instantaneously*.

"P-u-e-r-i-l-i-t-y!" drawled Mother Endor.

"Both of you, your minds are psychically puerile to my explanations." alleged Mother Endor.

"Can't you understand I don't know for sure what exactly happened to your daughter, let alone accusing anyone for it?" she added.

"Eh, I'd think there's an éclaircissement here, Mother." said Tisseewoonatis, as she held in her hands another image of the strange object she printed. She placed it on the table and they all lingered over this odd, self-revealing image.

"My intuition inkling me that these cowries on the bizarre image were designed for the modern man to understand." said Tisseewoonatis, pointing to the details she was trying to explain, with the pencil she held in her hand.

"Now, the patterned arrangement of the cowries on the pot portrayed the world itself, but in the sense of when the continents were one landmass." she analysed and Mother Endor was struck by her observation, but she hid her suspicion.

"The drooping cowries round the pot, extending below its bottom were evident of hidden messages or hidden power, or rather hidden secrets pertaining to the pot, or something, or someone or the unseen world, I guess." inferred Tisseewoonatis.

"Like a curtain's a form of veil." she added.

"Mother, what did you think?" inquired Tisseewoonatis *from Mother Endor* about her inference on this strange object. Mother Endor mused her eyes on the image, contemplating what Tisseewoonatis had just ratiocinated.

"Mother, can you communicate with the image?" asked Erin's father.

"No, sir, this image isn't a child's play. It restrains its aura and psychic energy, somehow, from any interference. I haven't seen anything like it all my life." answered Mother Endor.

"What a strange stuff!" she said with her eyes still on this odd image Tisseewoonatis caught on her camera.

After lingering awhile on the image, Mother Endor and her visitors went back calmly to their seats. Mother Endor relaxed on her armchair, looking at Tisseewoonatis.

"Are you prepared to go to Africa?" she asked and almost instantly Mother Endor's phone rang before Tisseewoonatis could give a reply.

"Excuse me!" she politely requested to pick her call.

"You're quite excused." responded Tisseewoonatis.

"Hello, Mother!" said Pott.

"How do you do, son?" asked Mother Endor.

"And how's Shea doing?" she asked quickly.

"She's perfect, Mother." said Pott.

"We're good." he added.

"Mother, we're trapped in a forest called Igbo, Ajala had

warned us it's dangerous to go outside the forest." relayed Pott to Mother Endor.

"I know what you're going through and I want you guys to know that I'm with you." empathised Mother Endor.

"Stay close to him and earn his trust, perhaps, he'll eventually lead us to the nitty-gritty of the whole purpose we want to unravel." encouraged Mother Endor *to her protégés.*

"And try to help him in any way you can, please!" added Mother Endor.

Detective Chief Inspector Briggs' gumshoes, who were exercising twenty-four seven surveillance on Erin Eyers parents couldn't wait any longer for them to emerge from Mother Endor's apartment. So, one of them went closer to listen to what was going on inside the house with his hi-tech, recording headphone, embedded with powerful microphones to catch and record suspected voices even from distance. He stood near the block, dancing with his head, as if listening to music, but he was in fact attentive to the discussion going on in Mother Endor's apartment.

"I'll go to Africa, Mother. Of course, I need to set my eyes on this lad called Ajala." interrupted Erin's mother the phone conversation of Mother Endor with Pott and she gestured to her to be quiet. As she was talking to Pott, Mother Endor looked at Tisseewoonatis, who also nodded agreement to go to Africa and this brought a broad smile on her face.

"Did you or Shea catch sight of any big, black pot, ornamented with cowries?"

"No Mother, nothing of such." replied Pott.

"Why?" queried Pott.

"Oh, never mind, dear Pott." said Mother Endor casually.

"The most important thing is, you'll be receiving some visitors from me in couple of days." said Mother Endor.

"But how you'll get them safely to you where you are is of paramount importance and you also have to protect them from any harm."

"Eh, Mother, call you back in a minute. We better talk to Ajala about this issue, don't you think so?"

"Okay Pott, I'll be waiting." replied Mother Endor.

Pott called Shea O'Shepherd to his side and discussed the coming of the visitors with her and how possible they could ensure their safety. While they were still discussing the issue secretly and trying to decide how best to inform Ajala to make sure they get them safely to Igbo.

"Do not worry, let them come." telepathised Ajala in the usual thought transference manner right into both Shea and Pott's psyche. Shea turned around to Ajala immediately she heard his psychic voice and found out the lad wasn't even looking at them and also wasn't within earshot of their discussion. Ajala was busy breaking palm nuts with stones, chewing the kernel and spitting out its whitish particles. Though, he could hear Shea and Pott's psychic voices in this matter, without them perceiving he heard them.

"What?" said Pott.

"You heard him, don't you?" answered Shea.

"He said we shouldn't worry about their coming." added Shea, still staring at Ajala and as Ajala perceived Shea's glare towards him, he held the stone in his hand on a palm nut and slowly turned his face on Shea too. He got up, leaving the stone on the palm nut, he gently walked the ground length to Shea and Pott and stood before them.

"Let them come, we'll receive them safely and I'm happy they're coming." he said.

"But you don't even know them!" asked Shea, in the usual extrasensory manner.

"You don't have to see or know someone to love them, you only have to see or know someone to hate them." said Ajala and Shea shook her head in acceptance of his pithy words.

"Can you sense their coming's for a good purpose?" asked Shea.

"Guess so!" answered Ajala, with raised facial expression. As Ajala's okapi strode to the entrance of the cave, he walked to the beast, jumped on it, looking at Shea and Pott.

"Let them come." he drawled and the okapi galloped away from their sight into the jungle, under the *heavy* typical African rainfall that began. Shea and Pott wondered, where Ajala could be going during this heavy rainfall.

Nevertheless, Pott dialed mother Endor again to finally approve of the coming of Tisseewoonatis and Erin's mother. Pott gave them the phone contact of the driver, who drove them from the airport and promised to inform him to drop them off *Tisseewoonatis and Erin's mother,* where he did alight them. He texted the phone contact of the visitors to the driver, after he spoke to him of the coming of Erin's mother and Tisseewoonatis.

While Mother Endor sat alone inside her house, starring at the printed image of the strange pot, Erin's father drove his wife home to begin preparing her visit to West Africa and Tisseewoonatis went back to her hotel room to analyse and make notes about the occurrence of the day, with her heart also focused on meeting Ajala.

Detective Chief Inspector Briggs' gumshoes wasted no time to hint him of Erin mother's plan to visit Africa and this indeed raised suspicion on his mind, when he couldn't rationalised why on Earth she would be visiting Africa, in middle of the investigation of her daughter's disappearance. *Perhaps, this woman knew more than what she's letting out.* Mused detective Chief Inspector Briggs.

Chapter Nine

THE metropolitan police had been struggling to decipher the *whodunit* conundrum behind Erin's sudden disappearance, however, no realistic result had come off their investigative and scientifically laden forensic effort.

Detective Chief Inspector Briggs had interrogated everyone to be questioned concerning the case, but his sleeplessness over this case was futile, as he couldn't just generate any credible lead and also explaining what happened to Erin, too, was impossible other than the only untenable option that the innocent girl *just* disappeared. The only thing sure and well established was that Erin was nowhere to be found and the much relied upon CCTV footages couldn't just give any clue as to how this happened. The investigation was frustrating for Briggs and his squad and the pressure to produce result was mounting *on them* day in day out.

"Erin on the damn morning of December 1st, along with her parents was visiting a team of psychologists, philosophers and scientists on the unusual issue surrounding her incessant dreams and her weird genetical features. The fucking rendezvous was in one of the NHS children's hospital, where Erin's General Practitioner referred her case, which to her did not only seem to defy scientific reasoning and logic, but also goddamn fucking common sense. At the meeting, while Erin was being examined through excellent series of bullshit clinical questions concerning her oneiric experiences, she requested to take a leak. However, the loo was just fucking next door to the damn meeting room and the nurse attending to Erin pointed her to the fucking door leading to the goddamn loo for Erin to get herself eased. She opened this damn ill-fucking door and entered into the children's loo. While Erin was in this loo, the goddamn question of Erin's unique genetic traits was raised amongst these experts, perhaps, as a godforsaken possible cause of her damn oneiric experiences. Though, Erin's General Practitioner, who was also present at this shitload of a meeting, made these experts understood that such damn possibilities had been fucking clinically examined and found to be of no goddamn particular effect on Erin's sleep, dreams or health whatsoever." detoured detective Briggs *in frustration* his usual repertoire, before his investigative squad. Nevertheless, unknown to him, Erin's mother was listening behind the door. She entered and focused her eyes on him.

"Holy shit!" murmured detective Briggs, as soon as he saw her. Erin's mother sat on a chair nearby her, looking at him while the investigative squad's eyes turned *briefly* on her. *What a motherfucker badass she probably think I'm!* Mused detective Briggs.

"The team of experts was examining Erin's parents to get more facts as they could, when Erin's mother noticed her daughter delayed coming out of the loo." continued detective Chief Inspector Briggs, pointing to Erin's mother where she sat. He was struggling to stay clear of cussing since she came in.

"Even the CCTV footage showed her viewing her wrist watch. She wasted no time to excuse herself and went straight after her daughter, just to come out empty handed. Why? Simple, Erin was gone! No blood traces, no suspicious foot print or shoe print or finger print, no skin flakes and no single hair strand. In fact, no DNA was left behind. The whole crime scene was swept clean and forensic investigation for the first time in my years of career was totally rendered nugatory by this crime. The CCTV recorded nothing other than Erin going into the loo and her mother coming out after. The outdoor CCTV that surrounds the whole hospital and the streets around had been examined, but they all yielded no lead. None the less, through the window of the same loo, a colourful, tiny, unclassified bird was seen going inside, and astonishingly, like Erin, no trace of this lovely bird coming out of the loo either. The CCTVs were neither in bad condition nor tampered with, according to technical examination." there was a pause. "Then, what the fucking hell happened to this innocent gal?" cried Briggs on top of his voice, banging his hand on the table so hard his wrist watch broke off and everyone shuddered, including Erin's mother where she sat.

"No bodies, no fucking leads." he said.

"This sucks." he sighed.

"I'm sorry!" he went to Erin's mother and muttered apology for swearing *despite that he tried not to*. However, detective Briggs, whom this whole puzzling circumstance was almost running him out of his mind, dismissed his investigative squad. He had audience with

Erin's mother, earnestly expecting her to inform him about her plan to visit Africa. After he was done with Erin's mother, who didn't mention anything about her going to West Africa, as his surveillance sleuths had inkling him, detective Briggs became strongly suspicious of her motive.

Instantly, he resolved to ask for the assistance of Intelligence and Espionage agency, MI6, *Military Intelligence, section six,* and counterintelligence agency, MI5, *Military Intelligence, section five,* to lend a hand by giving him and his trusted members of his squad access to their jointly developed superb hi-tech, surreptitious, genetically based programmed spying satellite, which was maneuverable to monitor more than one individual or groups concurrently, wherever they may be, anywhere in the world, even at different locations, countries or continents. The 'genomathics' involved in programming this spying satellite existed nowhere on the globe. Through this highly developed 'genomathics', this satellite could be manipulated by applied 'biogenoarithmetics' to locate and spy on anyone on the planet, wherever and whenever.

However, he knew this wouldn't be easy, because this was a top secret project that was instituted by the clandestine clique within the éminences grises and made available only to their authorised few. He was concerned about one thing and that was how he would explain the means by which he got to know about this classified, espionage satellite dubbed 'God'. Unbeknownst to detective Chief Inspector Briggs, by seeking the help of this clandestine 'God' his genuine search for Erin would eventually spiral into another phase.

Nevertheless, he was convinced this was the only way he could keep tabs on Erin's mother effectively, if actually she would be visiting Africa. Furthermore, despite his conviction to resort to 'God', he wasn't of any illusion that this wouldn't be an easy task because 'God' was an unlawfully instituted and operated spying satellite that he knew, even his bosses, perhaps, weren't aware this possibility existed. Therefore, he resolved it would be wise to act through his privy into the knowledge of this unprecedented spying gizmo.

Detective Chief Inspector Briggs was amazed when he was granted this access within six hours of contacting his informant about the issue. He still couldn't believe it until he was provided a monitor control system in a classified location, where Briggs could stationed two of his excellent and trusted gumshoes. By whom, with the help of this clandestine satellite's cameras would monitor and record Erin mother's activities right from her doorsteps. Wherever she would go on the planet and whoever she would come in contact with, her actions and words would clandestinely be filmed round the clock.

"C'mon, assholes, there's no losing sight of her whilst this investigation's inconclusive and thoroughgoing." remarked Briggs to his two sleuths that he stationed in the monitoring room, when he visited them for a briefing.

Chapter Ten

THE starry night over Eboru overwhelmed the whole village with its thick darkness. Of course, the moonlit season was over, yet the stars dazzled splendidly in their multitudes, but could do nothing to lighten up the pristine milieu of these lost tribes, other than the sight of their soul-stirring beauty that glazed *over* the sky.

Eboru people weren't known for putting their village on guard because it was a taboo to attack Eboru – *as the land of ascendancy to all the tribes* – in any form or pillage it and this traditional notion somehow prevented the tribes from attacking or pillaging one another. However, Eboru had hunters in strategic places – *like any of these lost tribes* – to protect the tribespeople from wild animals that sometimes strayed out of the jungle. These hunters were sometimes used by the king to deal with anyone or internal affairs that might demand some level of enforcement against *or in arresting* anyone who went against tradition and customs. They were loyal to the throne and the occupier of the throne solely controlled them by tradition through the 'OluOde', *generalissimo of the hunters*.

The *stationed* hunters in strategic positions or any hunter at all weren't allowed by tradition to kill any animal known to stray from Igbo, *the evil forest and the land of the gods*, as it was tabooed to kill or hurt any animal of this revered jungle. They were to use their hunting deterrence to drive these particular animals from the vicinity of the settlements, but any other animal aside from the ones out of Igbo, which strayed into the settlements could be hunted down for food.

That night, the regent of Eboru *village,* was lying down on his wooden, leather covered bed, musing over Ajala's exploits in order to figure out how to finally put him to death. As he lay on his back, with a big tortoise as pillow, in his head was niggling the advantageous way to get rid of the lad. Of course, he knew things were getting out of hand already, therefore, he had engaged himself in persuading the chiefs and elders of Eboru to endeavour unleashing the *invincible* Shigidi once again, either to capture, or preferably this time, to destroy *Ajala* the lad he *now* dubbed 'OmoOfun', *l'enfant perdu*, of the house Babalawo, since he ascended the throne as the regent of Eboru, proudly claiming he was publicly chosen by the fire of the gods and thus the first to be granted such honour by the gods.

However, the problem of whom would willingly volunteer to let go of his or her innocent daughter, as a voluntary *ad hoc* sacrifice for the *invincible* Shigidi to act against Ajala was unthinkable. The regent wasn't ignorant of the fact that without the blood of this voluntary sacrificial victim *of Ajala's age and sex* for the Shigidi to act, it would be impossible to unleash the *invincible* Shigidi against him.

The regent had confuted the notion everyone held that Ajala was male, hence his capture by the Shigidi did never occur in the first place, because the sacrifice of an innocent male child was offered to the *invincible* Shigidi instead of that of a female. Indeed, the chiefs and elders of Eboru *village* refuted this idea of involving the *invincible* Shigidi *once more* with the excuse that, if the *invincible* Shigidi couldn't overpower and apprehend Ajala in the first occasion, perhaps the Shigidi wouldn't work on him the second time. Though, the regent knew that the chiefs and elders of Eboru weren't willing to offer this *invincible* Shigidi's voluntary ritual, which might deprive whoever volunteered the life of his or her innocent daughter of Ajala's age.

While the regent was perturbed and unable to sleep in the palace, contemplating how to get rid of Ajala once and for all. Shea and Ajala on the other hand were sitting at the entrance of their cavern *home* at Igbo, admiring the starry night sky.

"There's reason for whatsoever happens in life." said Shea to Ajala, as they both were sitting, gazing at the starry sky over Eboru, but Ajala remained silent still, focusing his eyes towards the constellations.

Shea also had been persuading Ajala to help her in setting free the *untouchable* children in the dungeon, though, Ajala declined her request with the excuse that he wouldn't want to meddle in Eboru's affairs anymore. That very night, Pott had already slept off in the cavern, with a robust cobra that he did befriend through Ajala, lying on him for warmth.

Shea also went silent for some time, looking at Ajala, whose attention was fixed on the awe-inspiring starry night sky.

"What're you looking at?" asked Shea.

"They say that is where the Babalawo went." telepathised Ajala, pointing to the constellations.

"Who's this Babalawo?" asked Shea.

"My late father!" he replied, but Shea knew that something else was bothering him. Shea was also thinking of saving the *untouchable* children in the dungeon before it would be too late.

"What are you thinking, my friend?" she asked calmly.

"Nothing," answered Ajala briefly.

"C'mon!" said Shea with friendly gesture, as she placed her palm on Ajala's hand.

"Just thinking about my mother." added Ajala, after a brief silence that was followed by a heavy sigh.

"What about your mother, dear friend?"

"She gave her life for mine."

"Any good mother would do that for her child." remarked Shea.

"I want you to know that your mother was a great woman. You must stop blaming yourself for what happened and let me tell you, you've done very well to show your people that you're the true son of your mother, okay?" encouraged Shea.

"Yes, she was indeed a good mother, but I couldn't help her when I was supposed to. Does that make me a good person too?"

"What could you've done, Ajala?"

"You're only a kid!"

"At least ..." said Ajala.

"At least what?" interrupted Shea *gently*.

"Yes, you did all you could."

"All I could wasn't enough to save her and sometimes I did ask myself why?"

"There's a reason for everything that happens in life, my friend." said Shea.

"No, we find justifiable reasons for whatever right or wrong that happens in life." answered Ajala. She was silent, musing over he said and trying to see how he could sway the discussion towards the misery of the *untouchable* children *she met in the rock-cut subterranean dungeon.*

"Then, let's find reasons that justifies the plight of the

untouchables."

"No reason on this planet could ever justify that, my friend." responded Ajala.

"It's like saying there are reasons that could justify my people for rejecting, persecuting, castigating and condemning me, no matter what, as a forbidden soul?" commented Ajala.

"What reason could ever justify that, or the fatal lapidation of my innocent mother?" he refuted.

"Then, this is why you've got to liberate the *untouchable* children, even if this would inflame the heart of your tribespeople to hate you the more. Of course, you have to do what's right before it is too late." buttressed Shea.

Immediately, Ajala realised where Shea was steering the discussion and although he knew Shea was right, but the lad feared that the more he meddled in Eboru's affairs, the more his people would be convinced he was the forbidden soul. While Shea waited for him to reply, she knew he was thoroughly ruminating the matter within him.

"Those children are dying and remember your mother died for you and I believe, whatsoever, she'd be happy and proud if you try to set them free." persuaded Shea.

Suddenly, at the words of Shea, Ajala looked morose and Shea knew he was afraid, she got hold of his hands.

"You're like my mother, lady. You're indeed making me rebellious?" he asked.

"The two of you!"

"Me and your late mother?"

"Yes!"

"Why?"

"She also told me that the untouchables are to be set free and untouchability intolerable anymore."

"If it's for the sake of the truth and what's right, let it be!" responded Shea.

"It's one of those things she taught me before she died." said Ajala *about his late mother*.

"Then, what are you waiting for?" replied Shea.

"I'm afraid!" he said, with a forlorn glance and Shea held his hands more firmly to make him feel she was there for him.

"I know, but I promise I'll stand by you to the very end, like your mother did."

Ajala looked at Shea deeply in the eyes, when he heard these words.

"She also told me to be careful because our people would leave no stone unturned to hunt me down, like they did to her and I'm scared." he said

"Fear's the bane of the soul." remarked Shea.

"And one last thing she said to me was, 'Even if they'd skin you alive, pluck out your eyes, smash off your teeth with stones and get you circumcised, don't you ever be a coward, because you are my son'." explained Ajala.

He went dead silent for a while, as he was staring into Shea's blue eyes, remembering that very day his mother spoke these words.

"These were part of her last words to me before she bravely stopped breathing, clutching my hands the way you are doing right now." he said, as tears trickled his cheeks.

"I'll always stand by you." assured Shea, as she held on to his hands firmly.

"What did you mean 'circumcise you'?" asked Shea.

"I saw no regret of dying in her eyes and I'm still confused if she did put up such bravery, because she didn't want me to be scared or because she didn't want me to lose heart." reasoned Ajala.

He buried his head in Shea's arms and broke into tears profusely, successfully evading Shea's question.

"You're right, we find reasons for whatever happens in life." agreed Shea, as she was moved to tears.

"Of course, mother!" responded Ajala.

Shea was amazed he started calling her mother straightaway, therefore, she bursted into tears as she was holding him in her arms.

"I'm so sorry I'm making you do this."

"No, mother!" responded Ajala.

"Of course, you're right." he added.

"I said that because I knew my people should find reasons for love and empathy. It isn't worth it to murder the innocent for the sake of tradition. All these killings were because of me and I felt I'd give myself up, just to stop this carnage."

"No, my son!" opposed Shea. Ajala withdrew gently from Shea's arms and looked into her eyes *again*, when she heard her called him son. Their eyes were streaming with tears, as they continued to stare one another.

"My son, don't you agree with me it's worth it, even if we lose our lives, trying to save the innocents, instead of giving up?"

"Is this what Ayafa meant when she told me before she died that, '... let the gods believe in you ...' because she wanted me to stand up for what's good and right." interpreted Ajala.

"Even if it's against the tradition of my people?" he asked.

"Guess so." muttered Shea.

Shea knew he was trying his best to divorce his emotions from what happened to his late mother, in order to quench his own fear. Shea couldn't hold her emotions any further, instead she broke down in her own arms, sobbing silently. Ajala rested his head on her chest.

"You're my mother, now?" he said, as he felt her heart beating.

"Yes, my son. I'm!"

"Now I understand that the food of the truth is to do what is right, good or evil comes from the mind of men." remarked Ajala, drawing from his late mother's words.

"So you told me, mother." he added, referring to Shea.

Shea knew he totally invested his soul on her as his mother, by supposedly putting his late mother's words into her mouth.

While Shea was still weeping, Ajala turned his attention on the starry night sky again. Shea looked at him tearfully, thinking of what his response about freeing the *untouchable* children would be.

"But Yawa, the mad woman, said the gods are dead. I think she meant that looking up to the gods for help is futile."

"Who's this Yawa?" asked Shea, still sobbing.

"She's a mad woman and my mother used to make me understand whatever she said." explained Ajala, still starring at the constellation.

"I could remember my late mother trying to make me understand that Yawa's the most pure at heart amongst all our tribespeople, because she always spoke the truth as she sees it even if it would displease whoever. If only one could understand that she may be mad, but her words aren't insanity to the enduring ears." continued Ajala.

"But I think to uphold the truth, one needs some level of healthy insanity." he remarked.

"What did you think, mother?" he asked Shea.

"Anyway, I believe in you, son." said Shea.

Ajala was silent *again*, still gazing the starry night sky intently. She knew the lad was somewhat confused about all the happenings around his life.

"I'm sure your mother ..."

"I know what you want to say, dear mother." said Ajala.

"Would be proud of me?" he suggested.

"Yeah!" confirmed Shea.

Ajala turned his attention on Shea and while looking at each other directly, he reached for his flute, which always was hung around his neck. He blew into the flute the usual dirge and his okapi gently pranced out from the forest towards them.

"I'll do what's right for the untouchables now and not tomorrow, mother." said Ajala as mounted the animal.

"Tonight?" asked Shea *excitedly.*

"I'll go with you, son." she said *happily.*

Ajala took her hands with smile, pulled her up to sit behind him on his okapi and as they rode together towards Eboru *village,* Shea noticed movements everywhere in the forest. When they came to a broad, grassy plain, the stampede for the emancipation of these *untouchable* children started, with many animals rushing out of the forest to join the drove.

"Where are you guys from?" asked Ajala.

"We're from the United Kingdom." replied Shea.

"Where's that?"

"It's in Europe."

"And where's Europe?"

Shea brought out her phone as they were riding and googled world map to enlighten Ajala on world countries and continents. The lad was amazed and curious about these other lands. When it was some distance to Eboru, Ajala and Shea alighted the okapi and proceeded quietly on their legs, while wild dogs were quietly checking and sniffing out everywhere ahead of them, for whoever or whatever might constitute threat or danger, until they arrived the dungeon of these *untouchable* children. However, it was indeed frustrating for Shea, when she found out that the bamboo made ladder to enter this rock-cut subterranean dungeon was nowhere to be found. She communed Ajala that the ladder must have been kept somewhere away from their reach.

"*Perhaps, now they are thinking ahead of us.*" responded Ajala.

Ajala looked into the small entrance of this deep dungeon, he saw how far below it extended and he was disturbed right away about how inhumane it was to incarcerate children in this sort of place, all because of tradition. *This is where I'd have been confined, if my mother had given me up.* He mused.

"*What a horrible place.*" he lamented to Shea.

"*Every kid accused of witchcraft were sent here as untouchable, after serious torture and mutilation to make them confess. Indeed, it's my first time here all my life, although, I've heard of this place from my mother and I don't know why I haven't been caught by the destiny of this terrible place.*" muttered Ajala into Shea's *attentive* psyche.

"*No one's allowed to come here, except the hunters and none of the tribespeople will even dare come here, because they believe these children could bewitch them with their witchcraft demons.*" explained Ajala.

He told Shea he had not seen this dungeon before and that he also knew from his mother that there was another such horrible dungeon called, 'OmoAdanu', *les enfants perdus*, where the deformed children are kept, just to waste away without being fed adequately.

"We must find that place, my son." said Shea.

"*Not tonight, mother. We do it one after the other.*"

"They'll die without food." said Shea *pitifully*.

"*No mother, they were being fed, only the ones accused of witchcraft were left to starve to death here, after being tortured and mutilated, in order to purge the land of their witchcraft demons.*" said Ajala.

He signaled to Shea to stay put, while he walked to rear side of the drove, where a long boa constrictor was on guard. He patted the head of this boa and led the animal to the small opening of the dungeon. This huge and long reptile, on slithering to this opening, peeped inside the dungeon.

"*You'll go inside to call all the children, the boa will help you down into the dungeon.*" Ajala told Shea, as he was patting the boa's head again. The reptile, in its style, wound itself round Shea

114

lightly and gently uncurled down into the deep dungeon and quietly landed her on the dungeon's floor. Ajala also actuated an elephant to hold the boa by tail with its trump, for a perfect balance.

While the boa unwound its body into the dungeon, Shea switched on the LCD light of her mobile, waking up these children and they were indeed filled with happiness to see her again. Ajala, who watching from the dungeon's entrance, was so impressed at the warm welcoming attitude of these children towards Shea and he was bemused how this wasn't the case with his own tribespeople. The boa knew exactly what to do, as it picked these children – *who were initially scared when they saw the beast, but Shea got them under control that the animal was there to help* – one after the other, winding *its body* round them and began to curl up towards the opening, where Ajala was on hand *to pull them out*. The last of these children and Shea were taken together, as Shea cuddled the child, the boa wound round her and lifted them to the dungeon's entrance, where Ajala pulled them both to the open.

Shea introduced Ajala to the children and all together, with the hordes of animal that accompanied them, they began to *slowly and quietly* trek back to Igbo – *the evil forest and the land of the gods* – in the dead of the night, with these wild animals on guard against any possible threat.

Shea was so delighted with her son *Ajala,* and she took keen interest in him henceforth, teaching him everything he had to know, together with these *untouchable* children. Shea taught them how to read, write, and even operate mobile phones and a little bit of integrated science to spark their curiosity. Ajala always pestered to be taught more, despite Shea being exhausted. That very night, Shea and Ajala basically adopted one another as child and parent.

Chapter Eleven

THE evil Chieftain prowled around from one pyramidal castle of Aye – *the otherworld of the witches of blood underworld* – to the other, looking for Kowe. He rushed around haphazardly in every of these in this vast, *seemingly* endless otherworld castles, from one chamber to the other and after he had searched everywhere, yet, he couldn't find her.

"Kowe!" he roared repeatedly amidst the wailing hubbub of Apaadi.

Kowe was the name of the ostrich-like bird with human head. She was a bird of ancient magical power, who alone could navigate the great mystique called IyaNla by these lost tribes. Apaadi is the otherworld under Kowe's magical control, of which the only entrance into was the psychically sensitive black membrane on the witches of blood otherworld's coven chamber's wall, since Kowe had been under their captivity for aeon.

"Kowe!" he shouted deeply.

"I know you're looking at me!" he exclaimed.

"Stop this evil magic-play on me, now!" cried the Chieftain, after he had also searched for Kowe with his bizarre reptilian tail, but to no avail.

However, everywhere in this otherworld castles of Aye were in utter silence, except the wailing hubbub that was filtering in from Apaadi and the reverberation of the Chieftain's thunderous voice. The Chieftain gingerly walked down the stairs, looking here and there with the hope that Kowe would show up. Yet, till he got to the lowest underground shafts, Kowe was nowhere to be found.

He walked back to the peculiar Bony-Spiny, where the Chieftain expected at least to find Kowe, no matter what. This Bony-Spiny was a living, gigantic bony cage, where Kowe had been imprisoned for aeon and from where she was summoned *for her fateful errand* some days ago for the capturing of the sacrificial victim, by whom alone the witches of blood underworld could usurp the sovereignty of the psychic world. Of course, capturing this sacrificial victim, which only could be possible by navigating the great mystique called IyaNla by this tribespeople, of which only Kowe could accomplish successfully. Consequently, this would free Kowe herself from her age long captivity under the witches of blood underworld, if only she could replace herself in the Bony-Spiny with this destined oblation – *the sacrificial victim*. Some days ago, as soon as IyaNla was perceived in Apaadi, the Chieftain quickly summoned Kowe to her age long awaited mission of capturing this victim. Thereby, she would be set free from the bondage of Aye by successfully accomplishing this much awaited hunt.

The phenomenon called IyaNla, *the ultimate witchcraft power, as called among these lost tribes*, which to Mother Endor was known as the 'eternal bird', could only be usurped by the witches of blood underworld through the *unique* blood or soul of the destined sacrificial victim. However, these witches of the underworld of the otherworld amongst these lost tribes didn't know who this sacrificial victim was and how he or she looked like or where she would be from. However, this wouldn't make any difference to them, what's useful to them was her momentous sacrificial blood. Even as these witches vowed neither to taste flesh nor blood of any human, until they would feast on Ajala's flesh and blood, this avowal was in no way including the flesh and blood of the sacrificial victim. In fact, Kowe had been in captivity of these witches for aeon just for the purpose of apprehending this destined sacrificial victim *for them*, in order to usurp IyaNla, *the ultimate witchcraft power*.

To the Chieftain's amazement, as soon as he set his beastly, glowing eyes on Bony-Spiny, a young girl from nowhere began to slowly materialise, trapped inside the cage.

"Bony-Spiny!" he mouthed the name of this odd cage out of sheer astonishment of setting his eyes on the much coveted sacrificial victim that his psychic ancestors had foretold for aeon. Which Aye, *the otherworld of the witches of blood,* from generation to generation had persevered to usurp.

"The time is no more nigh. The time is now!" he muttered.

He shuddered with surprise at the sight of this innocent girl because he knew his much coveted, age long awaited and destined sacrificial victim for them to usurp the ultimate witchcraft power had arrived at last. And thanks to Kowe, whose psychic ingression into IyaNla made this possible. Instantly he saw her, in his memory were

117

flashes of the two strangers – *Shea and Pott* – who barged into Eboru's gathering on the day of public execution of Ajala's mother. While he was still staring at the girl, his memory ran a panoramic view through the scenes surrounding these two strangers and their eventual rescue by Ajala. Particularly, he noticed that this girl – *the sacrificial victim* – was of the same appearance with the strangers – *Shea and Pott.*

"So, they came to find their own." he soliloquised about Shea and Pott.

The girl in the bony-cage was terribly frightened to behold the hideous creature staring at her. She cried and struggled in vain, trying to get out of Bony-Spiny.

"Poor little cute thing!" muttered the Chieftain.

"No one can hear your voice, nor help you out of this place." he said, as he was still staring at the girl.

"Only you can hear your voice, my pretty little prize." he whispered.

The young girl covered her tearful face with her palms to shut her eyes from seeing the ugly beast that was staring at her. Nonetheless, fear still moved her to peep between her fingers to see if this hideous being was still there, looking at her.

The Chieftain knew forthwith that Kowe was successful in her search for the destined sacrificial oblation he craved to usurp the sovereignty of the psychic world. The Chieftain was happy to behold his chance to reign supreme over the otherworld, yet, his search for Kowe continued.

"Kowe, I know you're here!"

The Chieftain suddenly roared on top of his voice while his glowing eyes were still on the innocent girl in the Bony-Spiny and there was a diabolical cachinnation in response, reverberating all over Aye, *the otherworld of the witches of blood underworld.* While the evil cachinnation rocked the pyramidal castles, Kowe's make-believe psychic antics seemed unbearable for the Chieftain no longer.

"Kowe, stop!" cried the Chieftain, and the laughter stopped.

Instantly, the essence of the bizarre Kowe appeared ubiquitously, flitting here and there, as the Chieftain was trying to catch up with his weird eyes these repetitiveness and selfsameness appearances of Kowe.

"Yes, my Lord!" cried Kowe.

"I'm happy *the mystique of* IyaNla favoured me to be free from Bony-Spiny, I'm now on the threshold of my freedom." the husky voice of the eerie, grizzled haired, ostrich-like big bird with an aged woman's head rocked the castle. The grey hair on its human head was made into typical African cornrows and its long, fork-tongue was covered with live scales.

As Kowe flew everywhere helter-skelter, like a dashing shadow all over the grim castle of Aye, the trapped girl in the mysterious cage *Bony-Spiny* saw these flitting shadows and she had a memory spark of seeing the bird before, but somehow couldn't understand fully what was going on in her head.

"It's you!" she shouted *anyway*.

"How did I get here?" she cried.

While she continued to struggle inside Bony-Spiny, the Chieftain immediately ran to Apaadi.

"Show yourself now, Kowe!" the Chieftain commanded and there was a push that bulged Apaadi from inside. This psychically sensitive membrane bulged *elastically*, as the forceful push from inside somehow went on. This bulged took the shape of Kowe's *figure* and eventually, in the presence of the Chieftain, Kowe was spewed – *like a fetus during birth* – from Apaadi *by means of this bulge*. Apaadi neither showed any sign of breakage, nor were the wailing voices and the odd creatures carrying on their activities in Apaadi disturbed. Immediately Kowe was disgorged, the whole of her dashing essence all over Aye vanished.

"Yes, my lord!" cried Kowe.

The mysterious bird tilted a bow before the Chieftain, as soon as she emerged from Apaadi.

"Your magical hide and seek annoys ..."

"Isn't it puzzling, my lord?" interrupted Kowe, as she tilted a bow before the Chieftain again.

"It's the magic-play of the ancient." added Kowe.

"Aren't you baffled that even you couldn't find me, my lord?" asked Kowe.

"The smell of freedom's beginning to revamp my powers." remarked Kowe.

The Chieftain immediately blocked Kowe's mouth with his palm to show his displeasure for her comments about freedom and

Kowe blinked her eyes slowly to him in remorse. He gently let his palm off her mouth.

"Your prize and my price, I know you have seen her." said Kowe.

She walked towards the chamber where the beautiful girl was captured in the Bony-Spiny. The Chieftain walked behind her, with his magical staff dripping of blood as he followed. Though, this blood vanished immediately it spattered on the floor.

"Ah, ah, so – sorry for you!" said Kowe on getting to the beautiful girl, who was talking to her, but she couldn't hear her voice.

"I forgot that it's another world inside Bony-Spiny." muttered Kowe.

While the Chieftain stood watching, his snake tail, in excitement of this captured sacrificial victim, elongated all around the castle, charging, hissing, puffing and spitting blood everywhere and afterwards shrank back and curled round him.

"Kerekerekerikekerekerekerike!" cooed Kowe repeatedly.

While she was cooing this spell, beating her massive wings gently, Bony-Spiny responded. It opened up and began to fold itself up around this beautiful girl, splashing blood everywhere. Eventually, Bony-Spiny stood on its feet as one overly giant human skeleton, with a conspicuous elongated skull. The beautiful girl was shocked and transfixed, as Bony-Spiny that looked spider-scorpion-crab-like in shape was unleashing itself into another shape – *of one overly giant human skeleton.*

"Don't be scared, sacred one." said Kowe.

"My name's Kowe." she whispered.

"You're my price *to pay*, you're his prize *to usurp*." said the mysterious bird, pointing to the Chieftain, who elongated his snake tail to this frightened girl, where she stood transfixed.

"Never mind, it won't hurt you." said the Chieftain to the girl, but as soon as the snake tail curled all over her, she was terrified and began to weep. This snake tail of the Chieftain puffed open its horrifying fangs right before her face and she shrieked out of fear. Instantaneously, it struck her mercilessly right on the face, then, on the left shoulder *first* and after, on the right.

"But you said it wouldn't hurt me!" cried tearfully the fear struck girl, as the snake tail of the Chieftain continued to uncurl itself off her and withdrew back to the Chieftain.

"Of course, you're too precious a prize for me to waste." answered the Chieftain.

The Chieftain stood with Kowe, expectantly pop-eyed, waiting to see the result of the mysterious attack on this girl, nevertheless, when they actually found the attack was futile on her, they became boisterously happy and jolly hand in hand.

"She's the one, the chosen one!" they shouted to one another, while the girl stood helpless, distraught and wandering her eyes all over the grim, bizarre, fear inspiring pyramidal castle in which she was being held.

"Remember me?" asked Kowe.

"Take me home, please!" said the sobbing innocent girl.

"I'll take you home, but don't you think I'd meet you, my little sacred thing?" scoffed Kowe.

"I'm Erin Eyers." she said.

My parents would be terribly worried about me by now. She mused.

"How did I get here and since when have I been here?" she asked.

By mentioning her name, the weird creatures roving Apaadi jubilated and all over the castle, diverse, ethereal and creepy creatures began fluttering here and there like flashes of lightning.

"What's this place ... London?" she asked.

"What's she talking about?" whispered the Chieftain.

"What's London?" asked the Chieftain further.

"The name of Aye as she knew *it*, my lord." replied Kowe.

Erin was indeed scared and couldn't understand what was happening. She shuddered, screamed and panicked at every flitting, ghastly creatures that were dashing everywhere to take a look at her. She tried to hide herself, but wherever she turned, these creatures dashed past her eerily, putting her into deep fear, as everything was pervious to them.

"Freedom!" proclaimed repeatedly these fluttering creatures. Kowe was all smiles as these eerie, flitting things were proclaiming her freedom, while they dashed hugger-mugger all over the castles joyously.

Kowe knew what would guarantee her freedom had at last being delivered and therefore her Apaadi kingdom celebrated the would-be freedom of their leader and their kingdom – *Apaadi*.

"You can walk around the castle till when I'll take you home." said Kowe to Erin.

"I want to go home now, you liar!" shouted Erin at Kowe, but the Chieftain and Kowe had turned their back on her, walking away and not minding her plea of wanting to go home.

"That's your sacrifice, my lord, to become the sovereign of the psychic world, and the price for my freedom, remember?"

"There shall be no freedom until the sacrifice's offered and I ascended the sovereignty of the otherworld." the Chieftain exclaimed in anger.

"In toto!" he drawled and Kowe was amazed, but kept silent.

"But where did you get her?" asked the Chieftain, just to make her break her silence.

"I can't tell, my lord. I only followed the great phenomenon, the mystique of IyaNla, through which she could be discovered. It led me to her directly over the plain overcast." replied Kowe.

"I couldn't see anything else, except her sacrosanctity." remarked Kowe.

"But as you know, only Kowe can navigate such phenomenal, ancient psychic energy effectively." spited Kowe to remind the Chieftain that her freedom was meant to be guaranteed by delivering the sacrificial victim, but the Chieftain frowned at Kowe and she quickly realised his displeasure.

"My lord!" hailed Kowe to pacify him.

"But you're not giving me a scot free freedom?" said Kowe frankly and the Chieftain stood face to face with her.

"The lord of blood speaks, as soon as you conduct the ritual successfully, your freedom is guaranteed and the freedom of your kingdom." assured the Chieftain.

"You've been waiting for this day for aeon, I know this, my friend." added the Chieftain.

"The psychic progenitors of the witches of blood battled and conquered your kingdom, then imprisoned you *for aeon* till now and for the main reason that only you can navigate the mystique of IyaNla. You've done this successfully. You have proved them right, O Kowe! I promise I'll give you your freedom as soon as the ritual's over." said the Chieftain.

Kowe breathed deeply.

"I'll take you for your words, my lord." she said.

"And stop loathing me with your freedom, please!" added the Chieftain.

"But how sovereign can her blood make me?" whispered the Chieftain.

"As sovereign as the Arch-witch, my lord." answered Kowe.

"You'll become the ultimate ruler of the unseen world, as we all know the unseen world controls the real world. The entire unseen world, which goes beyond the realm of realities, will be under your dominion." added Kowe and a smile passed briefly through the ugly face of the Chieftain while its snake tail hissed and puffed happily.

"You'll become IyaNla, *the womb of creation and existence herself,* the ultimate veneration and fearful power." said Kowe further and the Chieftain went pop-eyed with excitement. As Kowe and the Chieftain talked face to face, they both noticed Erin walking around and the Chieftain's memory flashed the rescue of Shea and Pott by Ajala.

"We've got to be on guard, Kowe." whispered the Chieftain.

"Even in this Aye, you're doubting my competence to safeguard your priceless prize and my precious price?" responded Kowe.

"Aye's a hidden otherworld no son of man can infiltrate, hence, your hidden nature, my lord." boasted Kowe.

"I'm not talking about son of man, but the devil of lad called Ajala." replied the Chieftain.

"Are you saying Ajala isn't human, my lord?" ridiculed Kowe.

"No, Kowe!" said the Chieftain.

"I'm saying we've got to be cautious as the lad isn't dead yet." added the Chieftain.

"Even though we've thwarted his destiny from becoming the Babalawo, *the possessor of secret ancient knowledge and wisdom,* yet we have to be on guard." warned the Chieftain.

"Remember, this is your freedom." reminded the Chieftain.

"Remember also, my lord. This is your only chance to the ultimate sovereignty." said Kowe, looking askant at the Chieftain.

"Ajala rescued two of Erin Eyers kind from the palace of Eboru and I'd think they were here to find her." hinted the Chieftain.

123

"Where are these unhuman-kind untouchables coming from, anyway?" asked the Chieftain.

"From the gods to be ritualised." answered Kowe.

"Where else could they be from, my lord?" added Kowe.

"Anyway, you're dilly-dallying too much, Ajala's destiny's a dire enemy and I can exterminate him by my supreme ancient magic, only if I'm freed, not when I am held to ransom. Give me my freedom now and Ajala will be gone, forever!" grinned Kowe.

"Stop!" exclaimed the Chieftain.

"This isn't a laughing stock, Kowe." he said.

"I've said there shall be no freedom until the sacrifice to my sovereign destiny's successfully offered!" shouted the Chieftain at Kowe.

"Yes, my lord." responded Kowe.

"Henceforth, there shall be no talk of freedom until I proclaim it so." ordered angrily the Chieftain.

"But remember, Ajala the enfant terrible prowls around." scoffed Kowe.

"Ajala isn't any of your concern, the powerful invincible Shigidi will take care of him. The tribespeople will manoeuvre the Shigidi to exterminate him *for me*. He's just a child to be wasted in his due time." said the Chieftain.

"He's no more enfant terrible as you called him, but *'un enfant perdu'* of the lineage of Babalawo hierarchy." said the Chieftain.

"Evil, only evil thunders and changes destinies." riddled Kowe in a low tone.

"Yes, Kowe." responded the Chieftain with a gripped fist, Kowe's riddle no doubt sank into the depth of his plan.

"There'll be an evil guided disease that kills before sunset or sunrise, therefore, there'll be cries and wailing all over Eboru and the tribes and no one, no one I say, will neither be immune, nor will be cured of this mysterious disease, only death shall reign." soliloquised the Chieftain.

"Thanks, Kowe!" said the Chieftain in recognition of this evil plan Kowe did just spark within his psyche.

"I've got to hasten my ... my lord." pointed out Kowe, and the Chieftain glowered as he knew she meant to say freedom.

"Only evil thunders and changes destinies." retorted the Chieftain.

"And who's to blame for this?" asked Kowe.

"Who else?" replied the Chieftain.

However, they both knew in their mind who would bear the brunt of this evil scheme they planned to plague on Eboru *village* and these lost tribes.

"Then the whole of Eboru will leave no stone unturned to send him to the ancestors, forever." added the Chieftain.

"Kowe, convene the coven now, while I've another look on the sacred one."

Then the Chieftain walked back to have an observation of Erin again and as he walked tip-toed, peeping from one chamber to the other in order to behold his ultimate offering to the sovereignty of the otherworld in his entirety, Kowe was already in the coven chamber of the witches of blood underworld. She stood before Apaadi, raised her hands and spread her wings.

"Apaadi O!" cried Kowe.

Instantly, all the horrible hubbub in Apaadi went quiet at the voice of Kowe.

"Let the coven be gathered, now!" directed Kowe and at once a creature pushed out of Apaadi *like a fetus during birth* and stood before Kowe. It stood on two legs and tail *as that of* a kangaroo, but this creature was covered with scales rather than fur. Its bloody human torso was not covered with skin and all its stomach and intestines were bared. It had seven, varied beastly heads stalked on its *only* giraffe-like necks and its wings like that of bat were attached to its scaly human hands. As soon as it stood before Kowe, it spread its wings open like Kowe and bowed to the ground.

"Kowe!
Kowe!
Kowe!
The mystic bird of birds,
That flew beneath the earth.
You wrestled evil and conquered,
Still in your soul evil pitched,
Blood becomes your water,
Flesh your sweet bread.

125

Kowe!
Kowe!
Kowe!
Bird of the beginning,
The bizarre bird of the ancient,
Kowe, the wings of immortality!"

hailed the creatures in Apaadi immediately one of their members pushed out to attend to Kowe's call. Kowe lowered her wings as her praise resounded out of Apaadi.

"Arise, assemble the coven for the Chieftain!" ordered Kowe.

Forthwith, this strikingly, odd in appearance creature from Apaadi leapt into flight with its human-like legs like lightning, *through the roof* and shot out through one of the peaks of Aye's pyramidal castle and was directly teleported into the literal world. However, as soon as it hit the real world, it instantly travestied into a vulture.

It continued to fly over the settlements of these lost tribes like an ordinary vulture, making whispery buzzing sounds that only the members of the witches of blood underworld of the otherworld could hear, as it flew passed over their different houses or wherever it spotted a member. Only these members could hear this travestied vulture's cries, but unknown to these underworld witches, Erin, even though in the otherworld of Aye, too, could hear these buzzing cries that were hard to explain. When this disguised being flew passed Igbo – *the evil forest and the land of the gods* - the animals and birds of Igbo started their various distress cries and this attracted Ajala, Shea and Pott.

"What's happening?" asked Shea, but Ajala was staring at this soaring vulture without response.

All the birds in the sky had abandoned the air for the travestied vulture and only this dissimulated creature of Apaadi was in the air, roving pass confidently. Ajala continued to gaze at this bird, walking and running to a vantage position for a better viewing of it, as he tried to commune with it in vain, while Shea and Pott were following him to look at the bird too.

"When are the visitors supposed to be here?" he asked Shea, when this strange vulture finally got out of their view. He ran

back to the cave to get hold of his flute that he laid beside him as he slept, *when suddenly he had to respond to the distress calls of his animal friends against this dissimulated creature from Apaadi.*

"They'll be here today, I guess." cried Pott into Ajala's mind, as they ran back to the cave after him.

Ajala rushed inside, picked up his flute and blew into the object his usual dirge *for his late mother*. In no time, his okapi appeared, cleaning its eyes and ears with its *naturally* long tongue.

"I'm going to trail the bird, I can sense somehow that its presence is evil." said Ajala, as he mounted his okapi and the okapi sprinted off into the forest, away from Shea and Pott's sight.

All the members of the witches of blood underworld in Eboru and among these lost tribes, *in their different locations,* knew this was Kowe's call, therefore, an emergency call.

Certainly, it was just noon and they all wondered what on earth could have happened that warranted them being summoned urgently at this unusual hour. Nevertheless, they knew it was a call to be obeyed instantly and some of them that got caught up in a hidden place with this impromptu call, spied around to be certain no one was watching. Then, they simply placed their left palm before them like *a looking mirror*, breathed on it thrice and the surface of their palm turned to blood, and into this psychic palm portal they vanished as they gazed into it, only to be teleported and also concurrently metamorphosed into their hideous, peculiar otherworld nature, as they appeared before Kowe in Aye, *the otherworld of witches of blood underworld,* and immediately taking to their position in the psychical coven arrangement of the great heptagram within the circle of witches.

Notwithstanding, some were caught up in the midst of people by this unexpected call and they couldn't just travel straightaway like their fellow-witches, who were lucky to be alone when this unusual call came in. However, they still made it by passing out *invisibly* their otherworldly nature to go and attend to the call, while in their human nature they continued with whatever they were doing *as if nothing had happened.*

Kowe's errand didn't fly back into Aye until all the coven members were completed. Then, this Kowe's dissimulated errand flew into the midst of the coven like lightning through the pyramidal castle's tip, as it erstwhile departed. Immediately it touched down before Kowe, it metamorphosed back into its real nature from its feigned appearance.

"Kowe welcomes you!" said Kowe *to this just arrived errand that erstwhile came out of Apaadi.*

"Ajala stalked me, O great one!" reported Kowe's errand.

"Our freedom isn't yet, we can't do Ajala much harm by our secret ancient powers while we are in bondage." hinted Kowe.

"Go back to Apaadi, now." commanded Kowe.

This Apaadi creature that was sent to convene the coven, in twinkling of an eye, dashed into Apaadi and there erupted jubilation among its fellow creatures in Apaadi for its successful errand. The Chieftain was yet to ascend his throne in the midst of the coven. Therefore, the coven began to laud his absence in the usual manner, as acknowledgement of his presence.

> "You're the Lord of blood!
> The ruler of darkness,
> The axe of the god of thunder,
> The sovereign of witches!
> You're the vicar of death and disease.
> The only ones safe from your decease
> Are those who lack in blood
> And such souls no one have neither seen,
> Nor would ever see.
> O rider of Kowe!
> The evil bird of darkness,
> You own the blood of your enemies,
> You're the god of the otherworld,
> Reign over the land forever
> From seas to seas.
> O first born of Evil!"

"Kowe, I was carrying on my hair braiding trade according to our terms of barter, when I heard your call and I indeed had a lot of customers to attend to. Why this impromptu call at this unusual hour, O great One?" asked a member of the coven.

"I was working in the farm, gathering produce along with my family when your errand flew by, what's this call all about, O great Kowe?" asked another member of the coven.

"I didn't wake up from my sleep to be here, my husband was watching over me caringly because of my fever, but this unusual call at this unusual hour amazed me, Kowe." said another.

When all this circle of witches are done confronting Kowe with their queries, a member from the great heptagram order waded in.

"Kowe!" cried the member of the witches of blood underworld, whose hideous psychic nature was like that of a dragon, with huge powerful wings that were bigger than its whole body, having strong, pawed human leg.

"How many times did I call you?" riddled the member.

"You called me thousands of times, wise one!" riddled Kowe in response *also*.

"Thank you, O great Kowe!" responded the member.

"Kowe's call hadn't happen for aeon, therefore, indispensable." added this member.

"I'm sure there's an urgent mission for this impromptu convening of the coven and at this unusual hour for that matter. In fact, some of us were caught up unprepared, but we've to dispatch our Aye's psychic self to come on our behalf." acknowledged this hideous being.

"Where's my lord?" she asked.

"The throne's vacant, O Kowe!" she added.

"My thanks to you all for urgently honouring Kowe's call." appreciated Kowe.

"You're all welcome." she said to the coven.

"While we are waiting for the arrival of my lord to this *ad hoc* meeting, let us uplift our psyche." recommended Kowe, and sounds mainly of talking drum, gong, shaker-gourds and dreadful songs broke out of Apaadi.

> "We're the witches of blood!
> The blood of the old,
> The blood of the young,
> To us makes no difference,
> Both are delicacies we relish
> And that of embryos'
> Are even better off,
> And their guileless flesh

Is our potent psychic tonic.
Of course,
Human flesh is our bread
And their blood our wine.
We're the witches of blood,
Human flesh and blood alone
Is food for our psyche!"

Immediately, facing one another, the coven began evil dance, moving their feet to and fro on the floor briskly in response to the sound emanating from Apaadi, and at the periodical stop of this sound - *majorly controlled by the talking drum* – they stamped their feet on the ground instantaneously. The dance continued while the Chieftain in another domain of the vast castles was tip-toeing after Erin Eyers, stalking the straying girl as she walked round these mysterious pyramidal castles of Aye, apparently looking for means by which she could escape.

Through some spiral stairs that went upward, she actually got to the topmost floor. She opened the door before her and found it leading to the pinnacle of this pyramidal castle. She stood at the pinnacle, gazing the whole *seemingly* endless and gigantic pyramidal castles of Aye all over the expanse of this otherworld and she noticed that these whole castles were dazzling amidst the thick darkness around them. She couldn't see anything other than these gorgeous, pyramidal castles that seemed to be everywhere, in this sinister, grim and extremely quiet environment.

She fearfully shouted to see if there would be any response to her call for help and at the echo of her voice, she noticed multitude of glowing eyes of different sizes and shapes *around these pyramidal castles* converging on her from horizon to horizon. Immediately, she could hear horrible noises, dreadful sounds and as she was wondering where these might be coming from, fear and confusion took over her and out of anxiety, she reached for the tinted glasses on her face. As she attempted to remove it by chance, suddenly, she noticed that her left eye - *of which she almost lifted the spectacle off* – could see vividly another picture of the world around her. Concurrently, the right eye that was still covered by the lens of this spectacle, saw this otherworldly milieu as it was. She was terrified seeing Aye in two different senses – *one through her naked left eye and the other*

130

through her spectacled right eye – and quickly she placed the left eye spectacle back, rushed inside and shut the door after her.

"It's dangerous out there, but in these castles you're completely protected." said the Chieftain to her. He stood before Erin, staring at her, with his memory flashing back to Shea and Pott, as he noticed Erin was of the same appearance with them. Afterwards, the Chieftain turned his back and walked down the spiral stairs, and Erin realised he had been stalking her all along.

"Stay in the castle, it is lot safer here." he said. As he was walking down these spiral stairs, Erin was staring at him and her thought went back to what had just happened to her sight outside the castle.

She remembered her bared left eye without the spectacle's lens saw that it was raining blood outside and, when she looked at herself, her left eye saw her drenched all over with blood, while her right eye that was still covered by the right lens of this spectacle saw neither rain of blood nor any single drop of blood on her cloth. She recollected all the dreadful, grotesque multitude of flying creatures she saw with her bared left eye, pressing from all directions to assault her. Erin was confused by the unusualness of her eyesight and she wondered why her right eye under the lens saw a dark world of gorgeous, twinkling pyramidal castles, but at the same time her left eye without the lens saw a bright, bloody and uncanny world, teeming with ill-natured creatures and giant flying monsters.

While Erin was pondering her terrifying, bizarre eye sight experiences outside the castle, her left hand reached for the spectacle again out of reflex. Immediately she lifted it off her left eye, she found out that with her bare left eye, the inside of the castle wasn't as she previously saw it through her spectacle. She saw that the castle was psychically fig-leafed and it wasn't as it seemed. It was actually built of live, slithering reptiles, monstrous worms, terrifying insects and bizarre creatures she couldn't comprehend, as they swarmed around and over one another continuously. She saw that the human skeletons of different ages, she previously saw on the walls were real humans in agony of torture by these miscellaneous eldritch beings swarming haphazardly nonstop. The luminescent gemstones of different colours in strategic corners of the castle that brightened up the castle's chambers, weren't indeed gemstones but human fetuses, captured to radiate their pure, unblemished, innocent *effulgent* aura to lighten up the castle.

Erin was terrified as she heard the voices of these innocent unborn children and those people in agony of torture by these creepy, monstrous stuffs, calling on her for help. She lifted the lens of the spectacle from her right eye for another trial to see if she would have the same experience, yet, the same thing happened *vice versa,* and all of a sudden, she found these odious creatures crawling on her feet and her body. Though, this instantly stopped when she quickly wore her spectacle so that she couldn't see them anymore. Erin was indeed terrified by these eerie experiences and she looked at the castle with deep phobia because she found out already the true nature of its makeup.

Immediately the Chieftain appeared in the midst of the coven, Kowe brought the dance to an end and the coven hailed their leader in the usual manner.

"You're the Lord of blood!
The ruler of darkness,
The axe of the god of thunder,
The sovereign of witches!
You're the vicar of death and disease,
The only ones safe from your decease
Are those who lack in blood
And such souls no one have neither seen,
Nor would ever see.
O rider of Kowe!
The evil bird of darkness.
You own the blood of your enemies,
You're the god of the otherworld,
Reign over the land forever,
From seas to seas.
O first born of Evil!"

The Chieftain calmed the coven by lifting his staff up into the air and they all at once took to their cultic assemblage.

"We're triumphant!" exclaimed the Chieftain, after the coven went silent and there was a great cheer with each uttering different cries out of their hideous nature. These fear-instilling cries attracted Erin as she continued to wander around the castle, looking for a way to escape. She fearfully, but carefully walked to see for herself what these frightening cries were all about.

"The perfect oblation for us to reign supreme has come." announced the Chieftain, and the coven went spellbound at this announcement. They looked at one another with a surprise hue that this news was too good to be true.

"I promised some time ago that I'd present this to you, didn't I?" he reminded.

"Anyway, all thanks to the great Kowe." cried the Chieftain, and the coven erupted into horrible cheers that almost stopped Erin's heart out of fear as she moved closer, looking here and there, and tip-toeing to see what was going on.

"But there's work for us to do and an urgent one indeed." said the Chieftain, and paused for a while, looking at the coven and they anticipated what the urgent work could be after all.

"We've got to get rid of Ajala once and for all!" said the Chieftain.

"How, my lord?" asked Apepa, *the treacherous killer,* of the witches of blood underworld, who assumed the position of the late Apena, *the invoker*.

"We've tried several times, but the forbidden soul seems protected by fate." he added.

"Because we haven't tried hard enough." mouthed Kowe.

"We've to devise a strategy, my lord!" suggested Apepa, *the treacherous killer.*

"Don't patronise me, Apepa!" inveighed the Chieftain, and the coven knew something was wrong.

"What or who gave you the order to exterminate the priestess?" queried the Chieftain.

"I was Apaniyan, *the executioner,* and was initialised to Apena, *the invoker.* My lord, I'm now Apepa, *the treacherous killer,* and I'm just doing what I'm supposed to ..."

"You're trying my patience!" exclaimed the Chieftain in annoyance, as he rushed to pierce Apepa with his staff, but from nowhere – *though only visible to Chieftain alone* – Alupa, *the terrible* ..., appeared and blocked the Chieftain's fatal move.

"I warned you, my lord." said Alupa, *the terrible...*

"But you knew what he did, didn't you?" responded the Chieftain.

"Yes, I did." answered Alupa, *the terrible...*

"Shall we continue to fight ourselves, while the enemy's out there?" queried Alupa, *the terrible...*

"O great one!" said the Chieftain, in agreement with Alupa, *the terrible..,* and he immediately calmed down and Alupa vanished off as he appeared.

"Now, Apepa, *the treacherous killer,* there shall be no more killing outside the authority of the coven and you would neither shape-shift, nor soul-shift into any member of this coven to do anything without permission." expressed the Chieftain, and the coven knew Apepa, *the treacherous killer,* had violated those rules.

"There's no gain going the way of Apena, *the invoker."* warned the Chieftain.

"I'm quite sure my orders are clear enough, Apepa, *the treacherous killer."* he added.

> "You're the Lord of blood!
> The ruler of darkness,
> The axe of the god of thunder,
> The sovereign of witches!
> You're the vicar of death and disease,
> The only ones safe from your decease,
> Are those who lack in blood
> And such souls no one has neither seen,
> Nor would ever see.
> O rider of Kowe!
> The evil bird of darkness,
> You own the blood of your enemies,
> You're the god of the otherworld,
> Reign over the land forever,
> From seas to seas.
> O first born of Evil!"

the coven hailed the Chieftain, as he flew back to his throne.

Apepa, *the treacherous killer,* indeed shape-shifted and soul-shifted into Alupa, *the terrible...,* and the Chieftain, in order to muster unchallengeable psychic power to extinguish the priestess on the day she was trying to help Ajala.

"The time has come for Ajala l'enfant perdu to join the majority, there's nothing incorruptible, impregnable, or impenetrable and indestructible." said the Chieftain.

"The invisible and invincible Shigidi!" announced the Chieftain.

"This is his fate and the way for him to die." hinted the Chieftain.

"Ajala's a girl!" announced the Chieftain, and the whole coven was stunned, with a deep scowl at the Chieftain.

"Don't be taken aback, O Aye!" said Kowe to the coven and they all seemed simmer down to this fact the Chieftain shocked them with.

"You stunned us unbelievably, my lord." said Apepa, *the treacherous killer*.

"For the very fact that Ajala's a girl, however, everyone somehow misrepresented her pseudohermaphroditism *to be a boy*, due to the ambiguity of his features. Therefore, Eboru offered the wrong sacrifice of a male child to the invincible Shigidi instead of a female, hence, the Shigidi couldn't arrest him." explained the Chieftain.

The whole coven was still reeling in this alarming news from their leader and to hear the fact that Ajala was a girl all these while was something mind boggling to them, as they all wondered why no one ever thought of such possibility.

"Do not marvel, we also made the blunder of permitting his conception." commented the Chieftain.

"So many mistakes had been made about this child called Ajala." said Akoda, *the enforcer*.

"What shall we do next, my lord?" asked Akoda, *the enforcer*.

"Evil must thunder to move the hands of everyone in Eboru *village* to support the Shigidi against Ajala once again." announced the Chieftain to the coven and as he was speaking, he continued to have eye contact with Kowe.

Suddenly, the whole coven went quiet spontaneously, immediately Erin – *hid herself to spy on them* – tried her naked eyes on them to see what would happen. She frightened when she, with her naked eyes, could behold the person *human appearance* of everyone in the coven, except Kowe who remained as she had always seen her. Erin's eyes penetrated into Apaadi and she saw it as a vast otherworld *on its own* of benign atmosphere.

Instantly Erin's eyes struck them, the whole coven went transfixed, and to their consternation a strange feeling somehow went through them all.

"What happened?" queried a member.

"Something did happen." said another.

"I felt naked." supported the Chieftain.

"Everything's fine, my lord." said Kowe, who felt nothing, just to take their attention off this strange feeling.

The phenomenon of Erin's naked eyes *on them* eluded them all, not even the Chieftain or Kowe could decipher what had just happened. Erin from her hiding position noticed the puzzle on the coven immediately her eyes struck them and when Kowe's hunch moved her to focus towards Erin's direction, she quickly replaced her spectacle and the coven felt instantly comfortable again in their respective bestial *otherworldly* nature.

"Perhaps, it's time I present the surprise package Kowe had for us, our ultimate ritual to dominate the unseen world in its entirety." said the Chieftain, and the coven cheered, but Kowe's attention was still focused on Erin's direction and the innocent girl quickly crawled away from her hiding place into one of the inner chamber.

The snake tail of the Chieftain started to elongate from where he stood, and branching out *popping up* different, monstrous, snakelike-self into chambers, searching for Erin everywhere in the castles.

When Erin saw the snake headed tail of the Chieftain coming for her, she rushed for an escape, but the swift, uncanny tail instantly launched itself on her, curled round her and shrank back swiftly to the Chieftain with Erin. The tail landed Erin in the midst of the coven and straightaway, long feathers dashed from Kowe's wings and struck the ground around Erin in a circle, therefore, she wasn't able to struggle beyond this Kowe's feather *magic* confinement.

"Kowe, please take me home!" pleaded Erin with tears running down her cheeks from under her spectacles.

"You're home." answered Kowe.

"Kowe!
Kowe!
Kowe!
The mystic bird of birds,
That flew beneath the earth.
You wrestled evil and conquered,
Still your soul's evil pitched.
Blood becomes your water,
Flesh your sweet bread.
Kowe!
Kowe!
Kowe!
Bird of the beginning,
The bizarre bird of the ancient.
Kowe, wings of immortality!"

the coven hailed Kowe for fulfilling the lasting prediction to the glory of the witches of blood underworld.

The moment they have been waiting for had come and Kowe was the heroine of this achievement, hence her imprisonment hitherto.

Afterward, there was a solemn quietude as the coven was staring at the sobbing Erin. Erin saw Kowe's attention was on her spectacle and she thought perhaps the coven did found out the secret of her bare eyesight on them.

"Don't touch me!" cried Erin repeatedly, as Kowe placed her left hand slowly towards her spectacle to remove it. Kowe gently removed the tinted spectacle from Erin's face. Erin, aware of her naked eyes' effect on the coven, quickly closed her eyes before Kowe could take off her spectacle. Yet, while Erin covered her eyeballs with her eyelids, she could still see the human appearance of the coven members, though, without them perceiving *this time* any strange feeling, and still only Kowe remained the same.

"Of course, she's scared of us." commented Kowe.

"We're the Witches of Blood!
The witches that longed
Always to devour.
In everyone's psyche

137

We dine, wine and live,
For blood and flesh.
Of course,
Human blood is our wine
And human flesh our sweet bread.
We're the darkness that shines gloriously
And the whispering wind that never blow.
The closed eye in the expanse that sees everything
And yet not seen.
We're the glistering cloud that rained only evil and death.
We're the grave of life
And the life of grave.
And the day our one closed eye in the expanse shall open,
Nothing at all,
Nothing shall resist.
Yes, we're the underworld
Of the entire otherworld
And we've vowed,
That until the day we feast on Ajala's flesh and blood,
Neither shall we feast on any human flesh nor blood,
Except that of the ultimate sacrificial victim."

the coven lauded themselves, as the Chieftain sat on his throne, musing at Erin. Also, his mind continued to flash back to Shea and Pott and the eventual exploit of Ajala in saving them.

"Precious one, here comes your cover, so, don't be scared of us." said Kowe.

She placed Erin's spectacle back on her face.

"Here's the key to our sovereignty!" cried the Chieftain, as he stood on his feet, pointing to Erin with his vertebrae staff and immediately he said this, the coven erupted with cheers again, which the Chieftain quickly waved down to calm.

"I called this meeting today because of Ajala, the forbidden soul. He must be eliminated!" announced the Chieftain.

"Why this concern about a child, who can't even think of this place, not to talk of him coming here? This is the most impregnable place in the unseen world." said Akoda, *the enforcer.*

"According to the ancient prediction, only if the child becomes Babalawo could he be a disaster for us and if Ajala's a girl as you alleged, my lord, he'd never become the Babalawo of the tribes, because she's a girl. By tradition of Eboru *village* and the tribes, girls don't get initiated as Babalawo." said Apepa, *the treacherous killer*, and the whole coven murmured in agreement to this fact, but the Chieftain and Kowe looked at one another in disbelief of their notion.

"Firstly, if a girl can't become Babalawo, Ajala's disadvantaged because she's a girl and can never become Babalawo. Secondly, Ajala's disabled and can never be initiated as the Babalawo of the tribes." said Aye-Aye, the imp Apepa, *the treacherous killer*, gave birth to on the day he was given the witchcraft of the late Apepa. Aye-Aye was behaving naughty around like a spoilt kid, to the coven's delight. The witches nodded their heads in agreement.

"Above all, Ajala's the forbidden soul of ancient prophecy and can never be accepted by the people as their cherished Babalawo." he added.

"Therefore, I suggested we concentrate on other matters pertaining to the ultimate sacrifice and leave the issue of Ajala, at least for now." he concluded.

"I think Apepa's right." a member of the coven supported, while the Chieftain and Kowe remained silent and listening.

"We've got the oblation, now let the sacrifice begin." added the member.

"We can only perform this ritual at full moon." reminded Kowe.

"And that's even more than seven days to this present moment." buttressed the Chieftain. He walked down from his throne with a daring sight on Erin, who stood still on her feet within Kowe's feather *magic* confinement.

"Apepa, *the treacherous killer!*" called eagerly the Chieftain.

"Yes, my lord!" answered Apepa.

"Ajala, now!" he cried, with his staff pointed to the mystic column. His eyes were still fixed on Erin and immediately Apepa knew that Ajala's psyche was to be invoked. Apepa, walked slowly round the mystic column three times, he stretched his hand towards the column calmly and folded it to rest on his chest. He went into a deep cogitation, with eyes closed.

139

"Ajala, son of Ayafa O!" he invoked the name of Ajala emotionally and his mother's name with it, *as his sure abode into the world* and immediately the mystic column turned to a pillar of clear, sparkling water and in the midst of it Ajala appeared afloat. While the coven was shocked at this presage, the Chieftain bursted into laughter.

"I knew it! By no power could this jinxed and wild child be sent to the grave, except by the invincible Shigidi." said Kowe with her daring look focused at the mystic column.

"What an omen!" murmured Kowe.

"Let me my ... now, my lord." said Kowe.

"Ajala should be searched out for extinction immediately because water in the mystic column's ominous. I'll take him down in magical combat before it's too late." added Kowe.

However, to the Chieftain, the inaudibly suggestion of freedom prematurely *by Kowe* displeased him, at least for now and Kowe quickly noticed this fact.

"Your lordship!" said Kowe to pacify the Chieftain, and finally she realised that the Chieftain didn't trust her a bit.

Immediately Erin saw Ajala in the mystic column, she was aghast and spellbound at the appearance of her oneiric friend and all her dreams about this African lad that she had flushed into her senses. She was sure Ajala was the reality of this oneiric African lad. Afterwards, Erin's face was full of smiles when she finally convinced herself that the lad in the mystic column, so much was the same African lad of her dreams, who wrote the striking, tiny, rough and scattered oneiric handwriting – *hajahlah.*

The named Ajala pronounced aloud by Apepa, *the treacherous killer,* erstwhile rang in her ears again and her memory flashed and resurfaced in her mind the handwriting borne out of her dream.

It's him! Erin cried within herself, as she went pop-eyed.

"Hajahlah!" she screamed on top of her voice.

"O ho O!" drawled Ajala's essence to fade into the hearing of everyone in the coven through the mystic column, as soon as Erin called him, all the members of the witches of blood underworld were flabbergasted. They wondered how on Earth Ajala and Erin could communicate through their mystic column *and yet not a member of their coven.*

"Help me!" cried Erin.

"I'm coming!" mouthed Ajala.

The coven was all eyes on the Chieftain and Kowe, as Ajala's voice came into their ears once more, out of the mystic column and while Erin struggled effortlessly to get out of Kowe's feather *magic* confinement, Ajala also was struggling in vain in the mystic column to reach Erin forthwith he heard her voice.

The Chieftain wasted no time to signal Apepa, *the treacherous killer*, to do away with Ajala's essence in the mystic column. He hummed brief incantation and at the same time snapped his fingers thrice, as he walked round the mystic column and the strange, live, dragon winged rifle, out of nowhere flew towards him. He grasped it and aimed it up, pulled the trigger at the spot where the mystic column met the roof of the coven chamber and Ajala's essence in the mystic column vanished. As soon as this happened, the water in the mystic column that Ajala appeared in, dissipated into the coven chamber's floor from beneath the mystic column and this huge phenomenal pillar took on its characteristic grandeur again.

All the members of the witches of blood underworld gasped, as cold water ran over their feet and they all shuddered in amazement of Ajala's elusive fate that not only defied their powers, but also bamboozled their witchcraft.

"Ajala, please come back!" cried Erin tearfully.

"Where did he acquire such magical destiny?" a member of the coven, of the group of the young witches *that formed the circle of witches*, said in confusion. Kowe and the Chieftain stared one another at the hearing of this question. Kowe winced and then spread opened her hands to oppugn the Chieftain that he was the one delaying her handling of Ajala's extinction.

When the coven invoked Ajala's psyche into the mystic column, Ajala was asleep and dreaming somewhere at Igbo - *the evil forest and the land of the gods*. In this dream, he heard the voice of Erin calling on him and he responded, running here and there, searching for her at Igbo. While running helter-skelter around the jungle, looking for the person of the voice that called him *Erin Eyers*, he came in contact with Apepa, *the treacherous killer*, holding the odd rifle.

He saw Apepa, *the treacherous killer*, as a hideous creature with a buffalo's head and different, fierce snakes were embedded on his torso. He had only one human hand at the back of his buffalo head, which could be manoeuvred to any direction or part of his body or elongated to reach his target, just like the snakes embedded on his torso. His big wings of dragon allowed him easy and powerful flight. His strong, sinewy legs were partly human and partly like that of a hawk.

"Who're you?" asked Ajala fearfully, as he encountered this dreadful creature in his dream, but Apepa, *the treacherous killer,* instead of answering Ajala, unveiled the strange rifle in his bizarre hand and aimed it at Ajala directly. Ajala ran to escape from Apepa, *the treacherous killer's* onslaught and instantly the creature took to the air and his powerful, easily maneuverable dragon wings eventually enabled him quickly catching up with Ajala.

However, Ajala became defiant, as he had nowhere to run or hide from Apepa, *the treacherous killer,* anymore. He stood his ground and showed no more fear of the scary, live, winged rifle creature aimed at him by his grotesque assailant – *Apepa, the treacherous killer.* He started walking towards the grotesque creature before him with bravery that stunned Apepa. Instantly, Apepa pulled the trigger, the rifle surged on Ajala splashes of cold water that woke him into reality. While Apepa got confused how his strange rifle failed to kill him, Ajala saw the water on his when he woke.

Ajala woke up from his dream and he could feel Erin's presence around him.

"I've called this meeting today so that we could all see that we can't afford to let Ajala continue to live." said the Chieftain.

"And I'm sure you didn't only see the presage that we can't really afford to, you felt it too." added the Chieftain, while his attention was focused on Erin, whose eyes were still on the mystic column, expecting to see Ajala again.

The Chieftain gestured Kowe to take care of Erin, as he continued his words.

"Ajala's fated to die by the invincible Shigidi and we've to do everything to move the hand of Eboru *now* to support the Shigidi once more against him." explained the Chieftain. While Kowe was walking round Erin anticlockwise and as she walked, her feathers started returning to her wings from whence they came, one after the other. At the returning of these last feathers, Erin vanished from before the coven and she found herself in the chamber where she first met the Chieftain.

She saw the overly huge human skeleton before her and recollected how it restructured itself from a huge, bony, spider-scorpion-crab-like cage. Suddenly, the human skeleton with unusually elongated skull and bulged forehead started to restructure itself back into its spider-scorpion-crab-like cage. Erin knew she was about to be trapped again as the cage began to change shape. She ran frantically, but the mysterious skeleton was too swift for her to beat. She was captured and caged in a twinkling by the Bony-Spiny, as it swiftly unfolded on her. She couldn't believe it, as she found herself in the Bony-Spiny once again and her cries for help faded out from the ears of the coven immediately the Bony-Spiny encaged her.

"She's safe." assured Kowe, as Erin's cries faded off from the hearing of the coven.

"Now evil must thunder in Eboru and the tribes, let there be mysterious death in every home from the least to the great of all families." cried the Chieftain on top of his voice with his staff raised into the air.

"This is why I convened this ad hoc coven and all these discussions that Ajala should be left alone or Ajala can't become a Babalawo because he's a girl or disable is arrant balderdash." added the Chieftain. He lowered his staff and the coven looked at one another.

"Have we forgotten Apena, *the invoker,* was murdered by this evil child called Ajala?" he asked.

"You're well spoken, my lord." said Kowe.

"Why're we bothering Eboru for the voluntary ritual to unleash the Shigidi against Ajala once again? Some of us do have daughters of Ajala's mate that we can offer the invincible Shigidi for Ajala's destruction once and for all." suggested a member of the coven.

"No!" shouted Kowe.

"Have you forgotten that the Shigidi will not accept ritual from this circle again, we provided the first ritual, both." reminded Kowe.

"The Shigidi doesn't eat leftovers." added Kowe.

"Now, any ritual from this circle is considered leftover by the Shigidi." added Kowe.

"My lord has neither children nor wife left." said Kowe.

"Now, all we need to do is move the hand of Eboru to provide one of their daughters voluntarily to the priest of Shigidi, as voluntary ritual." hinted Kowe.

"Well, my lord." breathed a member from among the coven.

"I think it's a task perfect for me, my lord." she said.

"Arun!" called the Chieftain.

"This is a speedy operation, as we're already pressed with time." said the Chieftain to Arun.

"I'm aware of this, just accept me to handle the task." replied Arun.

"I'd be so honoured, my lord." added Arun.

"Before I accept you to handle this task, brief the coven of your witchcraft modus operandi to convey this task successfully." requested the Chieftain.

"I'll infect Eboru and the tribes with my invisible imps disguised as mosquitoes to cause unusual fever. Anyone infected in the morning dies before midday, and anyone infected by midday dies before sunset, as anyone infected in the night dies before dawn." informed Arun.

"Simple, my lord!" concluded Arun casually.

"Perfect!" said Kowe when the Chieftain turned to her for sanction.

"Simple and perfect!" added Kowe.

"Let the children of Ajala's mate be the first to be targeted in every home, so that the mind of the tribespeople could easily blame Ajala as the jinxed soul, who brought death on their children." suggested the Chieftain.

"Then let every age be struck in all over the tribes, even to the royal family of Eboru, so that they may be hit where it matters, so as to have a quick rethink." suggested the Chieftain and when the coven heard this they were pleased.

"The people of Eboru, in less than seven days will give in to the invincible Shigidi" declared Arun.

"I'm ready to infest Eboru, my lord! Commission me, now!" requested Arun.

The Chieftain got up his throne and javelined his staff right before Arun and the diabolical staff struck itself into the ground firmly before her. Instantly, the vertebrae staff continued growing its rib cage and as it remained stuck into the ground, all the human organs in the rib cage appeared gradually in their right places. The rib cage was full, dripping with blood. The skull that was on the vertebrae of this staff started growing muscles, the sockets grew eyes with all the essential nerves in place, but it grew no flesh to cover any of these parts. The tongue came up also with all its functioning muscles.

"Eat Arun." commanded the staff.

"What shall I eat, my lord?" replied Arun.

"The soul of your victims." answered the bizarre staff of the Chieftain.

Arun's eyes went over the coven, she stared at Kowe briefly and her eyes fell on the Chieftain, who nodded her to go ahead. Arun observed the diabolical staff painstakingly and finally she began to try with her hands to reach for the staff's conspicuously beating human heart, but the muscles protecting the organ were too tough for her claws to penetrate. The staff bursted into diabolical laughter, blood gushed out of its mouth as it laughed at Arun.

Arun was a hideous, grisly creature, having part-human and part-hyena-like face, but with the tongue that functioned like that of a chameleon. Her single, powerful leg, was avian-like, half of her body was covered with feathers and the other half with pores all over that oozed dirty pulses and worms in and out continuously. Her human arms had powerful claws that could be withdrawn into her body at will and this arms could be coiled up, as if they had no bones. She had one small, effective wing on the feathery side of her body and her tail feathers spread out like that of a peacock, as she was trying to reach the vital organ of this bizarre staff.

After some desperate trials by Arun to reach this beating organ in the rib cage of the Chieftain's staff without success, Arun stepped back a bit and stared at everyone before she sent forth her powerful tongue. It went forth into the rib cage and through the muscles, penetrated the beating heart of this odd staff and forcefully plucked it off into her mouth. Blood flowed from Arun's mouth, as she munched the heart for her commissioning.

"You're commission to go and prevail on your victims." said the staff to Arun, and all the parts that grew on the staff started falling off and the coven picked portions to eat one by one, except Kowe and the Chieftain.

"By this portion the disease of Arun won't affect you or any of your loved ones wherever they are, you're immune to Arun's evil

145

fever." declared the staff, as the coven were taking portions of the staff's fallen parts *to eat* and the Chieftain walked down from his throne to Arun's side.

"Arun, we're with you in this mission, show us what you've got in this race against our foe, Ajala." said the Chieftain, as he got hold of his staff while Kowe stood aloof, watching.

Arun stared the Chieftain briefly before she started beating her small wings against her body and out of the pores on her body came pulses with numerous egg-like organisms, they were dropping on the floor. Once on the floor, they immediately metamorphosed to a mosquito-like insects, but having scorpion's tail, and within seconds these tiny things swarmed around Arun in multitudes like fleas, covering Arun entirely from the coven's sight. These mysterious insects about to assault Eboru were sucking from Arun's dirty pulses. The more they sucked the evil pulse, the more it came forth and the more they multiplied around Arun. Arun was so happy that her laughter overwhelmed the castle.

"Good!" commended the Chieftain.

"I'll lead them to the literal world and overrun Eboru and the tribes." boomed Arun.

"Send them forth, you shall prevail." responded the coven.

Arun flitted off the ground with her single, but powerful avian leg, her small wing beating powerfully through the air and her swarm of tiny, lethal, diabolical mosquitoes enshrouded her, as she flew off through the peak of the pyramidal castle of Aye.

> "Arun O!
> The mysterious plague
> Cries of evil
> Tears of death
> Arun the subtle killer
> Arun the mysterious plague
> Arun go!
> Go Arun go!
> Arun go!
> Go Arun go!
> Arun go!
> Go Arun go!
> Arun go!

Go Arun go!"

the coven was ecstatic as they continued to hail her.

She sprinted of the ground.

"Now, the time has come!" said the Chieftain.

He continued to stare at the roof Arun flew through, with her swarm of tiny lethal creatures.

Chapter Twelve

AJALA was staring at Erin's mother, with the dream he had about her missing daughter calling on him niggling his mind. He was sitting with Pott beside him, making and designing gourd penis sheath together. And within him he was ruminating on how to break this oneiric experience to her.

"Your daughter's alive *somehow* around us." telepathised Ajala through Shea to Erin's mother, as he was taking Pott through the act of making gourd penis sheath and feathery headwear of his tribe.

"How did you know my daughter's alive, lad?" asked Erin's mother through Shea, who was *often* the medium between Ajala and the newly arrived visitors.

"When I went for fetching food for the *untouchable* children, I found myself exhausted and while I was resting, I fell asleep and had a dream of Erin calling on me. I was looking for her, but I got attacked by a strange being." related Ajala through Shea.

"I've the hunch she's alive somehow, but I don't know where?" he added.

"How did you know my daughter's voice?"

"How did your daughter know my name?" queried Ajala. Erin's mother smiled at his wits.

"My hunch told me it's her voice, anyway." he said.

Erin's mother, who was caring for these children – *the untouchables* – walked to Ajala and gave him one out of the fruits she was distributing to the *untouchable* children.

"From Erin, your friend." she said.

"Thank you!" he replied.

He walked to the inner side of the cave and sat secluded, facing the cave's wall, watching the shadow casted on the cave's wall by the burning fire. Tisseewoonatis went to him and sat beside him, staring at the shadow of the burning fire with him. Tisseewoonatis slowly turned her eyes on Ajala, whose unwonted eyes were fixed on the cave's wall still.

148

"What's your boggle, son?" she asked, but he remained quiet, musing his eyes on the shadow on the wall.

"What's it that you're staring at?" asked again Tisseewoonatis.

"Nothing, lady." replied Ajala through Shea, who was some distance away from them, but Tisseewoonatis could hear her shouting what Ajala said.

"But you're always enamoured for some days now by the shadow of the burning fire." said Tisseewoonatis.

"When you stared at nothing, you stared at everything within." opined Ajala, as he remembered Odu's emphasis on looking within, when he met the phantom. Though, he still didn't grasp the nitty-gritty of Odu's messages, he always ruminated on them and on those remarkable eyes he saw on the phantom.

"When you came, I could find your location from the actions of my animal friends, and without bothering Shea and Pott, I actuated my beloved owl and it led me directly to receive you. You both accepted me when you saw me, even with all my animal entourage, still you embraced me and on our way back, I could see you were happy with me. Yet, I am deaf and dumb, with unusual eyeballs and totally rejected by my own people. I've never felt so much love from anyone all my life, except from my late mother. You took me, as if I were your own child and you began showing me things that you carried with you, like your phones, pen, iPad, cameras and pictures." said Ajala.

"Perhaps, you thought I haven't seen them before, never mind, my mother had shown them to me." he said humourously, referring to Shea.

"But when I showed you the owl that led me to you and most especially, the wild animals around that were stalking us for safety, you feared and clung to me." he laughed.

"Yea, it was scary for us." chortled Tisseewoonatis.

"But you quickly trusted me and calmed down, when I gestured you and most especially, Erin's mother fell in love with these animals immediately." remarked Ajala.

"Of course, it's her discipline." said Tisseewoonatis.

"She's a zoologist." she added.

"What's that?" he asked.

"A zoologist is someone who study animals." mouthed

Tisseewoonatis *briefly*. Ajala turned his face to Erin's mother.

"I guess she has more than enough to examine here." remarked Ajala. There was a brief laughter from everyone over his remark.

"Then, her first words when she set her eyes on me, 'Where's my daughter?' continued to niggle in my head after Shea later told me what she was saying exactly." he said, still looking at Erin's mother, and slowly he brought his eyes on Tisseewoonatis.

"How would I know?" asked Ajala and Tisseewoonatis knew exactly that he had the urge for finding Erin and for the fact that he felt powerless to do this was bothering him.

"Nevertheless, this question affected me so much and when she showed me the image of the missing girl. I felt as if it's my responsibility to find her and that worries me." said Ajala, as his eyes were fixed on the cave's wall again.

"Why did it worry you?" asked Erin's mother.

"Because I don't know how I can find her."

Tisseewoonatis knew something positive pertaining to Erin's disappearance was going on in his nascent psyche and she resolved to stir his mind further.

"Can you fly?" asked Tisseewoonatis.

"Fly?" guffawed Ajala.

There was a brief laughter from Ajala over this question, but Tisseewoonatis knew this was the scariest ability for juvenescent witches to accept. She had studied all the designs and sketches Ajala made on gourds and his gourd art posters. She knew there was more to these drawings and posters, but she needed to interrogate him to know more of his psychicgenesis – *provenance of psychic power*.

"No, of course." replied Ajala.

"Who made those designs I saw on the gourds."

"I did, lady."

"Did you sketch what you saw or what you heard, or whatever came to your mind?"

"Sometimes, I couldn't tell how or when I did some of them."

"In one of these numerous designs, you drew a child standing on a flying flat gourd."

"Yes."

"Why did you sketch that?"

"I don't know, lady." he replied.

"Perhaps, some sort of deja vu?" asked Tisseewoonatis.

"What's deja vu?" he responded, with a puzzled look on his face.

"Deja vu's when you felt an experience had happened to you before."

"Oh, yea!" he smiled.

"You're right, wise one." he added.

"Are you a witch, too, like my mother?" he asked, referring to Shea.

"No, I'm not a witch."

"I've felt that way lot of times and I often drew what I felt." he continued.

"I mean, d-é-j-à v-u!" he drawled.

There was a brief spontaneous silence from everyone, as he was staring at the shadow on cave's wall again.

"But I'm learning some lessons from the shadow of this burning fire. Fire tries all things, destroy anything on its path and nothing changes things quickly like fire. I just wish I could be like fire, and that's why I'm enamoured with the shadow of the fire on the wall." revealed Ajala *finally* and Tisseewoonatis realised his psyche was yearning for evolution.

"My dear, fire's like us, both good and evil burns in us, but we all have choices to make, either good or evil." said Tisseewoonatis and Ajala mused awhile. Tisseewoonatis allowed him and when she noticed he was ready to continue talking, she began her discussion with him again.

"You also sketch a girl, snatched by a strange bird, how did you come about that?"

"I'm not sure, I guess some of those things just came to me, when I was doing the gourd works, I guess."

"I want you to think very well, Ajala." said Tisseewoonatis.

"Do you think you have any drawing on gourd that had come true the same way you portrayed it?"

"I think the animals protecting me."

"Yes, I saw the massive gourd art poster you made on that, where the animals stood guard on you."

"Yes, that came to be reality." he said.

"I also saw the phantoms you drew."

"Eh, that's Odu." responded Ajala quickly with a chuckle and

Tisseewoonatis could see the difference on his face. Tisseewoonatis knew perhaps this was his psychicgenesis – *the provenance of his psychic potential.*

"Who's Odu or what's Odu?"

"Odu's my friend." he said.

"And Odu can do all things." he remarked.

"But he refused to help me, I can't understand."

"All things?" queried Tisseewoonatis.

"Of course, he told me my name's Ilari."

"Where's he now?"

"I don't know."

"Then, where did you meet him?"

"In my eyes or imagination, or dream, I don't know, but I saw him."

"What did you mean you don't know?"

"Lady, that day I saw Odu, may be I was awake or I was sleeping or dead, I don't know, but of a sudden, somehow, I traveled with my animal friends and eventually I met Odu. He's a good friend, anyway."

"Why a good friend?"

"He told me my name is Ilari."

"What's Ilari?"

"I don't know."

"Do you wish to meet Odu, again?"

"Yes, I do wish I see my friend again, but also I don't know how."

"I'd like to ask you one important thing." said Tissewoonatis. Ajala looked at Tisseewoonatis with a smile.

"What?" he asked.

"Are you a witch?"

"No." he answered plainly.

"Witches are said to be evil by my people."

Tisseewoonatis was at least satisfied by Ajala's answer, because she knew by his response, his mind had no inclination towards evil.

"No, dear, to be evil's like the food we eat. It's by choice."

"Yeah, they told me evil's by choice." said Ajala, referring to Shea and Pott. There was silence in the cave, with all eyes on Ajala, as Tisseewoonatis brought out the picture of the strange pot for him to see.

"What's this?" asked Tisseewoonatis, as she showed Ajala the image of the strange pot that appeared when Mother Endor psychically reached Erin through the bamboozling, scattered handwriting borne out of her dream. Ajala shuddered at the sight of the picture, his unwonted eyes blinked repeatedly. He was silent, looking at Tisseewoonatis strangely and in his mind, the picture of the pot reminded him of the moment he *somehow* came across the exact pot, during his somnambulation at Igbo – *the evil forest and the land of the gods* – when he traveled with the animals, as led by the white tailed rat.

"Are you okay?" queried Tisseewoonatis.

"And you said you're not a witch?" he added.

"Yeah, I'm not a witch."

"Then, how did you come about this?" he asked, about the picture.

"I know where that is!" he added.

"Where?" asked Tisseewoonatis.

"But I don't know exactly where it is."

"What did mean by that?"

"Because when I went there, it was through an ant's hole."

"Ant's hole?" retorted Tisseewoonatis.

"But how?" she asked.

"I don't know, but I was there and saw it in a huge cave, it's a huge pot exactly like this one." said Ajala, pointing to the image in Tisseewoonatis hands.

"Deja vu, I guess!" he said *casually* and laughed.

"Hey, have you been there, too?" queried Ajala, and Tisseewoonatis noticed a sudden surprise look on his face.

"No, Ajala."

"Then, how did you get to have this?" said Ajala, referring to the picture.

"You must be a witch, too, if you can travel through ant's hole." said Ajala, and they all laughed.

"I'm not a witch, but I conduct deep researches into paranormal activities, trying to see if they have logical basis or at least, a rational explanation." said Tisseewoonatis and Ajala nodded his head couple of times.

"That's better than witchcraft." he remarked. Then,

153

Tisseewoonatis cued to Erin's mother to present the scattered handwriting borne out of her daughter's dream. Erin's mother took the paper from her rucksack and gave it to Tisseewoonatis. Immediately Ajala saw this handwriting, his psyche sparked a vision of Erin's predicament – *at the hands of the witches of blood underworld* – and he became terrified, as he saw Erin in a bizarre cage surrounded by these hideous evil beings.

Tisseewoonatis and the rest of the camp could easily notice that this handwriting had effect on his psyche, but were all unaware of his clairvoyance through the piece. Tisseewoonatis was about to fold the paper, when Ajala held her hands because he saw a huge ostrich-like bird with an aged woman's head, approaching and looking at him. While the camp was asking Ajala what was going on, he remained silent and focused on this paper and the vision it facilitated. Suddenly, the odd bird, with its shriveled hand, threw a blow of psychic current that instantly knocked Ajala into coma. Tisseewoonatis held Ajala and found out he was still breathing. They laid him on the ground and the camp was trying to wake him up, at the same time, wondering what had happened to him. While Erin's mother was patting his face with water, suddenly, Ajala got hold of her hands firmly. Gradually, he let go of her hand and snored into a deep sleep.

"He's sleeping, now." said Pott.

He watched over Ajala. Of course, they all knew he got some sort of unusual attack. However, it was about half an hour after he fell asleep, the camp was talking about the happening and the *untouchable* children were playing outside the cave, when Ajala got up and slowly walked to Erin mother's rucksack, trying to lay hold on the handwriting of Erin's dream. Despite that Erin's mother called on him through Shea, to let go of her rucksack, he seemed oblivious to Shea's telepathy.

"Noctambulation!" recognised Tisseewoonatis.

"What was that?" asked Erin's mother.

"Sleepwalking." she replied.

She quickly noticed Ajala wasn't in his real self and she cued to Erin's mother to remain quiet, as she began to televise him. Ajala scattered the content of the rucksack, but couldn't find the paper. Then, he left the cave and they followed him, watching every move he made to make sure he wouldn't injure himself.

Ajala somnambulated into a gourd field, fetched virgin gourds and sat under a tree, unaware of anyone's presence. He began to design on these gourds the vision he saw when the handwriting of Erin's dream was shown to him. Ajala's design was astonishing, as his hands moved with precision. Though, remarkably fantastic, yet, what he drew looked bizarre to them all. *An ostrich-like bird, with human head, again?* Mused everyone.

Tisseewoonatis moved closer to him, saw his hands moving with ease and precision, while he etched the images of a caged girl, as he saw it in his vision. When Ajala finished, he took the gourds to a nearby place, where he kept some gourd works and added them as part of his collection. Then, he proceeded back to the cave, lay on the exact spot where he got up before and snored back into deep sleep.

"He's a kind of noctambulo." remarked Tisseewoonatis.

To the surprise of Tisseewoonatis, who examined the drawing Ajala just made, she didn't only see the image of a girl among bizarre, grisly looking creatures, she also noticed Ajala drew up himself holding this girl's hand and running through these hideous beings.

Ajala also made the drawing of Tisseewoonatis, showing him the handwriting that was borne out of Erin's dream and the vision it facilitated, which eventually knocked him into stupor. Ajala depicted all these images clearly on these gourds and Tisseewoonatis was convinced Ajala needed help to realise the juvenescent psychic potentials in him, if Erin had to be found. Erin's mother was stunned and couldn't still settle with the thought of these paranormal activities surrounding the disappearance of her daughter.

Tisseewoonatis took the gourds and placed them beside him to test his reaction to them, when he would wake up. They hid themselves, watching over him. Howbeit, when Ajala finally woke up, he took the gourds and casually looked at them. Tisseewoonatis knew he didn't recollect when and how he made them. Though, he knew no one else worked on gourds, but him, therefore, he casually shrugged them off. Tisseewoonatis knew probably this was how Ajala designed almost, all the remarkable gourd works he made.

"They'll help you, my dear." said Tisseewoonatis, as she came out of hiding with the others, pointing to Shea and Pott, who went to sit close to Ajala, looking at him while Erin's mother came with a pure white cloth and unfurled it on him. They all began to laugh at her covering of Ajala with the cloth and he seemed to love the stuff, too. Of course, this was the first time he had ever been clothed and the first amongst his tribes *at least in this form.*

He blithely began to drape the cloth on himself to the amusement of his friends, but their laughter abruptly stopped when at last, his draping himself with this white cloth stupefied their fashion sense. He placed a cut out, well-designed, archly tapering gourd *he hung on the cave's wall* on his head cutely and wound the rest of the white cloth round its margin to hold it in place. The remaining of the cloth he hung over his left arm, eventually, furling this white cloth on himself like a toga.

Ajala looked great to his friends and they somehow beheld his panache in this simple act. They all admired him, as he stood before them. He began to pose for their mobile cameras, as they all scrambled to capture him.

"You have to help him realise his mind, I presume he has potentials he's not entirely ignorant of." Tisseewoonatis called Shea and Pott aside and informed them.

"And explain to him clearly who you're. Of course he trusts both of you. Let him know he can do better. I'm convinced his gourd sketches and art posters could be of help, too."

While Tisseewoonatis was talking to Shea and Pott, Ajala gratefully held Erin mother's hand and walked her into the forest, where his okapi was waiting. He wanted her to ride on the okapi with him because she had several time reasoned the animal was a fortunate nature's cross between an okapi and a wild horse, because of some distinctive horse-like qualities she noticed on this rare animal.

He mounted it, pulled Erin's mother behind him and sprinted off into the forest to show Erin's mother the awe-inspiring jungle's bountifulness. After he had toured Erin's mother around in this jungle, which she indeed relished, he came to the place where the travestied vulture – *Kowe's errand that she sent to convene the coven* – vanished. *That's where the strange bird vanished, after I stalked it to this point.* Ajala gesticulated to Erin's mother, by pointing his finger towards the sky, when he came to *a halt* at where this dissimulated Apaadi creature *he had stalked* vanished.

"Vanished?" said Erin's mother.

While he focused his frown towards that part of the sky, Erin's mother looked at him, trying to understand his thought.

Therefore, she could see the natural simplicity on his face, despite his bizarre eyeballs.

Chapter Thirteen

TRAGEDY had struck in Eboru and throughout these lost tribes. Arun, *the mysterious disease's* lethal mosquitoes were hardly seen, yet, they were ubiquitous, witchcraft guided and so much infectious that many children of Ajala's age caught fever and within twilight to twilight, many homes had their dead *children* to bury. These strange, swift, elusive and bewitched mosquitoes of the witches of blood underworld mingled with ordinary mosquitoes and were particularly bedeviled to target children of Ajala's age first, so that the tribespeople's mind could easily heap the blame on him.

Families, according to tradition, invited juju priest to initiate the souls of their dead children into the spirit world. It was rife among these lost tribes that dying young wasn't natural and the spirit world might reject the soul of such juveniles, except if the spirit world could be appeased, – *only then would these young souls be allowed into the world of the dead* – in order that more juvenile's death wouldn't result from the rejected souls of these children roaming around.

The appeasement ritual was casually wrapping the children's body in black leather and on each body would be placed a white pigeon or dove. Elders of all the families involved would sit, sympathisers and onlookers alike would also be present, waiting, not only for the arrival of the juju priest, *who was* to complete all ritual procedures, but also to hear the revelation that would follow – *the cause of these children's death, as revealed by the ancestors and the gods to this juju priest.*

As the bereaved assembly were waiting for this juju priest to arrive, they continued to weep bitterly for the loss of their sons and daughters. Then, faraway emerged a man, walking gingerly towards them, humming incantations and making purification by sprinkling everywhere with the horsetail in his hand, from the pot of juju water he was carrying *in his other hand*. This small black pot of juju water was marked with white dots all over. While he continued to approach this bereaved gathering, he was looking here and there, as if on the lookout for someone or something.

"The spirit of the ancestors commands silence!" he cried to stop the women and mourners *who were weeping,* from perturbing the brief ritual process.

"You're welcome, wise one!" said one of the affected families' elder to the juju priest.

"Please, do as tradition demands." he added, permitting the juju priest to carry out the custom of appeasing the spirit world to allow these souls of the dead youngsters into their midst.

The juju priest was wearing round his waist, a ragged leather apron of cheetah's skin and on his neck was dangling human skull, and his body was entirely festooned with all sorts of juju from head to toe.

He sprinkled on these children's body, from this pot of juju water in his hand, before he started walking round them, a ritual walk families affected had to partake with him after his seventh time *of walking around these bodies.* While these families continued this ritual walk around the bodies of these deceased children, then, the juju priest was staring the dove on each body one after the other and there was an effulgence from each *dove* that radiated all over the body on which it was placed.

This juju priest, who seemed to be in trance as he stared these bodies, saw revelation for the cause of the death of these children through this effulgence. Of course, Arun, *the mysterious disease,* of the witches of blood underworld was revealed to him in all of her evil glory *by this effulgence.*

Instantly, he was so alarmed that he woke out of his trance and the doves on these bodies flew off, out of sight into the clear sky, as a symbolism of the acceptance of these children's soul into the spirit world.

As soon as the pigeons flew off, there was an outburst of lamentation from mourners, but the juju priest shouted at them to stop, while the vision of Arun, *the mysterious disease,* that he saw was still boggling his mind. He allowed the people to settle and all eyes came to be on him to reveal what he alone saw while the ritual walk was going on – *the cause of the death of the children.*

"I want you all to be happy, of course, the souls of the children were accepted by the ancestors into the spirit world." the juju priest declared, as he was walking among the children's bodies and of a sudden, he stopped and went mused.

"Talk, wise one!" said an old man to him, but the juju priest remained mused, staring at the bodies on the ground. He raised his eyes towards the sky and pointed to the rising sun.

"There'll be more deaths like these *ones* before the sun set." he announced.

The families affected and their sympathisers were all together troubled and they began to murmur rejection for this bad message from the voodoo priest.

"What are we going to do to prevent this, O wise one?" asked an aged woman.

This juju priest quickly calmed the troubled people from jittering because of the revelation he gave.

"I'll declare the revelation of the ancestors and the evil doer behind these deaths!" exclaimed the juju priest.

He barely finished this statement, when, with the sound of thunder, audible to him alone, Arun, *the mysterious disease,* of the witches of blood underworld, travestied as one of her diabolical, lethal mosquitoes, swiftly landed *from nowhere* on the left ear of this juju priest.

"Greetings, wise one!" spoke Arun into the mind of the juju priest, as he went transfixed because he knew the secret he was about to reveal had displeased someone. He remained attentive, while Arun, *the mysterious disease,* of the witches of blood underworld was speaking right into his psyche. The juju priest could feel the enormity of the evil power vibrating through Arun, *the mysterious disease.*

"I came in peace to inform you that what had happened is our concern, and it isn't for you to expose." said Arun, *the mysterious disease.*

"Don't even dare open this can of worms." she warned.

"Now, the message of the witches of blood underworld is, 'Ajala, the forbidden soul is avenging his mother's blood.' This shall be your message and no more."

The juju priest nodded his head in agreement while the people watching him knew he had an urgent message in his mind to reveal.

"The secret you hear with your left ear should never be revealed to your right ear." instructed Arun, *the mysterious disease,* metaphorically.

"The coven of the witches of blood underworld hath spoken."

she warned.

"Greetings, once more, wise one!" thundered Arun, *the mysterious disease,* of the witches of blood underworld into the juju priest's left ear and flew off like lightning.

The juju priest shook his head and nodded again in agreement. As he stood spellbound, he gently raised his eyes towards the sky, and the people were puzzled by his prolonged moment of quietude. He thought of speaking the truth and dared the wrath of witches of blood underworld or rather complied with the message of Arun, *the mysterious disease,* and be free from any havoc they might wreak on him or his loved ones. When this juju priest imagined, as deeply as he could, the possible evils these underworld witches might visit on him or his loved ones, his imagination terrorised him because his juju manifested to him he wouldn't be able to save his entire family and loved ones from the wrath of these evil witches, if he dared them. At same time, he knew whatever he perceived was just a tip of an iceberg because he realised these witches would fight with everything they've got, if he wouldn't comply with them. Therefore, he resolved not to be gutsy.

"Wise one, elders are here to listen to you, let us know the cause of these youngsters' death." said a family head.

Everyone, out of desperation, *now* rose to their feet, looking at the juju priest. He turned his attention on them, too, and they could read on his face that he had a terrible message to deliver.

"The gods and the ancestors aren't angry with you, O Eboru!" declared the juju priest. The people were baffled and wondering. They continued to murmur, but an old man immediately waved down their agitations.

"If the gods and the ancestors aren't angry, then, who's angry?" asked the old man calmly.

"The forbidden soul's angry and had vowed to avenge the blood of his mother, whom he said you all murdered at the market centre." he declared.

"The bodies are ready for burial. Now, I take my leave." concluded the juju priest.

The juju priest departed with a heavy heart, as *he knew* he lied on his revelation about the cause of the death of these children and couldn't believe he was this much of a coward. The people shivered, murmured and argued among themselves, that they suspected the same reason all along as the juju priest had just revealed, because all the dead children were of Ajala's age. The families' elders affected beckoned to their able bodied men to convey the bodies of these deceased children for burial, while they communed together on the revelation of the juju priest.

"The gods and the ancestors aren't angry, Ajala the forbidden soul is?" surmised an elder to his fellow elders, as they deliberated together and suggested the terrible message *should* be passed to the chiefs and elders of Eboru immediately for a response before it would be too late.

Chapter Fourteen

IT was stark darkness over Igbo – *the evil forest and the land of the gods* – and all the tribal villages dwelt in the utter silence of the night, only Ajala and the nocturnal mammals of the vast Igbo were under their respective pressures. While the nocturnal mammals went around in search for food, Ajala was under intensive tutelage of Shea and Pott.

Since Tisseewoonatis made it clear he would need their help to be more conscious of his subliminal self *in order to be aware of his psychic potentials* and the psychic curriculum was inspired by Ajala's amazing sketches and designs that he made on different gourds.

Shea, Pott and Tisseewoonatis *had* gathered and studied all these wonderful collections borne out of Ajala's imagination and somnambulation and *had* resorted to the best way of applying them to his psyche.

They all agreed to use meditation to prepare Ajala's mind and also employed the psychical bountifulness of Igbo as a paradigm to spark his subconscious, so as to alert him to the potentials he could be filled with by his fate.

For Ajala to understand fully, Shea and Pott would even have to give him panoply of who they were. Though they had been with Ajala for a while, yet the lad wasn't fully aware of their witchcraft.

Also, Tisseewoonatis knew if the psychical potentials in Ajala had to be awaken successfully and effectively, it would have to be in line with his psychicgenesis, which she identified as Odu and the only way to achieve this was to follow majorly as guide, those things he drew, sketched and worked on gourds, even though some of these things were obscured to them.

They also knew his psyche had to be freed and evolved from the shackles of superstitious belief that witches were evil and afterwards would no doubt auto-didactically convince himself to live with his destiny as a witch without guilty conscience.

Tisseewoonatis suggested to Shea and Pott that Ajala had to

be helped to be able to wield the psychic potentials in him at will and effectively, if Erin would have to be found. Nevertheless, she assured them of speedy success, as she also noticed the lad had already been evincing some of his hidden potentials. Perhaps, due to his ostracism by his people and his deaf and dumbness that prompted him to look inward the more, rather than dwelling on his miseries.

So, every night, since Tisseewoonatis deliberation with Shea and Pott on this issue, Ajala was placed under mind control exercise and other psychic drills that would spark his subliminal self. Shea and Pott spared no nightfall without having séance with Ajala on a new psychic skill and they were both impressed with the alacrity at which Ajala was progressing with his learning. Also, he was engaged in how to read and write, rudimentary mathematics and science by Shea and Pott. In fact, he no doubt enjoyed these disciplines, as he always asked for more, even, when his mentors were tired.

Ajala was taken on Shea's broomstick one night and they flew him all over and around Igbo. He was excited, thrilled and amazed at how extrasensory the feeling was.

One night, after Ajala's psyche had been prepared for the final moment, Shea and Pott took him to the huge gourd that was full of his remarkable artistic works and was asked questions about all the works he *had* made on the extraordinarily big fruit. Ajala could explain some, but couldn't give reasons why he did many of them.

Shea told Pott to cut an opening into the gourd at the top, so that Ajala could go inside. Pott, who had prepared himself for this with all his camping paraphernalia on him, made a safety ladder first to climb on the huge fruit, took out his camping *battery powered* saw and painstakingly made an opening on the gourd, making sure Ajala's sketches weren't affected.

Ajala entered into the huge gourd and it was perfect nature's interior décor for him with the pattern formed by the fibrous tissues that were holding together the big seeds inside the gourd. All these fibers were so wound together and attached in forms that Ajala could sit comfortably on them for solemn cogitation. When Shea saw this, she realised her hunch was right and decided within her forthwith that Ajala alone would have séance inside the gourd throughout the night.

"Now, Ajala, the mantra is: 'Ilari and Odu are friends, Odu and Ilari can do all things, and my mind is Ilari Odu.' repeat this again and again until I come back." instructed Shea.

"I repeat, until I come back." drawled Shea.

"Good luck, son!" said Pott and he replaced the gourd's cut out lid.

Ajala *really* absorbed the importance of the mantra with his mind on Shea's drawling her instruction to him. The inclination he nurtured to find Erin motivated him, too. Therefore, he immersed himself obediently into anything he was asked to do.

He knew he needed this help from Shea and Pott, as he realised he had no other people in his life he could rely on and believe in. He was impressed at the encouragement he had from Shea and Pott, of course, he knew not even his own people counted him a persona grata, but these strangers around him were exercising faith in him. Thereby, he took every instruction from them as bona-fide.

"Ajala, as a witch, being at parity with your mind isn't enough, you have to be greater and be the god of your mind." communed Shea.

"Remember, '... let the gods believe in you ...' says your mother." added Shea.

Shea communicated Ajala's mind, reminding him of his mother's words and forthwith Ajala heard Shea, he squeezed his face, trying to hold back tears. None the less, his eyes lodged tears of determination. He seemed to be more resolved to achieve the whole process for the memory of his mother and perhaps to spur him on the edge was Shea's aim by reminding him of his late mother.

"Am I not my mind?" he cried.

"That's exactly why you're in there to realise that what your strength can't achieve, your mind is capable of doing." answered Shea, hinting at one of Odu's encouragement to Ajala when he met the phantom-like creature. Afterward, there was eye contact between Shea and Pott that signaled agreement. Therefore, Shea communicated Ajala's mind to start the mantra, which Tissewoonatis put together for them.

Though, the inside of the huge gourd was dark, but through some perforations between the lid Pott cut out and the gourd, moonlight filtered inside in three different directions. Ajala looked at these moon rays and sighed heavily before he kicked off with the mantra.

"Ilari and Odu are friends, Odu and Ilari can do all things, and my mind is Ilari Odu." continued Ajala his mantra inside the gourd throughout that night.

Even though he dosed sometimes, yet the lad held on till morning twilight started to show inside through perforations between the lid and the gourd. Ajala's eyes were bleary and sometimes closed out of sleepiness, however, he didn't give up and at a point the encounter he had previously with Odu started to replay in his mind like visions.

In this dreamy state, he saw the two amorphous, diaphanous phantom-like beings beside him inside the gourd, as he continued his mantra. Their attention were on the *somnolent* Ajala, and as one began to move clockwise round him, the other was moving anticlockwise. In his somnolence he watched these two creatures, as he continued his mantra, with the message of Shea, *'Repeat this again and again until I come back ... I repeat, until I come back.'* niggling inside his head.

The two opposing energies created by the phantoms' circular motion became stretching on Ajala's psyche, as the *psychic* pressures the creatures wielded increased. In fact, Ajala was terrified and felt as if his mind was about to explode. Then he was held aloft in his cogitative posture by this field of psychic energy created by these esoteric beings, but he continued to try his damnedest to achieve control. All the strong fibers and big seeds in the huge gourd were torn to pieces by this unbelievable field of psychic energy wielded by his mind. As he was held aloft, he was stretched into a unique posture, though, this special posture was not immediately registered on his mind, as his primary concern was to achieve control of the situation.

While he continued to resist this psychic energy, suddenly, he was thrown into a spin that almost torn him apart by this field of magical force Odu wielded on him. However, he didn't allow Odu to tame him, instead, he struggled to control Odu by holding on to the mantra, as Shea's words continued to echo again and again in his mind.

In a flash, he recollected all he had been through with his mother and her last words to him.

Eventually, as he didn't back down on chanting the mantra, despite all the difficulties he had with the forces from the two contrary motions around him, he was able to see and hear things in his mind. This *ad hoc* instant clairvoyance and clairaudience from his psyche was indeed didactic for Ajala.

At one point in his vision, he saw his drawing of depicting a flying lad, standing on a flat gourd, and he heard in his subliminal self the unique spell *'ofe'*. Instantly, he saw this drawing came alive and flew into the huge gourd and all around him at will. At this vision, he remembered how he flew with Shea and Pott on their broomsticks and knew probably he could do the same with the help of this spell. Henceforth, he realised this spell was probably for preternatural flight. He also saw the long neck bottle gourd he had adorn with cowries and beautified the stopper of it with colourful feathers *that he pinned into it*. At the hearing of the rare magical spell *'ase', divine energy,* he heard in his subliminal self, he saw the bottle neck gourd achieving magical feat at different strokes and angles of direction, and at a point the gourd's stopper opened up itself and silently began to devour everything; trees, mountains, rivers, sea and even the clouds in the sky, the moon, the sun and the stars, into itself with its stopper flying back into its place, shutting everything in and with this he suspected this particular spell could be for carrying out his wish.

Ajala witnessed many things in his *ad hoc* visions before the two phantoms suddenly vanished as he wouldn't stop his mantra after all, and the energy wielded around him, which nearly tore him apart, went calmed. He fell from being airborne unto the gourd's bottom, extremely exhausted and motionless, almost stripped naked of the white covering Erin's mother gave him, which had become his clothing since he received it.

"Are you okay?" cried Shea, when she opened the huge gourd in the morning and found Ajala motionless and the inside of the gourd entirely smoothened and cleaned up of its fibrous tissues and seeds, which were scattered on the numbed Ajala, as if someone had attacked him. Pott entered into the gourd and touched him.

"Odu!" he cried repeatedly with fear as he regained himself.

"It's me, Ajala." communed Pott with him to calm him down.

"What happened?" he asked Pott, as he looked up and saw Shea, who was standing on the wooden ladder made by Pott for entering into the gourd.

"I don't know, friend." answered Pott. He helped Ajala out of the gourd, while Shea received him outside.

"What happened?" asked Shea.

She sat him on the ground and while Ajala was staring at the gourd, wondering what had happened and trying to recollect his experiences during this meditation. Meanwhile, as his eyes caught his drawings on the gourd, instantly he had a reliving in his mind of every happenings.

As he was about to inform Shea and Pott of what he saw and heard, '*asiri*', his subliminal-self pronounced this peculiar spell, away from the perception of Shea and Pott and he remained mused and held back the disclosure of those words because he got the hunch that '*asiri*' meant his psychic secret.

"The whole thing came alive." he said, pointing to his sketches on the gourd.

Shea looked at Pott, who was climbing out of the gourd. Of course, they knew Ajala's mind was what came alive, and they knew the lad had begun realising himself and his potential.

"Everything is all right." Shea calmed him down and his white cloth was dressed on him properly, with the conical gourd placed on his head and the loose part of the cloth he wound round its margin to hold it in place.

Shea went into the gourd and examined it carefully. She wondered what had happened that swept everything off its place and smoothened the inside of the huge, extremely hard-skin fruit. She sat and tried to communicate with events that had taken place in the gourd while Pott helped the exhausted and weak Ajala proceeded to the cave.

Shea sent forth her psychic concentration to saturate the inside of the gourd to connect to what had happened to Ajala, and all Shea could hear was Ajala's psychic voice repeating the mantra. Shea couldn't perceive anything else other than how the lad had struggled to subdue to his will the psychic energy in his mind by maintaining the focus that eventually brought control and Shea was amazed how Ajala was able to control such powerful psychic energy.

Ajala was welcomed by Tisseewoonatis. Erin's mother took care of him with some food and drink *for* to regain his energy. The child of Eboru, dubbed forbidden, who had never known care and love from his own people, was shown the same by strangers. Ajala himself knew he did never have cause to expect such from them with the way his own people stigmatised, castigated and ostracised him.

Though Shea couldn't sense anything from inside the gourd that had happened to Ajala, but she knew something had taken place in him, even if she couldn't define what psychic uniqueness the child's fate just imbued him.

She came out of the gourd and examined all the markings and drawings Ajala made on them and the sketch of the phantom-like creatures struck her the most. She stared at these two phantoms drew by Ajala and noticed the binary eye patterns on them, and something struck her there should be more to those unique eyes.

Ajala was eating the food set before him and the *untouchable* children gathered around him. He called them to eat with him, and they dined all together from one calabash bowl. Pott and Erin's mother found out the food wouldn't be enough for them, they went and added more and Tisseewoonatis was watching Ajala, when Shea joined them in the cave.

"What happened?" Pott inquired of her, but Shea looked at him with a puzzling expression on her face, Pott knew she hadn't been able to harmonise psychically the event that took place in the gourd, which he believed, perhaps, Ajala himself might not be able to express with clarity.

"It's a positive awakening." said Shea to Pott.

"Sure?" asked Pott.

"Yeah." she mouthed.

Immediately Ajala finished his food, he laid on the ground and slept off. In no time he found himself in a dream riding his okapi for the rescue of his *late* mother, as at the day it actually happened. But the difference was that, this time, his dying mother, after he got her to Igbo – *the evil forest and the land of the gods* – said to him, "Find Erin quickly, she's in danger."

"You know this girl also, mother?" he asked.

"How can I find her?" he queried.

Then her mother pointed behind him and when Ajala turned around to the direction, he saw Shea, Pott, Erin's mother and Tisseewoonatis standing.

"Who're they?" she asked her son and the message sank into his mind straightaway.

"They love and care for me, mother." he said.

"As no one teaches the heart to love, so follow your heart to find her." she said.

Suddenly, Ajala awoke his sleep and found out it was a dream. Ajala got on his feet and quickly left the cave without saying a word to anyone. Shea got up to follow him, but Tisseewoonatis cued her to let him be. Ajala walked back to the huge gourd and began to examine his works of art that he made on it. While staring at them, his attention fell on the phantoms he drew and what really hit his hunch were the remarkable binary eye patterns.

The binary patterned eyes of Odu came to his senses and he remembered the first time he met Odu, these binary eyes were labile between different binary patterns. As he unwittingly folded his thumb, index finger and the pinky, pointing his middle finger and the fourth finger side by side towards the eyes of one of the phantoms he drew to demonstrate the pattern of the arrangement of the binary *eight* eyes, from top down *and left to right*. He was instantly fear struck when he felt somehow shocked by the psychic current that went through his body. Immediately, he withdrew his hands quickly and fearfully, but curiosity made him try again. Though, unbeknownst still, this time, pointing different fingers, the index finger together with the middle finger, these in effect attracted no psychic impulse.

He looked at his fingers and recollected he first felt, at the tip of his middle finger and fourth finger, the psychic current that shocked through his body and he realised perhaps he wasn't using the same fingers, that he used previously. He tried again his middle and fourth fingers on the binary eye patterns and instantly his fingers demonstrated half way, enduring the flow of psychic impulse that sent shock waves into his body, as he persevered to fully demonstrate the binary setting. Of a sudden, as soon as he finished, there was an explosion of the whole gourd into the air, in such that no piece of it fell on the ground.

"Is that atomic bomb?" asked Erin's mother *ad lib*.

"No, it's psychic explosion." responded Shea quickly.

Shea, Pott, Tisseewoonatis and Erin's mother as soon as they heard this terrible explosion, they ran hurriedly to the place and the *untouchable* children, too, ran from their different playing grounds to see what had happened. They met Ajala in a panicked state, his body extremely hot and given off smoke that the heat repelled everyone from coming nearer him.

Though, Ajala feared and was panic-struck, but indubitably the psychic powers of these eyes were unexpectedly and fortuitously discovered by him. In his mind continued to run all the uncountable binary eye settings labile on Odu, that he noticed when he first met the phantom in his somnambulation.

"What happened?" communed Shea.

"What did you do?" she added *quickly*.

"The gourd fucking disappeared or what?" queried Pott.

"No, it exploded into the air." communed Ajala to Shea and Pott.

They were all amazed and wondered if they hadn't awoken Ajala's psyche to the wrong side of magic. Tisseewoonatis nodded her head in satisfaction and a pleasant smile briefly shown on her face for Ajala.

"What did you do?" Shea asked Ajala again, he wagged his head in reply to assure her that all was fine because Ajala himself was becoming convinced he could do more than what had happened

However, Tisseewoonatis didn't understand what occurred exactly, though in her mind she knew the humble lad's powers were beginning to unfold.

That night, while Shea and Pott were in séance with Ajala, treating him into the world of advance witchcraft telekinesis. As usual and unknown to anyone at Igbo, except Ajala alone, one of the homesick members of the *untouchable* children used to sneak out of the jungle to pay his parents nocturnal visit. This dangerous, furtive visitation had been going on without anyone being suspicious of it, only Ajala would open his eyes and smile during this lad's creeping surreptitiously in and out of the cave *before day break*.

Ajala kept this awareness to himself all the while without anyone or the lad himself knowing it and sometimes, Ajala would muse at this occurrence with the imagination of himself as the lad, sneaking out to meet his mother, just to get home without any one waiting for him. Nevertheless, he would reimagine himself that if he were to meet his mother at home, how quietly and cozily she would receive him away from the suspicion of the villagers.

Therefore, Ajala realised how dangerous this underhand nocturnal journey into the village was for this nostalgic lad, if he were to be caught. So, whenever he set off on this surreptitious, homesick, nocturnal journey, psychically as he lay asleep, Ajala would actuate a lion, a cheetah, a tiger and an owl to stalk him, just to guarantee his safety from the villagers. Unbeknownst to this lad, these animals would slink after him painstakingly to and fro his dangerous journey.

One fateful night, Shea and Pott, under the view of Erin's mother and Tisseewoonatis, were taking Ajala into thaumaturgical training when this child sneaked out of the camp. Ajala's hunch got him aware and he sent after him for protection the usual animal guards.

It was a moonlit night, this homesick lad embarked on his dangerous hush-hush journey and as usual his parents had left the door open, awaiting their one and only beloved son to emerge quietly into their loving arms. It was always a quiet meeting, though joyous as food specially prepared by his mother would be set before him and at the same time, as he ate, he would continue to relate to his parents the care and benevolence of Ajala towards them and the strangers alike.

Indeed, this stunned his parents and threw their minds into the questionable confusion as to who Ajala was, *a forbidden soul indeed or a forbearing child?* As this nostalgic lad was reporting and demonstrating again to his parents how Shea with the help of Ajala rescued them and his outstanding love and care for everyone at Igbo, his mother broke into tears in the arms of her husband.

"O, what a child!" she wept.

It was about daybreak when this homesick lad bid his parents farewell and set out to return to Igbo – *the evil forest and the land of the gods* – even though he spied to be sure no one saw him, yet Ajala's body guards were steadily at alert for his safety.

As soon as he stepped out of his parents mud shack, one of Arun's witchcraft guided lethal mosquitoes spotted him and suddenly glided towards him for a bite of death. However, Ajala's psychically actuated owl, which perched on a tree, making sure the lad wasn't out of sight, quickly swooped into action to save the unaware lad from the menacing, diabolical, lethal mosquito of Arun, *the mysterious disease.*

The tiny, almost invisible mosquito engaged the owl in the air within the viewing sight of the lion, the tiger and the cheetah that stood guard, and at the same time helplessly watching the lad and the battle going on in the air between the owl and the unusual mosquito of Arun.

The mosquito retreated, recharged on the owl and as it flitted towards the bird in a superb-gliding flight that beat the owl hands down, it bored into the owl's right eye straightaway and erupted through its left eye. As the owl lost control of itself, the mosquito attacked vigorously that it shattered the owl's feathers entirely into

172

the air in a twinkling, before it fell the earth, perforating its body into shreds.

Immediately, the wild animals exchanged glare and the cheetah made its swift run to Ajala, while the lion, the tiger and the jaguar stayed on guard for the lad.

The mosquito, defeating the owl handily, made its glide again towards the unsuspecting lad before he could enter Igbo and gave the unaware poor lad a painless bite of death under the full glare of the *helpless* lion, tiger and cheetah. On the spot, this unsuspecting lad took ill, but he managed to stagger into Igbo, struggling his way towards the camp.

Suddenly the cheetah sped into the cave, waking up the camp and Ajala knew there was problem. As if his okapi knew what was going on, before Ajala could make his way to the entrance of the cave, the okapi already stood at the entrance, making itself available for the emergency. Ajala mounted it without a word to anybody and dashed off with the cheetah leading the way while the remaining members of the camp were wondering what was going on. They all stayed perplexingly to the entrance of the cavern, waiting for the outcome of this emergency.

As soon as Ajala found the dying lad, he placed him on his okapi, mounted it and hasted back to the camp with the lion, the cheetah and the tiger with him. At the entrance of the cave, he laid the lad on the ground, looking at him with had-i-wist attention.

"Did you know anything about this?" communed Shea to Ajala.

"Yes." he answered.

"How could you?" reproached Shea.

"Of course, you're aware of the danger to his life if the villagers caught him." she added.

"But he's to visit his family." responded Ajala.

"No, Ajala!" cried Shea.

"No! No! No!" she raged.

"Don't be mad at me, please!" pleaded Ajala.

"Mother, please!" called Ajala on Shea.

But Shea was too distraught to remain calm and Ajala felt he had hurt her very much and everyone in the camp, as his somber eyes wandered from one person to the other.

"Must you put his life at risk because he's to visit his family?"

queried Pott.

"We're all together in this predicament and we must stay together. How could you do this without letting anyone know?" ranted again Shea.

Ajala looked at the dying lad and bursted into tears, Erin's mother found the lad had temperature and thought it was only fever, she went to his backpack and brought out some medicine for him. Ajala with his hand, out of remorse and annoyance with himself, struck the medicine off her hands.

"Please, help him!" begged Ajala.

"Please, mother!" he cried, begging Shea.

"Mother, please!" he retorted.

Shea looked helpless too, as she knew her magic wouldn't be of any effect on the lad's *Arun* inflicted disease.

"I'm sorry I let him go, I'm so – sorry, I'm so sorry, I'm sorry, mother, please!" cried Ajala repeatedly with profuse tears, pleading to her for help, but Shea wagged her head to Pott in hopelessness of healing the child.

Ajala got to his feet and held Pott's hands, crying to him for help apprehensively. While Tisseewoonatis brought out her tiny stethoscope to feel the child's pulse and heartbeat, Erin's mother was picking the medicine Ajala struck off her hands. Tisseewoonatis had already had her thermometer in the lad's armpit, reading the body temperature she found out that though she felt with her hand it was extremely high, yet the thermometer wasn't affected by the lad's body temperature.

"The unusual fever's killing him, it isn't ordinary." said Tisseewoonatis.

Ajala clung unto Shea when he found out he couldn't get the help he needed from anyone. As he held unto her, with his head on her chest, he heard her heart beating and he at once remembered when he rested his head on his mother's chest as she laid dying and felt her heart beating.

"Be strong, my son." he remembered his mother's words.

"Mother." he looked Shea in the eyes and called.

"Yes, my dear son." answered tearfully Shea.

Ajala turned to the lad as he got his inner compos mentis out of Shea's psyche. While he was looking at him, in his mind began to run the binary eye patterns of Odu and, as he remembered what *had*

174

happened to the huge gourd that exploded into the thin air, he walked to the lad and crouched beside him. He raised his right hand's middle and fourth finger together – *folding the rest* – and made the sign of Odu's binary eye pattern that he demonstrated on the huge gourd some days ago.

Suddenly, the ground started to shake and at the same time in Ajala's mind, he had a recurrence of when the phantoms were pulling him apart in the huge gourd, he remembered he heard the magical spells 'ejiogbe' and 'oyeku' from each of the creatures respectively.

While the ground continued to quake, he yawped 'oyeku' in his subliminal self, and everyone present went aloft topsy-turvy. Therefore, he quickly realised he perhaps mentioned the wrong spell for Odu's magical binary eye pattern *that he signaled*.

In his subliminal self, away from the perception of Shea and Pott, he calmly and with inner compo mentis mentioned, 'ejiogbe'. Then, everyone went calmly and peacefully to their original position and concurrently in Ajala's subliminal self was opened the revelation of what to do to counter Arun's mysterious infection on the boy.

Immediately *he knew what to do*, he rushed into action, running to one of the thin, tall palm trees and climbed with his bare hands as usual. He brought down the calabash of palm wine on it and signaled *'ejiogbe'* magical sign spell of Odu's binary eye pattern on it to bewitch it for the healing of the lad *against Arun's disease, as it was revealed to him in his subliminal self*. He rushed back to the view of the waiting camp and gave the lad the palm wine to drink and also sprinkled it all over his body.

It was all joy and laughter as the lad got well immediately, after sneezing and vomiting worms. However, the vomited mixture incinerated the worms as soon as they touched the ground because of the presence of the bewitched palm wine of Ajala's magic.

Tears of joy ran down Ajala's cheeks as he embraced the lad passionately, cheers of hope brightened up everyone's face. One after the other the camp embraced Ajala for this breakthrough and the healed lad for his magical recovery.

Unknown to the camp, while Ajala casted the spell 'oyeku' wrongly *on Odu's binary eye pattern he made* and things got to start working adversely. Yet, by chance his clairvoyance was opened in a flash by this magical sign of Odu's binary eye pattern to see the missing Erin Eyers still confined in a weird cage. Anyway, he

175

pondered this in his mind without telling anyone.

When the camp saw him dressing his white cloth properly on himself, Tisseewoonatis was wondering where he could be preparing to go.

"Where are you going?" asked Shea.

"Eboru, of course." he communed.

"Why?" queried Shea and he turned to look at everyone.

"I sent an owl, a lion, a cheetah and a tiger to stalk the lad for his safety. The lion, the tiger and the cheetah came back to me, where's my owl?" said Ajala and Shea saw on his face a kind of chutzpah she hadn't seen before, as they both stared one another quietly, and Ajala understood her glare was one of caution against overconfidence.

"Mother, did you trust me?" he said to Shea.

"My son, my dearest son." nodded Shea to him.

"Thanks, mother." he appreciated.

"I'll never rest, mother, until I find my owl, dead or alive." said Ajala, as he mounted his okapi.

"I'm coming with you." said Shea, who was still not comfortable with letting Ajala go alone.

"No, mother, I think it's dangerous out there for now, I'll be back." he said to Shea, but he found on her face a kind of dismay about him going.

"You're my promisee, mother, I won't take unnecessary risk." he pledged.

"Please, my son!" urged Shea.

"I'll be back." he assured her.

She stretched her hands towards him and Ajala got hold of them and as they stared one another, they hardly could let go.

The lion, the tiger and the cheetah sped towards Eboru with Ajala, the cheetah before him, while the lion and the tiger followed behind. The cheetah led Ajala to where villagers had gathered, looking at the owl's devastated body and they were wondering what on earth could damage the owl to such horrible death. As they gathered around this owl's shredded body, discussing among themselves that the bird was an imp of witchcraft, suddenly, they spotted Ajala speeding towards them together with his friends and out of fear of these wild animals with him, the people remained transfixed in total reverence before him.

He calmly bounced off his okapi and walked towards the villagers with the animals on guard and they began to make way for him as he approached. When he eventually set his eyes on the bird and saw the damage done to its body, he crouched beside the bird and wept deeply. As he was weeping his heart out, he raised his tearful eyes on the villagers, who were all bemused and nonplussed by what was going on right before their eyes. As he was looking at them round, his eyes caught a piece of leather on the ground. He walked gently to it and picked it up. He gathered the body of the owl into the leather, all its feathers he picked up also and wrapped it up before he mounted his okapi and with heavy heart, galloped towards Igbo – *the evil forest and the land of the god* – through the roads of Eboru *village,* with his white cloth windswept after him *as his okapi galloped on*, a peculiar sight to these villagers that somehow instilled his admiration, reverence and hatred, too, in the mind of everyone present *as the forbidden soul they all dread.*

The news of Ajala and the dead owl incidence spread like wild fire over Eboru *village* and among these lost tribes and coupled with the evil campaign of Arun, *the mysterious disease,* Ajala was no perceived hero, but the villain of the piece, even by the villagers that had just admired him.

Moreover, the clarion call by the tribespeople for his head after this occurrence overwhelmed the chiefs and elders of Eboru *village* and this pressure couldn't be condone any further. Therefore, the chiefs and elders of Eboru *village* quickly summoned the priest of Shigidi to deliberate on expediting action of the invincible Shigidi against Ajala. Exactly this was what the witches of blood underworld planned to achieve through the *false flag* plague campaign of Arun. In fact, Arun's psychic crusade of death strategy worked effectively as she promised her coven and many children of Ajala's age had died from Arun's inflicted disease and eventually Arun would visit her killing escapade on all age groups and sexes, if the chiefs and elders of Eboru dawdled to expedite the Shigidi action *against Ajala.*

These tribespeople began to complain to one another that if their Babalawo, *the possessor of secret ancient knowledge and wisdom,* were to be alive, he would have proffered solution to this mysterious plague ravaging them. The fear and pain caused by Arun's witchcraft-guided plague so much gripped them that they heaped the blame on Ajala being alive still. Wherefore, they pressured their leaders that if nothing was done on Ajala's issue, he would kill them all. The chiefs and elders of Eboru *village,* bowing to this public pressure, were now more than ready to offer the voluntary ritual for the invincible Shigidi to exterminate Ajala. They reasoned that it would be better if they give one soul to save many.

The regent was pleased to hear that the chiefs and elders of Eboru were prepared to offer the voluntary Shigidi offering to destroy Ajala.

However, when Ajala came for the owl's body, he noticed many children were lying under trees at the front of many mud shacks with the same illness that struck the homesick lad. As his okapi strode through Eboru *village,* his eyes prowled over these dying children as their parents were totally helpless to do anything to help them. Therefore, one night, together with the homesick lad *he healed of the same disease*, they both sneaked into Eboru *village* carrying with them the healing palm wine *of Ajala* that he hallowed by his magical sign of Odu's binary eye pattern. When they got to the boy's parents, who were scared of Ajala's *unexpected* presence, though their son helped calm the situation by letting them know Ajala wasn't atrocious as alleged. He related to his parents how Ajala saved his life from the same mysterious, lethal epidemic ravaging Eboru *village* and the tribes.

"I'm Ajala, charge no price on this cure because these are my people and tell no one how you came about it. When it's about to finish, add more content of palm wine to it and by that means this can last you forever, so far you follow my instruction." said the nostalgic lad to his parents, as Ajala had instructed him through Shea before they set off from Igbo.

Ajala handed over the cure for Arun's mysterious epidemic to this boy's parents and left with the boy to Igbo. During this visit, they inkling their son that the following night would be the last time Ajala would be alive, because the preparation to send the *invincible* Shigidi after him had been concluded.

While Ajala was feeling utterly despondent, since the nostalgic lad through Shea broke the news of the *invincible* Shigidi against him, also the cure he gave against Arun's disease was getting famous in Eboru and amongst the tribes in just some hours. Incredibly, people began to flock from all over the tribes, bringing their sick ones for healing.

Though, the parents of this nostalgic lad didn't disclose how they came about this effective cure, yet they doubted that perhaps Ajala was the originator of the disease, hence, he could easily find the cure. Unbeknownst to them that for this reason Ajala warned them never to disclose the source of this cure that would earn them fame and respect among these lost tribes. Certainly, this Ajala's Arun *disease* magical antidote didn't only cure, but immune the tribespeople, too against Arun's killing spree, instantly they used it.

Ajala wasn't able to sleep throughout that night because he was worried about the news of the *invincible* Shigidi coming against him. Everyone in the camp noticed this and were affected by Ajala's bad mood. Early in the morning, Shea approached him.

"What worries you, my son?" she asked.

"The invincible Shigidi is coming after me tonight. You don't know this warrior of the gods."

"Do you think this report is true?"

How I wish it isn't. he thought.

"Why would they lie, anyway?" he communed.

"If it's true, then, we've to do something." suggested Shea.

"There's no chance against the invincible Shigidi, mother." said Ajala and remained mused awhile.

"This is my tradition and I know what I'm saying." asserted Ajala.

"This is no child's play, I'm dead. Tonight maybe the last time you'll ever see me." he added.

"Stop it!" cried Shea repeatedly. She got hold of him tightly in her arms.

"I'll not lose you, my son." she moaned.

"I'll never lose you, not even to the Shigidi!" she cried, but she felt Ajala seemed resigned to fate. He held on to Shea also, like never before.

"Mother, let's focus our energies on finding Erin." he surmised. Ajala instructed Shea to inform the camp of the urgency to attempt finding Erin that night, before it would be too late.

Tisseewoonatis was stricken that Ajala simply embraced the fact that he was going to die by this Shigidi thing. She knew his mind wasn't entirely independent from the shackles of superstition and that in itself could limit the extent for him fathoming and exploiting fully his hidden extramundane potential.

"Fuck this Shigidi stuff!" she raged.

While Shea was still speaking to them about Ajala's bad mood concerning the Shigidi, Tisseewoonatis walked into the inner compartment of the cave where she lodged and dressed herself up in her typical, elaborate, feathery Native American powwow outfit and rushed out of the cave. She continued to run haphazardly through the jungle, looking for Ajala and finally met him where he sat meditating. She went and sat beside him in the same posture, meditating along with him. Suddenly, as she couldn't hold her cool any further, she gripped Ajala's hand, they both slowly turned their heads and threw their eyes open upon one another. Her outfit and the glare Ajala saw *on her face* spoke for itself. It was more than a thousand words for the dejected lad, who was struggling with the bad news of the *invincible* Shigidi. *Yes, I'll not give up the fight*. Mused Ajala. He could perceive the daring message from her glower and they gently nodded courage to one another.

As Ajala continued to stare into her eyes, he actuated his zebra and the animal eventually searched him out where he was in the jungle with Tisseewoonatis. Immediately he saw the animal coming, he signaled with his eyebrows to her. Tisseewoonatis looked back and when she saw the zebra, she knew Ajala understood why she came and wanted her to go back to the cave. She let go of his hands, as he noticed he wouldn't let himself be distracted from his meditation and Ajala calmly got back to his session.

Tisseewoonatis went back to the cave on Ajala's zebra and instructed Shea to persuade Ajala to be courageous and dismiss the shackles of superstitious belief of his tribespeople about the invincible Shigidi and rather trust in himself.

Shea and Pott too had witnessed firsthand the otherworldly power amongst these lost tribes, they understood what the Shigidi did with Ajala's mother, but it was Ajala who felt this loss the most. So, to them it was thus understandable if Ajala got struck by fear. Yet, they assured Tisseewoonatis they would do their best to support him. Of course, Shea knew that Ajala had made up his mind on nothing, except to find Erin Eyers.

Shea informed Pott to be prepared, because Ajala would need their help in the search for the girl. Erin's mother, too, came looking for Ajala to comfort and encourage him. However, he had wandered into the jungle after his meditation to reflect on the whole process of finding Erin and to behold the beauty of the forest and his animal friends he loved so much, because he feared he might never see them again.

There were unusual cries from all these animals at Igbo, as if they could perceive Ajala's sorrow. Birds flew around him and many of these animals came closer and he still tried to play with them as usual. Though deep down his soul, he missed them to tears as they huddled around him en masse.

At eventide, Ajala entered into a small cave for further meditation and while meditating with eyes closed, he spontaneously raised his right hand and folded other fingers of the same hand, except the middle and the fourth fingers, which he pointed forward side by side. He maintained the two fingers side by side and made the binary pattern of Odu's eyes in the air – *from top down and from left to right* – of four columns aligned in four lines, and after this magical sign spell, calmly from his subliminal self, he pronounced the spell, "iyerosun", which he believed was a peculiar magical spell for invocation of vision cloud and to his amazement it worked. He then opened his eyes slowly on the white cloud that forthwith precipitated peacefully right before his eyes, and the magical sign *oyeku* of Odu's binary eye pattern he made shown on it.

"Erin Eyers, where art thou?" pronounced Ajala in his psyche.

"How dare you venture into my territory, O forbidden soul!" replied Kowe, as she appeared on the magical white cloud instead of Erin. Immediately, he realised he saw this peculiar avian creature, when the handwriting born of Erin's dream was shown to him.

"Behold, the invincible Shigidi will cease your soul tonight." revealed Kowe.

"And who revealed these secret ancient magic to you, little boy?" queried Kowe.

Ajala was shocked and shuddered at the sight of this bizarre human-headed avian creature, but he had resolved to fear nothing as he already resigned to fate on the invincible Shigidi *coming after him*. None the less, he quickly regained his confidence as he recollected the embolden glare he witnessed on Tisseewoonatis' face and the filial love he had for Shea, with the adage of his mother running through his mind, *'as no one teaches the heart to love, so follow your mind to find her.'* Even if it was the last thing he would do, Ajala focused his energies on one thing and that was finding Erin. This positive poise within Ajala to find Erin actually quantum leapt him into the threshold of his destiny, serendipitously discovering his fate through curiosity and intuition.

"Who're you, O great bird?"

"Kowe, my name is Kowe!"

"I'm Ajala, I've nothing to do with you, O great one! The one I seek is Erin Eyers."

"I know you, Ajala." replied Kowe.

"She's beyond your powers, boy. The blood of the one you seek is sacred enough to be offered as ritual for the ultimate sovereignty of the witches of blood underworld." she said and bursted into laughter. But Ajala remained poised and on his face arouse deep determination.

"Even tonight, before daybreak, she must be inevitably sacrificed and you too, extinguished by the invincible Shigidi. The two of you'll never see daybreak." asserted Kowe.

"O great one, seeing the daybreak isn't the beginning or the end of life, but Erin Eyers won't be sacrificed."

"O forbidden soul, we'll see about that!" communed Kowe daringly and gusto into a solemn evil chuckle.

"Thank you, great one!" communed Ajala.

However, he wondered Kowe was the one who appeared and not the invoked Erin. This magical savvy to invoke Erin came to Ajala spontaneously from his subliminal self and thereby realised that if he kept his confidence clean of fear and any other emotional and feeblish stumbling block, this composure would aid his subliminal self and his psyche would be more supportive to his will.

Ajala's serendipitously finding his psychic fate made him confident and believe more in himself and realised he should be more grateful to Shea and Pott for their help, because he knew without them no one would ever hear his voice. Immediately, he made up his mind to make his gratitude known to Shea and Pott, and the camp all together before the attack of the Shigidi.

None the less, after he communed with Kowe, he became gutsier about finding Erin Eyers and was even ready to confront the Shigidi, even if it wasn't going to be successful. Of course, the glare he saw last on Tisseewoonatis face spoke volumes *of audacity* into his being.

As he prepared himself for the worst, he continued to think more of his first encounter with Odu and this encounter continued to run in his mind. As he walked back to the camp, he remembered his discussions with Odu. Also, his encounter with Odu in the huge gourd he recollected and was trying to expiscate valuable lessons from these experiences. He remembered the bottle neck gourd he saw when he was under the pressure of Odu's metaphysical energy inside this gourd. He went straight and picked the bottle-neck gourd, looked at it very well and adored the beautiful and colourful long feathers he pinned to its stopper.

Afterwards, he proceeded straight to the camp with the gourd tied to his waist. When Shea saw him coming, she was troubled because she could see he wasn't happy and he was only trying to hide from himself and from others.

"Where have you been?" asked Shea, as all the camp stood looking at Ajala. He remained silent, staring at them one after the other, down to the *untouchables* children.

"Shea!" telepathised Ajala.

"The thought of having a mother like you did never cross my mind, but here we're, me and you, mother and son. No matter how we look different and no matter the disability we carry on our being, we'd understand that we can love one another truly and are capable of taking care of the needs of one another without malice or detestation. We can all leave in peace together, over whatever we are tempted to believe should alienate us. Mother, I do love you and I'm happy to have you as my mother."

At his speech, Shea broke down to tears and was struggling to communicate Ajala's words to the camp. Pott held the distraught Shea in his arms and took over the interpretation. They were all staring at Ajala where he was, standing on a small hill, talking to them.

"Pott!" he added.

"I thank you for your care and love for me. If it hadn't been for you guys, I wouldn't have found myself that I may be able, at least, do something in my life. I thank you very much for your strength and for making me know and acknowledge that being a witch isn't evil in itself, but that what a witch uses her powers to achieve is what matters. I couldn't thank you enough."

As Ajala was speaking through Pott, they all could feel the

atmosphere around them was one of no solace. The untouchables were sobbing and some of them clung to Erin's mother, as the whole camp was listening to Ajala through Pott, who also was struggling with his tears.

"Tisseewoonatis, your in-depth observation, knowledge and experience had really been of benefit here. I thank you, my dear wise lady and I believe you're here for more discovery. However, you think you aren't a witch, but your witchcraft is more glaring to all of us. Thank you and I will never forget your glare of encouragement and most especially, that beautiful outfit you're wearing." he communed with his hands towards her, as she stood in her gorgeous powwow apparel.

"I've learnt that all humans are equal, no matter who they are or how they look like, their skin, hair, eyes, nose or their talents or ability. Therefore, my dear precious ones, they call us the untouchable ones, but today I call us the infrangible ones. The rights of every child should be inviolable and that's what we should begin to look into amongst our tribespeople. Any power that failed to protect children's rights does not fit to exist and such power we should resist unto death."

When Shea heard this, she stopped weeping because she realised the lad isn't giving up struggling, until the very last end.

"We aren't guilty of anything, we're the innocent ones, but a victim of our people's status quo. You've to stand up for yourselves in any way you can and change this unfairness. If I die tonight, you'll live to tell this story to our people that Ajala the son of Ifa is neither the forbidden soul, nor a castaway." he paused.

"Erin's mother, I know how the passion of motherhood burns. I know how you feel because I was with my mother all along in our misery before she was murdered by my people. I've nothing much to say to you other than to promise you that either I'm alive or dead, you'll see your daughter alive, even if it means my life in exchange for her life."

"Oh, don't talk like that!" responded Erin's mother with outbreak of tears, as she felt Ajala was given a farewell speech rather than pep talk.

Ajala addressed his gratitude and empathy to each and every member of the camp, his sadness was felt by all, despite that he tried not to show it, but also his urge to find Erin.

"There's no time for tears and sadness, friends" he said as he walked down the small hill where he stood and they all could feel the immediate change in the atmosphere to one of determination.

"The time to find Erin has come and I'd be proud of everyone's help, most especially Shea and Pott." he communed

"How do we find her?" asked Shea, as she was wiping her tears with her hands, like a child.

"We've to employ the magic of all the elements *on which everything was created.*" answered Ajala.

"We'll all understand, when it begins. I'll tell everyone what to do as my hunch unveils." communed Ajala.

"We've little time." said Ajala, looking at the awe-inspiring crepuscule and pondering Kowe's words.

"I've little time." he muttered.

"Get Erin's picture, now!" cried Ajala through Shea *as usual* to Erin's mother and she went into her bag and presented the picture to him. He took the picture, look at it awhile.

"We flood the Earth." he said.

"What?" asked Pott.

He could neither understand what Ajala was talking about, nor the magic behind it.

"Flood the Earth, the whole world?" retorted Shea.

"Are you crazy, we'll all die?" said Erin's mother.

"Everything and everyone." she added.

"How and what'll happen, during and after?" queried Tisseewoonatis.

"He can't do that, you believe him?" Erin's mother asked Tisseewoonatis.

"I don't know, I'm just curious." replied Tisseewoonatis.

"Curious about what?" asked Erin's mother.

"Have you lost your mind?" she added.

"Let's wait and see." replied Tisseewoonatis.

"I know it's a dangerous magic and two of us will have to stake our lives, we might not come out alive." announced Ajala. The camp began to contemplate his words seriously.

"Oh, no! There must be another way!" said Erin's mother.

"Erin was abducted by the powerful witches of darkness, who'll sacrifice her before daybreak to become the sovereign of the otherworld." hinted Ajala.

Erin's mother surged into tears forthwith she heard this. While Ajala took another look at Erin's picture that was in his hand, the camp looked at one another pensively.

"Why they chose Erin, I don't know and the only way to infiltrate their otherworld realm of operations' through the ancient magic of uniting the elements of life." Ajala told the camp, who're still wondering about the idea of flooding the Earth.

"This is a dangerous magic, Ajala. Are you sure of what you're doing?" queried Shea.

"No one teaches the heart to love, mother." answered Ajala.

"What did you mean by that?" queried Shea.

"I'll follow my hunch in this matter. You taught me always to do just that." said Ajala, staring at Shea.

"I love you, mother." he said.

"I love you too, my son." replied Shea, staring into his eyes too.

"I tried to contact Erin, but Kowe blocked me and warned me of the dangerous territory I'm venturing into. She told me Erin won't see daybreak." said Ajala again through Shea.

"Who the hell's this Kowe?" asked Erin's mother emotionally.

"I felt she's a great, extramundane witch of ancient powers. My hunch told me she isn't supposed to be where she is. Anyway, we've to get Erin out of their grip before it's too late."

"Where exactly is she?" asked Erin's mother.

"I don't know, woman." responded Ajala.

"You don't know, then, how'll you get to her." she asked.

"We flood the Earth." repeated Ajala.

"Oh, Jesus Christ!" yelped Erin's mother.

"Flood the Earth, Flood the Earth!" she repeated.

"How the heaven are you gonna do that?" she cried.

"And fish Erin out of the flood even if you're able to do it, isn't that what you telling me?" she suspired.

"Yes!"

"Now, you mean my daughter is turned to a fish by your witches of …?"

"No!" interrupted Ajala.

"I never said that." answered Ajala.

"How're you gonna do this?" asked Pott quickly, gesturing

Erin's mother to keep calm.

Tisseewoonatis was already making ready her cameras to capture whatever action that would come out of this occurrence that Ajala was suggesting he could put up. Erin's mother looked at her and shook her head.

"You're going nuts, Tissee!" she drawled.

"Shut up, please!" shouted Tisseewoonatis at her.

Ajala smiled to Tisseewoonatis and felt encouraged that she totally trusted him to achieve what he proposed to do.

"Just-simmer-down!" drawled Tisseewoonatis to Erin's mother, as she was skeptical about Ajala's witchery.

"When we flood the Earth, Erin will lead us to Erin." said Ajala gently, raising the picture of Erin in his hand. Though, everyone was yet confused how Ajala would achieve this magical feat.

"Who's ready to stake his or her life with mine?"

"I'm with you, my son." uttered Shea

"Me, too!" volunteered Erin's mother, almost at the same time as Shea.

"No, you're not a witch." responded Ajala to her.

Shea and Pott looked at one another, they knew what Ajala meant was directed at them. All the while, Tisseewoonatis was busy capturing the scenes in her camera.

"I'm with you, my son." volunteered again Shea.

Instantly, without tarrying, Ajala gathered the camp into the cave. He told the camp not to leave the cave until sunrise and when they see the flood coming, no one should be afraid because it wouldn't be real, but it was the only way to reach Erin where she was being held. Ajala made the camp aware he didn't know where Erin was and assured them that, nevertheless, Erin would lead them to Erin. Even though, no one in the camp understood a bit of how he would have to achieve this magic, yet the urge to find Erin made them willing to partake in this dangerous witchery. He told Erin's mother to stay in the camp and make sure the untouchables weren't out of the cave until it would all be over.

Ajala continued to give instructions to everyone in a hurry as he walked around. He told them the whole world would be submerged, but no one would see it or know it, except those who knew about it or heard of it like them. He told them if they feared, the waters would become real and such a person might be in danger of being drown, but as soon as he or she could dismiss the fear, the waters would become unreal again.

"Even you'll see and feel the waters, yet it isn't real. So, there is no time for fear." explained Ajala to the camp and they all marveled how he came about this magical idea and the newly found temerity behind it. In fact, Tisseewoonatis knew her erstwhile embolden glare into Ajala's eyes worked as expected.

Ajala instructed them to be alert because he would continue to give on the spot instructions, as the magic would proceed. He placed Erin's picture on the ground inside the cave and covered the picture with fine ashes that he took from the cooking *fire* spot inside the cave. On the ashes he made Odu's binary eye setting of '*oyeku*' magical sign.

"*Oyekuyeku.*" he uttered thrice from his subliminal self his unique spell, as he was making the sign with his magic finger. It's a spell he understood would connect Erin to Erin, for her ultimate escape, thereby, she would be cheating death as planned for her by the witches of blood.

"*Parada!*" cried Ajala on the magical sign spell to manifest his thought-form on the picture.

The pre-physical realm of existence responded to Ajala's thought-form. Immediately, Erin grew out of the picture exactly as she was dressed in it. Erin's mother was confused and rushed to hold her daughter.

"No!" cried Ajala, *through the voice of Shea,* as usual.

"She isn't your daughter yet! She's our guide to her, wherever she's on this planet or in the otherworld." hinted Ajala.

"If you touch her, she'll disappear and there'll be no means, as far as I know, left to get to Erin." warned Ajala.

"This is not your daughter, this is Erin's quiddity from pre-physical realm of existence." maintained Ajala.

"Everyone, remain where you're and wait for my instructions." added Ajala.

"No one does anything without my consent, okay?" he instructed.

He took out of the ashes on the picture of Erin, which was before the conjured Erin's *essence's* feet. He spread the ashes on his left palm and made Odu's binary eye pattern of '*ejiogbe*' magical sign on it with his magic fingers – *the middle and the fourth fingers placed*

188

side by side.

"*Eji O!*" he cried.

Ajala cast his magical spell *inaudibly* once more from his subliminal self on the *ejiogbe* magical sign to make his good intension known and to befriend water essence from pre-physical realm of existence to yield to his command.

He looked back at Erin's quiddity, as it was standing motionless. He turned back to the ash powder on his left palm and blew it into the air.

"*Eji O!*" cried Ajala once again on the magical spell to invoke the deluge. He blew the ash into the air and it vanished.

Everyone was looking into the sky awfully to see what would happen next and they were amazed when, shortly after he blew the ash powder on his palm into the air. There came around Erin's feet, a pure white cloud that rose from the ashes and began to struggle quietly. He looked at the cloud and smiled, because he knew he was on the right track, as his hunch did inkling him.

Ajala turned to the camp, but, before he could say a word to them, the white cloud breezed out of the cave into the atmosphere and it started to rain. When Erin's mother peeped out to see the sky out of sheer surprise, her eyes caught an unbelievable sea of waters from afar, approaching them violently. This wall of water and waves was so high and turbulent, that everyone in the camp feared from the sound of its turbulence.

Ajala encouraged them through Shea to remain steadfast because the deluge wasn't real and it could only be real through fear, which could be dangerous to the person in question. So, everyone in the camp trusted Ajala and awaited his instructions in due time. Ajala told Pott to hide the untouchables away from the sight of the magic and instantly Pott led the untouchables into the inner side of the cave, where they were totally out of sight of the entire magical scenario.

Of course, the two sleuths of Chief Inspector Briggs, entrusted with the monitoring of the happenings around Erin's mother could see and hear all that was happening at Igbo through the eyes of "GOD" – *the sophisticated clandestine global satellite monitoring system.* Therefore, they were also able to see Ajala's magical deluge on their monitor screen because they heard about it too, as Ajala said to the camp that whoever knew about the magic would be able to see and even feel the magic. They were puzzled about what was happening on their monitor screen and were struck with fear and panicked, contrary to Ajala's warning to the camp. For that reason, the deluge hit their monitoring room immensely and dashed into pieces the glass windows as water gushed into the room.

"What the hell's happening?" one cried.

"Hurricane?" asked the other.

Their cries for help were heard and the door was forced open, but as soon as the door was opened, the whole unusual scenario suddenly became unreal to them and instantly their monitors went off, though their clothes remained drenched. The two sleuths were bemused and didn't know how to get their head around this incidence or what to make of the peculiar experienced. They looked through the shattered windows again, but no sign of raging flood outside as they did just witness.

"What the fuck is happening here, guys?" asked one of the MI5 agent, who forced the door opened.

"Everything's fine, sir!" answered Briggs detectives with a troubled frown. The security agents that opened the door looked around and found that there was no evidence of water in the room that could get these detectives' cloths wet.

"What the hell's happening here, pee-fighting?" mocked an agent.

When everyone left, they looked at one another in disbelief of what had just happened, but they don't know what to make of it. They turned to their monitor and found it off, one of them immediately put it on and the deluge was in view again on the screen. They were puzzled as to what was happening to them and they quickly radioed for a covert rescue mission, to which within minutes the authorities responded by sending well equipped, combat ready, battle tested, Royal Marine officers, accompanied by four military medical experts and a team of military fire men, to whom Briggs' sleuths were also responsible to guide to the destination in question. Despite warnings of raging hurricane and tsunamis by Brigg's sleuths to the rescue team, these covert rescue officers in their hi-tech combat helicopter were surprised they could neither see with their eyes, nor experience anything of such on their monitors.

"How did you come up with this?" asked Shea.

"Thanks to you, lady. You thought me to believe in myself and to dig into the core of my psyche. I did just that." answered Ajala.

While Shea was looking at the raging wall of waters, storming towards them, the wind of the waves were now hitting them in the cave and they began to panic. Ajala told them to remain courageous because it wasn't real and that no one in the world could see it, except them. Amidst this skepticism and panic to douse their fear and hold their ground, Ajala's doughty spirit kept them going still as the sea of high and raging wall of waters was about to overrun the cave. Before them was standing, cool, calm, serene and motionless, the figure of Erin Ajala conjured through the picture he had from her mother. Tisseewoonatis was busy taking pictures and making video of the entire incidence.

"Here comes the moment, everyone hold on and be brave!" shrieked Ajala, as this raging sea of waters overran the cave.

Though, waters didn't fill the cave, but feet level water rushed into the cave.

"But you said this isn't real." cried Tisseewoonatis out of panicky, when her feet got wet.

There were sea creatures passing along the entrance of the cave. The camp was spellbound and struck with disbelief, when they also felt cold water on their feet and beholding sea creatures – *through the dazzling moonlit reflection* – passing along the cave's entrance. However, Ajala encouraged them to remain brave and trust him.

While saying this, Erin's figure moved gently, for the first time, to the entrance of the cave. Ajala beckoned to the camp to be still and quiet, as the image walked to the entrance of the cave and dipped her left hand into the deluge.

"It's time, mum." muttered Erin's magical quintessence.

Ajala was elated that the quiddity recognised Erin's mother, because he knew this was a step forward in the magic.

"Quickly, snap her and make sure your camera flashes on her brightly." said Ajala through Shea to Tisseewoonatis.

Instantly, the ever ready Tisseewoonatis flashed her camera on Erin's quiddity and as she turned to the direction of the flash.

"Ina tan!" pronounced Ajala this spell in his subliminal self to brightened up Erin's quiddity he conjured and this figure became luminous, the luminescence of her body brightened up the inside of the cave.

"Now, get on your broomstick and follow her to wherever she goes. As she goes, she'll cast the trails of her luminescence after her

and only travel within this stream. I warn you not to deviate from the stream of her luminescence." instructed Ajala.

"Yes, my son." answered Shea.

"Mother, she'll be faster than you can ever be, don't forget, only follow the path of her stream." informed Ajala.

"It's time to cook the goose of these evil witches, friends!" cried Ajala.

However, before Ajala realised it, Erin's figure plunged into the deluge and flitted off scene, but the stream of its luminescence was on the waters as it goes.

Shea's broomstick appeared, she mounted it and stared at Pott. The reminiscence of the training by Mother Endor came to their senses at once, their elated flying on broomstick with Mother Endor through the sea and the instructions she gave them.

"Don't you even think about it that I'll let you go alone?" said Pott.

"Yahoo!" he cried to conjure his mobile with clapping of hands and his broomstick appeared. He mounted it beside Shea.

"Do not leave the waters." said Ajala to Pott.

"I repeat, do not leave the waters, only Shea can follow the quintessence wherever it leads. Now go, I'm with you." instructed Ajala.

At his words, Shea and Pott flitted off – *after Erin's quiddity through the stream of her luminescence* – like lightning. Ajala himself was amazed at their speed. The ethereal image of Erin had travelled far beyond their reach, but Shea and Pott followed her stream as they were travelling at extraordinary speed after her.

They saw sea creatures swimming across the stream of the luminescence as they journeyed and were manoeuvring their flight passed them. However, there were astounded, wondering how Ajala came about this mind boggling magic and as they flew further, they realised Erin's quiddity had gone *in toto* out of their sight.

They journeyed heavenward as the stream of the luminescence led them and suddenly thrust out of the deluge into the sky, though, yet in the stream of the luminescence of Erin's figure. They were flabbergasted when they had the aerial view of the magical deluge. They found the whole world, as far as they could see, entirely submerged and as they flew over cities through the stream, they saw reflection of city lights twinkling in the deluge. They were also amazed that they went through the waters, yet their cloths weren't soaked and their bodies remained dry.

"This is awesome." said Shea.

"Is it really happening?" asked Pott.

What an amazing magic. Mused Shea.

"This lad's wonderful, his psyche's a treasure of magic." added Shea.

Shea and Pott became thrilled when the stream again descended into the deluge, jauntily they dashed towards the deluge on their mobiles and one after the other they plunged into the flood again, as the stream of the luminescence descended, until they came to the depth of the deluge, where the stream terminated.

Ajala in the cave, who was monitoring them under cogitation, had the hunch something had happened. While Shea and Pott were still contemplating what to do, the echo of Ajala's psychic voice resounded into Shea's psyche.

"Mother, it isn't the end of the road, it's just the entrance into the destination." said Ajala.

"Mother, proceed through the stream until you enter the hidden destination of the underworld of the otherworld. Go now, but be careful." directed Ajala.

"Do not leave the waters, I repeat, do not leave the waters." telepathised Ajala to Pott, to remind him of his earlier instruction to stay in the waters.

After Ajala telepathised Shea, she flew some distance away, recharged her broomstick and plunged to the end of the stream at the depth of the deluge and straight into the earth. She instantly vanished from Pott's sight to find herself thrust through Apaadi into Aye and from thence she flew the path of the stream of the luminescence through the castles of the witches of blood underworld.

Shea had a creepy feeling about this strange place the stream led her. The luminescence led her to the chamber where Erin was held in the bizarre Bony-Spiny. When Shea got into this chamber, she saw Erin in the bony cage and she also saw her quintessence standing beside this cage, beckoning her to Erin. Then, the quiddity vanished on the spot, as soon as Shea set her eyes on Erin herself, though the stream of the luminescence remained.

Shea flew round the bizarre, gigantic bony cage and was amazed, when she realised Erin wasn't aware of her presence and couldn't even hear her voice. Therefore, she alighted her broomstick and walked towards the dangerous cage. She couldn't see any space of entrance or exit on it.

"Intruder, I can smell you." muttered Kowe in disgust, when she sensed intrusion, as she was strolling around in Aye.

"Erin!" called Shea repeatedly on her, but she was entirely oblivious of her voice and her presence.

As she moved closer to the strange Bony-Spiny, the long, numerous, and invisible threadlike projections that were all over the strange cage struck Shea, impaling her at once as it lifted her off the ground, drained her blood to the last drop into the cage's marrow and extinguishing her instantly.

Immediately Kowe flew directly to Apaadi. She stared the stream of the luminescence left behind by the quintessence of Erin and she was bewildered who could have such powerful magic to infiltrate Aye, *the otherworld of the witches of blood underworld.* She started to coo *incantations*, beating her wings on the stream, right from Apaadi where it emerged into Aye and to the spot where Erin's quintessence disappeared and the stream of the luminescence went darkled and vanished.

"Pott, I can't perceive her." Ajala telepathised Pott about Shea.

"You think there's problem?" replied Pott

"If I can't reach her, then, there's problem." responded Ajala.

Forthwith Pott heard this, he wasted no time as he with anger directly plunged to the end of the stream and vanished also into the depth of the deluge, but instead of him thrusting through Apaadi into the castle of the witches of blood underworld, he got stuck in Apaadi because the stream that was the portal for transmigration through Apaadi into the castle had been ward off by the great Kowe.

"Pott!" shouted Ajala repeatedly.

"Pott!" he called again emotionally.

"Do not leave the waters." drawled Ajala with frustration finally, in his subliminal self, as he realised Pott had went after Shea.

"I'll have to go after them." cued Ajala to Tisseewoonatis and Erin's mother.

"What's happening?" asked Erin's mother, but they could neither understand Ajala, nor perceive his psychic voice and Shea or

Pott that could interpret weren't within reach.

Therefore, without mincing words, Ajala got hold of his bottleneck gourd and tied it to his waist, he went inside the cave and brought his flat gourd *the size of a skating board*, its edges he accurately lined with cowries round and Odu's magical binary eye setting made on it with mollusks, *'ejiogbe' binary eye setting at the front and 'oyeku' binary eye pattern at the rear side*.

He threw the flat gourd on the ground and it floated on the feet level waters that filtered into the cave's floor. He looked at Erin's mother and Tisseewoonatis and to them his face suggested to them sort of courage and determination that he would be back.

Erin's mother went towards him and embraced him in her arms emotionally and this gesture filled Ajala eyes with tears. Ajala gently stepped on the board, which his weight at once pushed to the depth of the feet level water and he went into deep concentration, standing on this unique flat gourd.

"Ofe!" casted Ajala in his subliminal self the unique magical spell for flight and in a posthaste propulsion that beat any human senses, he flew off the cave into the deluge through the stream of the luminescence, standing on the flat gourd, his white garment windswept as he was flying. He quickly learnt to control this transport at will, as he saw it in his vision when it came alive on the night of his mantra. In no time, he was at the depth of the deluge where the stream terminated. While he was thinking of how to go further, a whale came so close he stroked its head with his hands. He gasped at the sea creatures around him. Of course, he knew going through the stream was now dangerous, yet he was so desperate that he decided to try. *Oh, Pott!* He mused within him pensively, knowing that Pott had disobeyed his psychic advice.

"My dear friend, I'll always be proud of you." he added.

As Ajala tried to further his journey like Shea and Pott, through the depth of the deluge, his body hit the earth and couldn't go further. Of course, Kowe's extirpation of the stream in the otherworld of Aye would gradually continue to wane the aptitude of the psychic portal of the stream. Hence, Ajala's erstwhile inability to perceive and reach Shea any longer. Since Kowe tampered with it, it could only transmit one person through, which Pott hard used up. Ajala was bamboozled and was looking around, while thinking of any other means of travelling further. His sight he could only see as far as the stream of the luminescence brightened.

Somehow, he remembered his meditation in the gourd and the energy wielded around him by Odu. This brought to his senses his friendship with Shea and Pott, all the good times and their care, their help and the love they showed him. He looked back through the path of the luminescence's trail or stream and remembered Erin's mother and Tisseewoonatis were earnestly waiting and counting on him to save, not only Erin, but also to protect Shea and Pott. Of course, he knew this was his magic and thereby his total responsibility to see it to a conclusive success. He tried to reach for his bottleneck gourd and found out it was missing. Unbeknownst to him, it fell off him in the cave when he got projected into his extraordinary flight. However, before Tisseewoonatis and Erin's mother could alert him, he was gone.

Ajala was worried and his black unwonted eyeballs blinked forlornly. Definitely, he felt as if his magic was frustrating him. He looked here and there and realised no help would come whatsoever. He was totally confused, wistful and disenchanted as he hit the earth *at the depth of the deluge* repeatedly with his bare hands.

Nathless, of a sudden, the hunch hit his psyche that he should stay focused and concentrated to perceive his subliminal self.

"... being at parity with your mind isn't enough, you've to be greater, be the god of your mind." he remembered Shea's words and he calmly maintained composure.

"Odu is my mind, Odu can do all things, and my mind is Odu." he reused the mantra Tisseewoonatis formulated for him to suit his psyche. He continued to recite it in his subliminal self.

"Repeat this again and again, until I come back, I repeat, until I come back." he remembered Shea's instruction and thereby made up his mind that until something would happen, he wouldn't stop the mantra.

As he composed himself and went into deep cogitation, with the mantra on his mind, he remained tranquilly concentrated and focused. When he found out the meditating posture he learnt from Shea and Pott seemed not to be helping fast enough to simmer down his psyche. Then, he remembered how he was taken aloft in the huge gourd and at a time reminisced he was straightened by Odu's magical pressure. Therefore, he stood straight on his feet as it happened in the gourd, his arms spread out sideways with his fingers folded, but his magic fingers he pointed outward – *the middle finger and the fourth finger of both hands side by side*. However, Ajala found this cogitation posture really effective for him more than the kneeling, sitting and the cross-legged poses Shea and Pott taught him. Sooner, he could feel the field of his psychic energy within and around him.

Tisseewoonatis and Erin's mother, who were sitting on a big stone side by side in the cave, awaiting the outcome of Ajala's magic, suddenly saw the floating bottleneck gourd moving towards the entrance of the cave. Erin's mother rushed to get hold of it.

"No, let go, please!" cried Tisseewoonatis and Erin's mother withdrew herself.

The magical object wielded itself into the luminescence's trail or stream, being attracted by the psychic magnetism from Ajala and it traveled straight into the field of psychic energy wielding around him.

As he remained in his newly discovered cogitation pose, with his eyes closed, he got hold of this gourd out of the gyrating field of psychic energy around him and his mind instantaneously went to his first serendipitous discovery of the secret of Odu's binary eye pattern and the explosive effect it had on the huge gourd. He wasted no time to signal the magical sign of 'ejiogbe' *the first binary pattern of Odu's eyes* on the earth at depth of the deluge. Instantly, there was a quake that blasted opened the ground for him and the stream got pepped up immediately. It continued its journey through the opened earth under the deluge, though, the deluge *waters* didn't rush into this opened ground through which Ajala continued to journey by the stream of the luminescence.

Ajala on his flat gourd mobile was flying in the stream, through the vacuum of the magical tunnel that blasted open for him, which finally led him to the castle of the witches of blood underworld. He touched down as soon as he flew into the castle through its wall, as the stream of the luminescence transmitted him and in his psychic instinct was the feeling of the sinister energy of this freaky place.

While he was sneaking around, he came across Shea's body, cocooned in an unusual big egg. This peculiar egg was sparingly overgrown with feathers and through the two, translucent, oval ends of its spherical shape, Ajala saw Shea inside in completely hog tied position. He was stunned. He was trying to commune with her, but his thought was being prevented by the aura of the odd egg.

197

Ajala closed his eyes in deep concentration and his psychic energy hit the egg. The egg countermanded his interference with a diabolical aura that took over his mind. This psychic energy forced him to lay his hands on the strange egg, contrary to his will. Ajala struggled to hold his hands back, so as not to yield to the evil psychic current of the egg. None the less, the evil aura of the egg overwhelmed him and instantly his hands touched the odd egg, he got psychically electrocuted. Although, he refused to give up his psychic will-power, despite being devastated by the egg's terrible magical shock. He continued to resist the stream of fatal, powerful, metaphysical force being ejected into him by the terrible egg.

"I'm Ajala!" he groaned from the depth of his psyche, as he was getting dazed.

"I'm Ajala!" he cried again, as he opened wide his unusual black eyeballs on the bizarre egg, but it had no effect on it. Instead, his eyes and nose started to ooze his blood, out of the damage the evil transmission from the egg was discharging into his psyche. Ajala's white cloth was heavily soaked with his own blood.

However, he remembered how he resisted to the end the psychic shock from Odu's eyes the very first day he discovered the secret of these binary eyes. He remained resolute, as he began to try his damnedest to clutch at one of the feathers on the egg and with all the strength left in him, he fortunately plucked one off. The egg's potent psychic force responded by throwing him high off the ground.

While airborne the bottleneck gourd fell off his waist from where he hung it and he watched from above it, as this gourd hit the ground. It opportunely rolled thrice on its feathers and at its round-bottom side, it projected magical rays, conforming to one of the binary eye pattern of Odu, which Ajala designed on it with cowries. Fortuitously, as it slanted towards the direction of the egg, these *psychical* powerfully projected ray splat the egg opened.

This unexpected discovery *of the use of this object by Ajala* popped up his eye, as he landed on the floor beside it. While he was staring at the object, Shea came out of the egg, sneezing and coughing.

"Shere, magic wand!" pronounced Ajala in his subliminal self. He picked up this bottleneck gourd and it glowed thrice in response to his call.

"What the hell happen to you, my son?" cried Shea

enthusiastically.

"Are you okay, mother?" he asked Shea.

"Yes, I'm fine."

"What happened to you?" asked Shea worriedly again, trying to examine his body.

"You're blood-soaked, son!" she cried.

"I'm fine, mother." said Ajala.

Shea was holding his hands.

"Tell me what indeed happened here?" he asked.

"I don't know, for sure." said Shea.

"As I was about to approach Erin in a bizarre bony cage, my hunch inkling me of the impending, fatal danger of going nearer to the cage. I stopped as my sixth sense continued to hint me of this immediate danger. At the same time, I applied my psychic motility and *immediately* sent forth my pseudo-self to approach the cage and my seity I hid away safely in oblivion. While my sixth sense was still unveiling to me what was just about to become of me if I had taken a step further, of a sudden, something searched out my seity and I got overwhelmed by a strange power unfathomable for me – *who was able to search out my psyche*. I felt as if a bird brood over me and all I could see and hear was total darkness and cooing." narrated Shea.

"Kowe!" murmured Ajala.

"Where's Pott?"

"No idea, son."

"Okay, take me to where you saw Erin."

Ajala and Shea proceeded to save Erin, but Kowe had known her egg had been tampered with and she was already on her way to find out.

"The quintessence *figure of Erin* vanished as I set my eyes on her." Shea informed Ajala, as they both were sneaking around the castle to save Erin.

"Yes, it has finished its part, the rest is for us to accomplish or to die." answered Ajala.

"I'm with you!" pledged Shea.

"I know, mother." he replied.

"It seems we're lost." said Shea after a while of wandering around Aye.

"You mean you can't find the path to where Erin is or what?"

"I think so."

Ajala quietly held Shea back, when his psyche perceived some sinister current. He stopped and beckoned to the direction of the unwelcoming current.

"The only thing I can perceive is danger, I can't perceived we're lost." he said.

He looked at the 'shere' on his waist and got hold of it, twist it round clockwisely thrice as he saw it rolled on the ground erstwhile. The bottom of the object was glowing.

"Oyela!" casted Ajala in his subliminal-self this secret magical spell for apocalypse, then, he pointed his 'shere', *magic wand,* forward. There was glowing on the 'shere', in holographic form that brightened up and opened Ajala and Shea's eyes to the looming danger approaching them. In this hologram they saw Kowe in three dimensional model, coming against them and at the same time the round bottom of the 'shere', *magic wand,* revealed to them Erin, as she was being placed on an altar, about to be immolated.

"This is some sort of magic wand?" asked Shea, when she saw the display the 'shere' performed.

"I'll stay to engage the evil bird, you'll go and save Erin." instructed Ajala. He taught Shea the magical sign spell to apply, as soon as he got sight of Erin.

"But if there's any problem, telepathise me and I'll answer, if I'm still alive." urged Ajala.

"How do I find my way to her?" asked Shea.

"Trust your mind, so you taught me, mother." said Ajala.

Shea conjured her broomstick and mounted it fast, Ajala pointed his 'shere', *magic wand,* to her.

"Touch it with your left hand." said Ajala and Shea's left hand was glowing immediately she touched the 'shere'.

"Onala!" cried Ajala his secret magical spell in his subliminal self, out of Shea's perception. He directed her to point her glowing left hand forward. Instantly, the glowing on her hand shot off like a meteor.

"Now, fly after the magical incandescent, it'll lead you to Erin and when you're able to save her, there's only one way out of this place, the way I came in, a vacuum tunnel that'll lead you to the stream of the luminescence in the deluge and back to the cave. The glow will lead you there before it darkle. Of course, we can't leave this castle without the stream of the luminescence, so hurry!"

While Shea blasted off after the glow, Ajala came to be face to face with Kowe.

"O Ajala! Of course, you kept your words." remarked Kowe.

"I did never think you're capable of such magic." she added.

"Thank you, great one." replied Ajala.

"I'm not only my father's son because I kept my words, I'll be proud to be his son when I finally save Erin."

"Forbidden soul of Eboru, I warned you, but you dared me!"

"I do not dare you, O great one!" responded Ajala.

"What would I gain from that?" reasoned Ajala.

"I'm only here for my friend."

"She's not your friend, you don't even know her." said Kowe.

"The gods send her to us to be immolated for our psychic aggrandisement." affirmed Kowe.

"She's the only ritual of such that the gods would accept for the achievement of our goal." she pointed out.

"Tell your gods that preying on human beings, either dead or alive, is Ajala's abhorrence."

"Haha! Haha! Haha!" cackled Kowe.

"What imprudence!" added Kowe.

"By the way, where did you learn those ancient spells of the gods?" inquired Kowe, before Ajala could respond.

Of course, she overheard Ajala's psychic voice when he casted the *onala* magical spell on Shea's hand, even when she wasn't within earshot and even Shea herself wasn't aware.

"The gods are dead, O great one!" replied Ajala sharply.

Immediately, Kowe heard this from Ajala, she realised his determination and readiness to confront her. She looked at Ajala deeply and found his psyche serene, but somehow mean towards her.

"Is it because of the girl?" she asked.

"Are you in love with her?" asked Kowe.

"Don't tell me you're in love with her!" cried Kowe. Ajala knew what she was trying to insinuate."

"Love's neither male, nor female, love has no sex." he responded.

When she found him incommunicado no more and somehow musing on her, she quickly took to flight, flapping her massive wings swiftly. Ajala suddenly found himself encircled by feathers from Kowe's wings.

As the strange bird hovered around him, he was struggling in vain to get out of her magic. She laughed thunderously, when she realised he got him magically trapped within her feather magic confinement. He wasted no time to maintain his newly discovered cogitation posture. He closed his eyes and was standing straight on his feet, with arms spread open a bit and his magic fingers pointed sideways.

Kowe bursted into a sinister laughter on this strange posture, but he maintained concentration and focus still. Then, an invisible field of powerful, psychic energy whirled around him like he had experienced in the huge gourd some days earlier. Though visible to Kowe, as she saw this psychic energy as innumerable, extraordinarily agile minuscule form of Ajala spinning haphazardly in a terrible tornado-like form around him. These minuscule figures of Ajala were covered only with fronds round their waist and as innumerable as they were, each had double edged cutlass. Kowe saw that these restless innumerable, invisible, magically gyrating minuscule figures *of Ajala* in twinkling of an eye, with their two-edged cutlasses shattered into thin air the feathers she casted around Ajala, setting him free from her magical feather confinement. However, Ajala himself remained calm and tranquil in his cogitation posture, unaware of Kowe's clairvoyance of the effect of his psychic energy.

On Kowe's face were both surprise and displeasure because there was something about Ajala that eluded her. These minuscule figures of him that she saw and the form she saw them was remarkable to Kowe.

While Ajala was in cogitation, in a flash of clairvoyance, he saw Shea on her broomstick, still being led by the shooting glow, descending *posthaste* far below into the underground of Aye. He saw that the farther below Shea went, the darker it get, but the shooting glow brightened up her path through the spiral stairs that led her into a shaft. Shea followed this shaft into a hall where the coven of the witches of blood underworld assembled in utter darkness, their sundry, beastly eyes glowing through with evil.

Suddenly, the shooting glow penetrated the coven, its brightness revealed the dazed Erin on the altar of the witches of blood underworld. She was motionless, *seemingly* lifeless and about to be immolated.

Shea saw the Chieftain raising his evil staff against Erin's chest and before she could do anything, he struck it into her in desperation of immolating her before it was too late.

"No-o-o!" screamed Shea at the Chieftain. Immediately he stabbed Erin with his mysterious staff.

"Odu's magical sign, now!" said Ajala.

He telepathised Shea and quickly Shea raised her fingers according to Ajala's instruction and made in the air the mystical sign spell of 'ejiogbe', *Odu's first binary eye pattern.*

"Ejiogbe gbe mi, Imole de, okuku parada!" communed Ajala from his subliminal-self to Shea these spells and she instantly pronounced it on this magical sign spell. These spell literally meant, *favour me, ejiogbe and let this mundane darkness (evil) be undone by celestial light (good).*

Instantaneously, each marks that represents Odu's eyes in the binary pattern Shea made, ignited and flickered into the eyes of all members of the witches of blood underworld. While they were supposed to attack Shea, they became temporarily blindfolded, dazed and confused.

"Get her and follow the shooting glow, leave now!" telepathised Ajala.

Shea quickly flew her broomstick beside the altar, got hold of the dying Erin and dragged her on her broomstick and the shooting glow sped off before her, as soon as she got Erin. Shea followed and up they flew out of the dark underground of Aye of the witches of blood underworld.

Instantly, these witches took to flight after Shea and they swarmed with fury behind her, though, still dazed by the magical sign spell of Odu that flickered into their eyes. They began to collide with one another, smashing against walls and hitting floors in confusion, only for these rugged witches to struggle into flight again.

Kowe heard Ajala's subliminal-self casting those unique spells and was astonished.

"How did you come about these stuffs?" inquired Kowe, about Ajala secret, ancient, magical spells of Odu.

"You know who I'm already, why bothering me?" replied Ajala.

"You amazed me, lad."

"Sorry, if I did!" he responded.

"As I said earlier, I'm only here for my friend, Erin." he

added.

"She isn't your friend, can't you understand?" cried Kowe.

Then, Shea came on the scene with the dying Erin, she was now conscious of what was going on around her, but also in pain of the injury inflicted on her heart by the Chieftain.

"You!" cried Erin.

"At last!" she sighed.

She pointed to Ajala with a troubled smile on her agony ridden face.

Kowe got annoyed when she saw Erin, of course, she knew her freedom was at stake. Kowe took to air again, beating its massive wings on the spot.

Ajala quickly raised his 'shere', *magic wand,* against her before she could display any magical attack, he rotated the 'shere' anticlockwise thrice and the object projected on Kowe a cobwebs-like psychic current, capturing the huge bird to a standstill in the air.

Ajala pulled to bring down the strange bird, but he couldn't, as he tried with all his psychic strength. Shea helped him and their combined effort yielded no result.

"Wizardry is in the mind and not in strength. Just look within always and the without would yield." he remembered Odu mentioning to him these words. Therefore, he held on to the 'shere', *magic wand,* with his left hand and posed a brief concentration.

"Ile!" communed Ajala this psychic spell to bring her down and the bizarre bird was thrown against the wall *by the shere's super force*, freeing the 'shere' from the psychic static current from the powerful Kowe.

Ajala quickly used the opportunity to attend to Erin's injury. Ajala looked at the Chieftain' staff that was stuck in Erin's heart and found out the hideous staff was draining her blood. He closed his eyes awhile and he saw the secret of the staff – *his clairvoyance showed him an old man – Oleobugije - confronting a strange sword that blazed into the gathering of Eboru and he heard the psychic name the old man called the sword.*

"Apasa yo, epon da, egbo di." he pronounced these spells on the staff to stop draining Erin's blood and for the removal of the strange staff *by itself* and also for Erin's wound to heal magically. The vision he saw made good his psychic instinct on what to do with the evil staff.

"Yes, my lord." responded the skull on the staff.

"Now, take her to her mother, do not allow anyone to remove the staff, it'll remove itself and the wound will heal magically. Go now, follow the shooting glow to the exit from the castle, go, go, go!" instructed Ajala.

"What about you?" asked Erin.

"Don't worry about me!" boomed Ajala.

"We can't leave him here!" shouted Erin, as Shea blasted off after Ajala's shooting glow.

The shooting star-like incandescent led Shea to the vacuum tunnel, where Ajala had entered into the castle. Shea flew through the wall after the glow into the tunnel and by the stream towards the cave, with the recuperating Erin, who was still looking back to see if Ajala was coming after them.

"You nearly killed me, Ajala." said Kowe as she came out of coma.

She teleported herself behind Ajala and got hold of him. Her grip miniaturised Ajala into powerlessness immediately.

"Thank your destiny, I'm in captivity." commented Kowe.

She was holding him in her hands when the coven furiously fluttered to the scene and onto Kowe, colliding with her en masse. Ajala fell off her powerful grips and straightaway regained his stature and psychic mind instantly he hit the floor. He realised he was pressed for time already and wouldn't delay any more in the castle because further waste of time could cost him his life.

"My staff!" cried the Chieftain, as he arrived on the scene.

"Where's my staff?" he raged in confusion, while trying to get up on his feet.

"You!" he cried, pointing to Ajala. Immediately, his snake tail and the entire members of the witches of blood underworld charged on Ajala.

"Iji gbe mi, O psychic eddy, take over!" pronounced Ajala.

This eddy spell responded before they could reach him. On the instant, he started swirling in rapid psychic eddies. Ajala's psychic eddy wound round the Chieftain his snake tail and threw him off the ground and against the wall. All the members of the witches of blood underworld were put into complete disarray by Ajala swirling in psychic eddies. The magical eddy spun him around the castle to the pandemonium of the members of witches of blood underworld. They were disoriented and couldn't comprehend this strange magic.

However, Kowe had warned the Chieftain that her captivity was an affront on her psychic powers. To the dismay of these witches, Ajala's magical eddy spun him through the wall into the vacuum tunnel, after ravaging the coven into total disarray. They all seemed to be drunk, as a result of Ajala's psychic eddy's effect. Ajala knew he had no time to waste in the Aye confronting these witches. Then, he tried to get out as fast as he could. As soon as the members of the witches of blood underworld followed him into the vacuum tunnel, they were thrown back *en masse* by the withstanding psychic field in the tunnel.

Of course, forthwith Shea and Erin touched down in the cave, the stream of the luminescence would start disappearing towards its source and the deluge also would magically recede, the Earth also would revert to its normal state, as if this deluge never happened.

When his psychic eddies swirled him onto his mobile, he flew posthaste so as to catch up with the stream. When he got out of the vacuum tunnel into the deluge, he found the stream of the luminescence vanishing away already towards the cave where it began. Though, Ajala knew this was a sign that Erin had reached the cave safely, consequently, he realised it was the end of the road for him because he already missed *by a hair's breadth* the stream of the luminescence by means of which he could travel through the deluge. Despite this magical blowback, his face radiated thorough satisfaction that he indeed kept his promise to Erin's mother.

In his mind was the joy going on in the cave as he was drowning in his own magic, while his remarkable activities from childhood till date and the memory of his mother began to panorama through his senses. He knew Shea was waiting earnestly to see him and would be shattered by his death and as also everyone in the camp would be devastated. Therefore, he clutched to his 'shere', even as he was drowning and tried some magical effort, but his psyche remained powerless for the stronger reason that his own magic lapsed on him.

"Mother, I'm sorry." he groaned *about Shea*.

As Ajala was drowning, the magical deluge continued to recede and he could perceive the hullabaloo going on in the castle of the witches of blood underworld. The stream of the luminescence was indeed the lifespan of the deluge and the haecceity of the whole magic. Since it started to darkle before he could catch up with it, there was no other way of transmission left for him to reach the cave through the flood.

He was thinking of his mother, his animal friends at Igbo, Erin's mother, Tisseewoonatis, Erin and Shea, and was contemplating what might have occurred to Pott. He was in deep remorse he couldn't help him.

As his body was descending helplessly to the bottom of the deluge, he saw that every application of the magical sign spell he had used were live representation of Odu's unique binary eye settings and in his memory he saw these strange, innumerable binary patterned eyes, blinking all around him.

Chapter Fifteen

IMMEDIATELY Shea and Erin touched down in the cave, the deluge began to recede turbulently and they were all worried about Ajala and Pott.

However, Erin too began to recuperate from the harm the Chieftain inflicted on her by his odd staff. While the whole of the camp where earnestly focused towards the caverns' entrance expecting Ajala, Shea was tending to Erin personally, making sure the staff wasn't forced out of Erin's chest as Ajala had instructed her. Everything Erin would say was Ajala's name on her lips repeatedly and it suddenly dawned on Shea that she probably had lost Ajala and Pott forever.

In a wild doleful loss for Ajala and Pott, Shea broke into tears of bereavement. Shea rushed towards the receding deluge to plunge herself into it, but she was held back by Tisseewoonatis.

"Don't do that, it's deadly!" cried Tisseewoonatis, as she let go of her camera to hold her down.

Erin's mother was full of both tears of joy and mourning, as she held her daughter after the Chieftain's staff fell and vanished into the earth.

At day break, the Earth had reverted to its previous stage as if the deluge did never happen and straightaway the camp flocked out of the cave in search of Ajala and Pott. They all ran helter-skelter around Igbo, looking for them, despite that they knew it might be impossible to find them. After searching everywhere, they came back into the cave tired and empty handed, where they met Erin weeping. When she saw them and the look on their faces revealed no trace of Ajala, she almost screamed herself to death.

As her mother and the camp were consoling her, Ajala's okapi galloped out of the jungle to the front of the cave and everyone was transfixed, staring at the okapi with utter quietness. At first they didn't know what to make of the action of the animal.

"Do you think he's actuating the animal to lead us to him?" Tisseewoonatis asked Shea.

Shea got up and approached the animal quietly, but it reared backward on its hind legs. Shea held herself back and called on Erin to approach the animal.

Instantly, the okapi walked to Erin on its own as she was approaching the animal. She began to pat its mane. She was helped by Shea to jump on its back and as she held the cowry lined bridle her mother made for Ajala to saddle the animal, it began to gallop away. The whole camp hurried after her, but the animal outran them.

The okapi eventually took her to where Ajala's body lay motionless on a flat rock surface.

"I've found him!" screamed Erin.

She jumped off the okapi as soon as she set her eyes on his body. She crouched beside him, pulling him to wake up.

They all flocked to the direction when they heard her screaming. They gathered round his body, while Erin continued to pull him to wake up, but Ajala's body yielded no sign of life. Shea placed her ear on his chest to listen to his heartbeat.

"He's dead." she said and bursted into tears.

"What?" exclaimed Tisseewoonatis.

"Can't believe this!" sobbed Erin's mother in tears.

Tisseewoonatis reached for her backpack after she snapped couple of pictures of his body, brought out her special first aid kit. She took the portable stethoscope out of it, had it on her ears and tested Ajala's pulse and heartbeat. Afterwards, her mind went numb. Erin's mother moved close to her, placed her hand on her shoulder and she raised her eyes towards her as she was kneeling beside Ajala's body.

"He's gone!" she said to her.

She brought her eyes back on the body, her stethoscope drooping from her neck as she lingered over Ajala's body with profound grief.

"Tissee!" called Erin's mother repeatedly, when she found her deeply affected.

"He's dead!" she mourned and began to weep thoroughly.

"Pull yourself together, please!" cried Erin's mother.

In no time Tisseewoonatis regained her composure and began to take photographs of Ajala's lifeless body again. She gazed at the terrains that looked so perfect, as it was before the magical deluge of Ajala. Yet, on her life she couldn't believe she witnessed this global flood personally. She began to ponder the correlation between the metaphysical and science, that though hidden and complicated, yet, with time it could be in toto comprehensible or forever incomprehensible at the absence of chronic scientific study. However, she understood magic transcends matter and particle or whatever the most brilliant of boffins could ever conceive.

"What's going to happen, mum?"

"Sweetheart, let go!" replied Erin's mother emotionally.

"What?" asked Erin.

"Let go of him and just walk away?" she queried.

She bent towards her daughter, placed her palms on her cheeks, wiped her tears sideways with her thumbs and slowly withdrew her hold on the lifeless body of Ajala. Instantly, Erin perceived her mother's intention to take her away from the body.

"No, mum!" she wept profusely.

As her mother dragged her away from Ajala's dead body, she was frantically trying to free herself. While stretching towards the body with all her strength, the grief-stricken *untouchable* children were also being held by the distraught Shea.

"My son, my son, I'm so – sorry I failed you!" screamed Shea in bereavement of Ajala, as all the remarkable moments they had together panorama through her senses.

"Eh, put yourself together!" encouraged Tisseewoonatis.

She tried to comfort Shea.

"We can't just leave him here!" cried Erin.

"It's okay, sweetheart." said Shea.

She went and embraced Erin.

"Yes, we'll bury him, of course!" responded Erin's mum.

"We'll bury him?" retorted Erin.

"Yes, that's all we could possibly do now." buttressed Tisseewoonatis.

"No one knows he's dead and is burial ground unknown?" asked Erin.

"He's dead, sweetheart. We can't take him to his people, they'll harm us or even kill us." Erin's mother pointed out to her daughter and Erin gently freed herself from Shea's embrace and walked to Ajala's body again.

"Get up, please!" she cried repeatedly, shaking the body.

"Wake up!" cried Erin innocently.

"He's dead, can't you see?" whispered Erin's mother.

"He isn't dead, mum!" responded Erin.

"He can't just die like that!"

"He's gone, sweetheart!" said Erin's mother.

She continued to call on Ajala to get up and everyone went silent and were captivated by her innocent passion, with which she was agitating the lifeless body to wake up. None the less, the futility of urging a dead body to wake up, suddenly dawned on Erin and she sadly let go of the body. As she continued to sob quietly, she sank her head in her chest. Everyone looked at her and nodded to one another that she was finally realising the fact that Ajala was dead. Erin's mother became tearful, watching her daughter coming to term with the reality on ground.

"It's alright, sweetheart." she said.

Yet, Erin remained indifferent towards everyone and her mother, staring at Ajala's body.

"You see now, sweetheart, he's dead and ..." commented Erin's mother.

"He isn't dead, stop saying it!" shrieked Erin before her mother could finish her remark and everyone was astounded at her fervent outcry.

Instantaneously, a superb hi-tech military helicopter hovered above them from behind a huge mountain. In a swift combat ready military antics, four well-equipped, battle hardened soldiers abseiled simultaneously with breathtaking military expertise.

"British Royal Marine!" cried one of the soldiers.

"I'm Major Steel and my colleagues are Captain Ed, Bill and Ball." the soldier quickly introduced himself and his colleagues to the camp.

They watched in disbelief as these soldiers took their precisive, *military style* vigilant postures as soon as they touched down.

They were all dumbfounded at the sight of these well trained, battle hardened military men. They wondered how on Earth these *military* guys tracked them down to Igbo – *the evil forest and the land of the gods*.

Unbeknownst to them, detective Chief Inspector Briggs wouldn't even spare the *classified* "God" to make sure they weren't out of sight.

"We're taking you home, guys!" announced Major steel.

"And him?" asked Erin's mother of a possible burial for Ajala.

"Dead or alive…" responded Major Steel.

He paused, while making sure Ajala was actually dead, as he was trying to feel his pulse and heartbeat with his right fingers, holding his sophisticated rifle in place with his left hand.

"I've got order for his arrest, anyway." he added.

Olodumare, *the personal name for the supreme God of these lost tribes. This was the only deity they had no idol to designate, because they believed Olodumare's forever invisible intelligence, formless, infinite, innocent, immutable, omnipotent, omnipresent and absolute. He would neither take on any form whatsoever, nor could he be appeased by any material rituals at any point in time, other than moral ritual of goodness, in all aspects of life. They believed that for the sacrosanctity of Olodumare to be preserved, he created, accorded and authorised different orisha into jurisdictions in his creation.* **Olorun,** *the generic name these tribespeople used for God.* **Orisha,** *primordial beings, spirits or energies, created by Olodumare. They were endowed with special qualities and sometimes freewill for good or evil, just like humans that these orisha created in their own likeness.* **Ogun,** *primordial being whom these lost tribes believed presided over iron, hunting, reconnaissance, politics and war. He was believed to be the patron of smith for these tribespeople and according to their oral history, he was the primordial being sent to assess and confirm, if the Earth was suitable for human life.* **Obatala,** *these tribespeople believed this primordial being was sent to preside over the creation of planet earth. He designed the brain, created the body and this was brought to life by the breath of Olodumare (the supreme god). Therefore, as the designer and creator of the brain and human body, Olodumare (the supreme god) accorded him the ownership of the head or rather, the brain, as this was deemed the masterpiece of his creation on Earth.* **Shango,** *the primordial being whom these tribespeople believed presided over fire, lightening, thunder and all forms of energies around the planet.* **Babalu-Aye,** *transliterated 'father, lord in the Earth', was believed by these lost tribes, as the primordial being who presided over the creation of the energies in the Earth.* **Jakuta** *was the primordial being believed by these tribespeople presided over the hurling of fire stones from the sky - thunderbolts and meteorites – to destroy enemies of Olodumare (the supreme god). He's the annihilator of the evil one.* **Orunmila,** *the primordial being and grand priest of Ifa revelations, whom these tribespeople claimed taught them the exposition of Ifa binary savvy.*

213

Osun, *primordial being who presided over love, intimacy, beauty, sexuality, maternity, marriage, wealth and the creation of the sea and according to these tribespeople, this primordial intelligence was female and her essence was believed to reside in water.* **Yemoja,** *the goddess of depths and patron deity of children, the spirit protector of the sea or the primordial being that these tribespeople claimed was spirit protector of the ocean.* **Esu,** *called the divine messenger, the primordial orisha of all transformation and the intelligence gatherer for Olodumare. He's the prime negotiator between good and evil and a staunch supporter of 'law of being'. Esu was believed by these tribespeople to be capable of speaking any language, in fact, he was believed to be the primordial intelligence, who taught humans to speak. In primordial times, he was considered to be the closest to both Olodumare and mankind out of all orisha.* **Legba,** *another transformation of Esu and here he was the sexy orisha with huge manhood and his shrine was always outside vicinities, at the entrances of settlements of these lost tribes and his ritual could be left at junctions, where these tribespeople believed his presence resided.* **Oduduwa,** *the primordial being these lost tribes believed was sent to lend a helping hand to Obatala in making the planet Earth suitable for life-forms.*